"This is not a night for thinking…"

He cupped her cheek and turned her face toward his. "That is good." His breath whispered across her lips.

Placing her hands against his chest for balance, Catheryn leaned closer. "Gerard?"

This time it wasn't his finger that silenced her, it was his kiss. His lips, so warm and gentle against her own, took away her words, her thoughts and her breath.

When he stopped his soft caress, Catheryn rested her forehead against his shoulder. "Who gave you this power over me? Surely I am bewitched. You touch me and I cannot think."

"This is not a night for thinking." Holding her in his arms, he slowly moved them back toward the bed. "Tomorrow you may think all you like. But tonight, Catheryn, let it rest. Let everything rest."

DREAM KNIGHT

by

Alexis Kaye Lynn

NBI
NovelBooks, Inc.
Douglas, Massachusetts

This is a work of fiction. While reference may be made to actual historical events or existing locations, the characters, incidents, and dialogs are products of the author's imagination. Any resemblance to actual persons, living or dead, is entirely coincidental.

Copyright © 2001 by Alexis Kaye Lynn

All rights reserved. No part of this book may be used or reproduced in any manner whatsoever without written permission of the publisher except in the case of brief quotations embodied in critical articles and review. For information, address NovelBooks, Inc., P.O. Box 661, Douglas, MA 01516 or email publisher@novelbooksinc.com

NBI

Published by
NovelBooks, Inc.
P.O. Box 661
Douglas, MA 01516

NovelBooks Inc. publishes books online and through print-on-demand. For more information, check our website:www.novelbooksinc.com or email publisher@novelbooksinc.com

Produced in the United States of America.

Cover illustration by Ariana Overton
Edited by Laurie Alice Eakes

ISBN 1-931696-19-5 for electronic version
ISBN 1-931696-80-2 for POD version

Dedication

Thank you to my family for never telling me I was nuts when at times I obviously am.

To my friends and critique partners who have labored so long with me—blessings to you.

To my husband, who accepts my dreams— keep dreaming with me.

And finally, to Jasper and Angie—Huzzah!

Prologue

"Nay!"

Catheryn's scream of terror failed to stop the advancing horror.

Battle-clad warriors astride Satan's own destriers raced through the fog toward her.

Mail, as black as the starless sky, covered each battle hardened warrior from helmed head to leather-booted feet.

Paralyzed and unprotected on the open moor, Lady Catheryn could only tremble at the coming onslaught of impending doom.

The mighty warhorses with their deadly mounts charged ever closer. Iron-clad hooves pounded in perfect unison with the heavy thudding of her heart. Swords, pikes and axes raised, the men rushed nearer. The leader of this demonic army ensnared her gaze. Dark, glowing eyes held no sign of mercy. There would be no quarter given if captured by this unforgiving force.

The cloying smell of death permeated the air, broken only by the acrid scent of smoke and destruction. The vile stench seared her nostrils. She shuddered with revulsion.

Catheryn fought to calm her racing heart, forced her trembling limbs to still. She would not cower before her enemies, nor would she kneel in the cold mud and beg for mercy. With a hushed voice, she prayed, *"Lord, give me strength."*

The leader of the pack of death-hungry wolves stopped before her as the remaining warriors raced past. A thunderbolt lit the sky. Raindrops rolled down the mailed arm reaching for her. The tears from heaven shimmered over an emerald and gold ring on the hand that grasped her shoulder.

Lifting her hands before her face in a feeble attempt to ward off the brutal end to her life, Catheryn begged, "Dear God, have mercy on my soul."

Catheryn bolted awake, frantically looking for her enemy. A draft of air blew across her naked body, creating goose flesh on her sweat-soaked skin. She blinked away the last traces of her dream and sighed with relief at the familiar sight of her own chamber.

The sight of the crumpled bed curtain still entwined in her fingers made her laugh. She remembered what had caused such a nightmare and retrieved the yarrow-filled dream bag from beneath her pillow. The words of the sachet's promise came back to her. *"Thou pretty herb of Venus's tree, thy true name is Yarrow. Now who my brave, true love must be, pray tell thou me tomorrow."*

A cold chill not caused by the night's breeze sent a shiver down her spine. She'd asked for a dream of true love and had instead received a vision of terror and death.

Chapter One

Brezden Keep, England—The Year of Our Lord 1142

"He is out there." Catheryn, Lady of Brezden, whispered into the empty darkness of the night.

Between her walls and the forest nothing moved. Only the cold spring rain fell on the ground surrounding her keep. She felt his nearness in the chill of the night air. The rustle of the trees vibrated with his strong, steady heartbeat. The blustering wind carried the scent of a man bent on destruction. A destruction that she had unwittingly called forth. A simple spell, meant only to give her a glimpse of the man who would be her life's love, had worked well.

Far too well.

She shivered. Not from the cold or the rain, but from the knowledge that soon her nightmare would come to life. And not in the manner she had envisioned in her waking hours.

"Milady, you should be abed."

"He has come, Agnes." Catheryn despised the alarm she heard in her simple declaration. A fear she would never show to anyone else. She knew she could never successfully hide the emotion from Agnes. Since the murder of Catheryn's mother, Agnes had been more than just a servant. The woman had easily slipped from being a nursemaid to being the strength that kept Catheryn from falling into an abyss of despair.

"Who is here?"

"My true love." She turned the sachet over in her hands one more time, she then handed it to Agnes. "The dark knight of my dreams has arrived."

"Fie. That isn't possible. It was just supposed to be a dream, nothing but a dream of love."

"You think I don't know that?" She peered deeper into the darkness of the night. His heartbeat drummed in her blood. "Regardless of what was *supposed* to happen, I cannot deny what I know without doubt *will* happen."

She resisted the urge to give into the hysterical laughter threatening to bubble forth. Catheryn turned away from the window and lit the tallow candles ensconced on the wall.

"This is impossible. Mistress Margaret said..."

"I don't care what the woman said." Catheryn pulled a gown from the clothing chest and tossed it atop her bed. "All I know is that the good mistress's spells must be stronger than we thought."

Agnes grabbed the gown before Catheryn could slip it on. "What are you doing?"

"Preparing to meet my destiny."

"You are not going to go meet him at the gates?" The maid's voice rose with each word.

"What else can I do?" Catheryn retrieved the dress with a gentle tug and slipped it over her head. "Shall I let Brezden's people be attacked without giving them notice? Shall I stay here in my chamber quivering like a coward?"

"Pike is the master here. Let him deal with the invaders."

This time Catheryn did let the laughter spill forth. "Pike? What do you think the baron will do? He will consult his minion, de Brye." A shiver coursed down her spine. "Then the two of them will save their hides first, using whatever means they can."

"But what about—"

"No!" Before Agnes could say anything reasonable that would sway Catheryn from her purpose, she strengthened her resolve. "I must do this. Don't you see? No one else is aware of his presence. It is my responsibility to warn our people to seek safety."

Catheryn opened the door to her chamber, resisting the urge to soothe the worry lines from her nursemaid's brow.

She walked down the dark corridor and fought the need to return to Agnes and provide reassurance. How could she ease the concerns of another when she didn't know herself what this night would bring?

~*~

Castle Brezden looked almost invisible in the curtain of rain falling from the sky. A bolt of lightning streaked, giving a glimpse of stone walls in its glare.

From his vantage point beneath the shelter of trees, Count Gerard of Reveur noted few men pacing the front wall. How many more would be concealed in the towers?

Gerard knew the keep's defenses were sadly lacking. For over a year he had waited. And planned. Gathering every piece of information he could about Brezden and its holder.

In a time when brother fought brother and nothing was as it seemed, paid spies came easily. They had supplied him with details he'd not have been able to garner on his own.

Fate smiled on him, proving his long wait advantageous. William, the Earl of York, needed help to secure his land from traitors. By ignoring the earl's call for arms, Baron Pike had added Brezden to the list of those disloyal to Earl William and King Stephen.

Ready and more than willing to assist the earl, Gerard volunteered to capture Brezden. As long as the keep fell into his hands, no one would care if his own schemes found fulfillment.

The sound of wheels clattering over a stone road gave him cause to smile. He reached out and patted the thick, wet neck of his destrier. The twitching ears and bulging muscles of the black war-horse informed him that the beast had also heard the wagon's approach.

A wagon driven by his men.

"Nay, not yet. Can you not be patient just a little longer?"

Gerard rolled his eyes when the animal bobbed his great head up and down in what seemed to be an answer to his question.

As the wagon drew closer he heard shouts, and the gates groaned slowly open. A frown replaced his smile. The guards had allowed the hay wagon entrance without so much as a second glance. At the very least he had expected the men to be stopped and questioned. An event that would not stop him. Gerard had taught two of his men how to pick a lock—a skill that came in handy more times than naught. If the wagon had not gained entry, the two would open the postern gate.

His spies hadn't been totally accurate. While it seemed true that the keep was lightly guarded, they hadn't mentioned it being garrisoned by fools.

A drop of cold rain found its way through his mailed coif to trickle down the back of his neck. Who was he to call the men sitting warm and dry behind those walls fools? Any sane person would think the man preparing for battle in the middle of a storm was the real fool.

But they'd be wrong in their assumption.

He'd played the simpleton once. And his misjudgment had cost him a beloved wife and a newborn son.

Gerard glared up at the steady downpour of rain and wondered if the bad weather was an omen of things to come. The storm had been with them constantly for the last three days. And for each of those long days he'd relived his wife's horrible death.

He crossed himself, cursing his apprehension. He cursed life and God. He cursed the man who had caused his idyllic world to turn into a nightmare. Gerard closed his eyes against the sickening memory of Edyth's twisted and broken body and swallowed his pain. "I swear to you, beloved, I will satisfy our revenge this night."

Gerard joined his captain Walter at a break in the forest.

"The fires will start slowly tonight, this rain has surely soaked the thatched roofs," he muttered to the older man.

Blue eyes, encased by a weather-beaten face lifted briefly to look up at the dark sky. "Aye. But we expected little else."

Gerard snorted at his captain's disgruntled tone. He knew Walter disliked this northern climate more than he did. After nodding toward the keep, he told his man, "The wagon gained entrance. I think a little too easily." He glanced back at the walls and weighed his options. There was but only one choice. "If anyone within had decided to stop the wagon after its entry, we would have seen more guards attend the walls." By now his men already inside would be anxiously waiting for their signal to open the gates.

He took one last look up at the keep before making the final decision. "Go. Take your group of men and proceed as planned. As soon as I hear your commotion, I will lead my group to the wall."

While Walter and his men approached the keep under the cover of night, Gerard's trained gaze kept track of their forms in the blackness. Lightning cracked through the sky like a whip. In its eerie light he thought he could see someone watching him as closely.

The stare fell upon him with a certainty he could hardly understand. It was as if someone inside eagerly awaited his arrival and the salvation they thought it would bring.

How would they feel once they realized his only offering would be death?

He shook the strange thoughts from his mind and the dripping rain from his nasal plate. Peering back at Brezden, he reassured himself that his flight of fancy was no more and shouted for his men to advance. "*Avancer! Reveur!*"

~*~

Catheryn watched the wagon enter her bailey with little more interest than she would watch a flea bite a dog. *He* would not enter concealed in a wagon. No. *He* would ride a destrier as black as himself through Brezden's gate. *He* would charge forward bravely, brandishing a sword before him.

A bitter satisfaction fell upon her soul. Men would die this night and she truly did not care. Her men, Brezden's faithful few, were safely away through the tunnel entrance hidden within her chamber's alcove.

They hadn't sought concealment meekly. She laughed at the recent memory. It had come down to her will against theirs. Her orders against their pleas. But at last they had gone grumbling to their safety.

Somewhere along the river gliding silently past Brezden her men watched and waited. She'd ordered them to hide far away from the keep, but Catheryn knew they would disobey that order. Her only hope was that they weren't found.

She glanced around at the remaining men stationed on the wall walk. These were the baron's men—and de Brye's. She cared little what happened to them. They were the scum and dregs of the earth and deserved whatever fate held in store for them this night.

How many times had one or more of them held her arms pinned while de Brye tormented her? How many nights had her cries gone unanswered while these men drank and played cruel games with her maids?

After her father's death over five years ago no one had spent a pleasant evening in this keep. And after her mother's death last year, the days and nights had become even worse.

"*Cease.*" Catheryn silently bid the memory not to overtake her now. She needed to remain in control. Having held off her grief and terror this long surely one more night would not make any difference?

De Brye grasped her arm. She jumped. Despite the pain,

she tried to jerk free.

"That's right, sweeting, fight me. You know how I so enjoy your struggles." His evil smile revealed graying, broken teeth behind the curled lips.

Her guardian's minion nodded toward the gates. "You think this force will deal more gently with you than I?"

Catheryn refused to rise to his bait. She knew he would twist her words around until she no longer knew exactly what it was that she thought, or felt.

He grazed her cheek with his lips. It took every ounce of willpower she possessed not to gag on the smell of his fetid breath. "No, my darling, they will gleefully enjoy your flesh." De Brye dragged her back toward the keep. "But do not worry. When they are through using you, they will pay with their lives."

She had no choice but to follow where he forced her to go. But Catheryn knew a level of fright she had never before experienced when he pulled her into her own chamber.

De Brye tossed her onto her bed. Catheryn rolled to the floor. She landed on her hands and knees, then scrambled toward the door. De Brye grabbed a handful of her hair and dragged her back onto the bed. He loosened his leather belt and waved it before her face. "Move again and your tender skin will feel my wrath."

Without turning her head, Catheryn frantically searched the room. Agnes had hidden herself well and for a moment Catheryn breathed a measure of gratitude.

But it was short-lived.

De Brye reached into the curtained alcove, grasped the maid by her hair, dragged her to the chamber door and then pushed the woman into the corridor. "Keep yourself beyond my sight else you'll watch your lady die."

Catheryn's heart froze. She knew his threat was not made in jest. "Agnes, go. Do as he says."

While Agnes scrambled to do Catheryn's bidding, de

Brye swung back to glare at Catheryn. "Open your mouth again and I'll close it for you permanently."

In hopes of gaining enough time for her dark knight to attack the keep, she bit back a scathing retort. If pressed too far, this insane monster would kill her and all would be lost.

A sly smile twisted his face into a mask of pure evil. "That's right, my sweeting, do as you are bid and it may go easier for you." He then turned back to the door and shouted for Pike.

Catheryn prayed for her avenging angel to hasten his attack. *Angel? When has the angry visage from my nightmare become a celestial being?*

Within mere heartbeats, Pike arrived. Chain mail askew, helmet held in one shaking hand and a wavering sword in the other, the baron's disheveled appearance belied his position. This was no commander of men and most certainly no leader for Brezden.

"What do you want?" Pike spared but a glance at Catheryn. "I have no time for your games at the present, Raymond."

"Games? I play no games during your moment of truth, milord."

Had she been anywhere else Catheryn would have laughed at the tone of abject disrespect de Brye used toward her guardian. But she wasn't anywhere else and she was well aware this was no game to de Brye.

"Then I ask again, what do you want?"

While pulling off his long tunic, de Brye slowly approached the bed.

The fear that had kept her limbs frozen, now propelled her from the mattress. Pike and de Brye blocked any escape through the door. Racing toward the long, thin arrow slit, she hoped to capture someone's attention.

Before Catheryn could scream for help, de Brye wrapped his hands around her neck, effectively cutting off her cries.

She clawed at his fingers. It did little to loosen the vise-like grip. De Brye only laughed and squeezed harder.

Her vision clouded. Her lungs burned with the need for life-sustaining air.

De Brye released his grasp and tossed her back on the bed as if she were little more than a child.

Catheryn's chest heaved with the effort to breathe.

De Brye reached down and wrapped her hair around his hand. He looked at Pike and smiled before stating, "I thought perhaps you'd enjoy being witness to your ward's first bedding."

Catheryn glanced around the chamber, seeking a knife, willing to cut her own hair off if it would free her. Before she could find a way to escape his hold, de Brye launched himself atop her. He moved with an agility she had not realized he possessed.

Shuffling from one foot to the other, Pike asked, "Really, Raymond, do you think now is the time to be satisfying your urges?"

"Urges?" De Brye's face was so close Catheryn could feel his hot breath on her cheek. "Not urges, milord." He grasped the back of her head. "It is only right that her future lord and master have the honor of taking her maidenhead."

She heard the baron approach the bed and nearly screamed when he ran a gloved finger across her cheek. "He is correct, my dear. It will be much better this way."

Catheryn kicked and twisted beneath de Brye's weight. "Let me go. Dear Lord, do not allow this to happen."

The sounds of battle drifted in through the window. Pike sighed and patted her cheek one last time. "I am sorry it had to be this way. I can hold him off no longer, my dear. Had you agreed to become the Lady de Brye your fate would be different." He turned back to de Brye. "Now, Raymond, I must make an appearance as the lord here. Try not to be too unpleasant. You'll want her to be willing later."

De Brye smiled. "Close the door on your way out."

Catheryn stared at the man above her. She had not the power to stop him. But she'd not be a willing victim. Keeping her voice steady, she ordered, "Get off of me."

After releasing her hair, he rolled to one side, grasped the front of her gown and rent the fabric to her waist. "I only want to prepare you for the night to come. It is proper that I have the honor before they pass you from one man to the next."

She tried desperately to close her mind to what was about to happen. But something, either fear or anger, kept her from escaping inside herself. She tried to slip away from him. She slapped his hands away. "You are worse than a swine! You have no right."

De Brye pulled her back to him and stopped her accusations with a stinging slap to her cheek. Her mind screamed with pain as his fingers squeezed and prodded her exposed breast. Her soul cried out with terror when he shredded the rest of her gown down the front.

Unmindful of the reprisal sure to come, Catheryn spat in his face. "Regardless of what you do this night I will kill myself before becoming your wife, de Brye."

She watched in mute horror as a stark, insane rage covered his features. Before her mind could scream for her to seek safety, his fist closed in on her face.

~*~

Men and horses rushed out from the woods, surprising the lax force stationed behind and on the thick stone walls. Swords drawn, Gerard's men poured through the open gates.

"Remember the Lady of Reveur and leave no traitor alive!"

The men who had ignored King Stephen's call to arms

would regret their decision.

But they would not be as regretful as the men who had killed his wife.

As Brezden's unsuspecting guards fell from the walls and towers, their screams of astonishment and pain mixed with those of the animals stabled in the outer bailey.

Gerard remembered his promise to a broken and battered Edyth as she took her last breath in his arms. He shouted a final order to his men, "The baron is mine alone!" The force charged across the outer courtyard. With heavy swords and two-headed battle axes they instantly dispatched anyone who offered the slightest resistance.

When they reached the wall that separated the inner and outer yards, Gerard offered a silent prayer of relief and gratitude as he watched the iron-shod portcullis rise. His advance men had performed their duties to perfection and had already gained control of this last barrier to the keep itself.

Certain that his men were capable of taking possession of the inner ward, Gerard tightened his grip on his sword and turned to look up the motte toward Brezden.

He swallowed the bitter taste of iron and urged the destrier up the man-made hill. The metallic taste of blood before a battle was nothing new. It only served to strengthen his resolve to be the victor.

He sucked in his breath with a hiss when a bolt of lightning, streaking across the sky, outlined the stone keep at the top of the earthen mound.

At the base of the keep, Gerard dismounted and slapped his horse on the rump. "Go." He shook his head at the departing animal, knowing there was no need for concern over the beast's welfare. "Do not hurt too many." The clad hooves and strong teeth would easily maim, if not kill, anyone who came within reach.

Gerard turned and raced up the stairs leading into the

keep. The narrowness of the stairway permitted only one person at a time to try to hold him back. Each slash of his sword, and every contact he made with an enemy fueled his desire for battle.

By the time Gerard reached the great hall he could hear his heart pounding in his ears. He felt the blood course through his body. He wanted to take Pike now while he was primed and ready for a fight.

Gerard entered the hall and stopped. He searched for the lord of this holding. Edyth had described two men before she died. One was old, fat and balding—Pike. Her description of the other had been brief. *Satan. The devil.* He had little doubt which one had sent her to an early grave.

After spotting a portly older man on the upper level, he ran up the steep, curved stairs at the side of the hall. "Pike!" The man stopped and turned to look at Gerard. "The time has come to pay for your act of cowardice."

"Come, pup, who ever you may be. Try to wrest Brezden from my hand."

Gerard knew then he had one man—the baron—within his grasp. Turning to defend himself, Pike drew his sword and beckoned Gerard forward. "You, a nameless scum, think to challenge me?"

It would take more than a simple taunt to sway him from his mission. "Nameless scum? I need no name to avenge my family."

He lifted his sword and swung at Pike's blade. "It was my wife you killed a winter past. My child, fresh from her womb, whom you slaughtered."

When the baron appeared unable to remember the act, Gerard stepped back and bowed. "Count of Reveur at your service, Baron."

Pike blanched and tossed his sword over the railing to clatter on the stone floor far below. Smiling, he spread his arms. "Forgive me, milord. But would you kill a defenseless man?"

Gerard chose the spot on Pike's chest where his sword tip would do its final work and smiled back. "Yes, I would." In that same instant, he remembered the oath he had sworn as a knight.

Valor.

Honor.

Pike spun around and raced down the long hall. Gerard charged after him and wasn't surprised to hear footsteps behind him.

When the baron reached into an alcove for what Gerard instinctively knew would be another sword, he turned and rammed the tip of his own weapon into the treacherous knave who thought to take him from behind.

Before Gerard could turn fully back toward Pike, the baron slashed at him. Gerard's blood trickled down his arm. Had it not been for the double-linked chain mail he fought in, he would have lost a limb.

Unwilling to chance another injury, he grasped his hilt in both hands and plunged it into Pike's chest. Exactly on the spot he had chosen only moments ago.

As the older man fell, Gerard jerked his blade out of the unresisting flesh and wiped the bloody sword on his tunic. He looked down and crossed himself, resisting the urge to do the same thing for the dead man on the floor.

A soothing peace briefly flowed through his veins. He closed his eyes and saw Edyth bless him with one of her sweet smiles. Yet he knew he'd only accomplished one of the vows he'd made to her. He still needed to find the other man.

The one she'd called Satan.

Gerard forced himself away from the image of his wife, strode back to the steps and yelled down at his men. "Hold your swords! Secure the rest of this keep and gather the survivors in the hall." As an afterthought he ordered, "Make sure they see their previous lord's fate."

When the men rushed to follow his bidding, Gerard paused long enough to allow his pounding blood to slow, but only slightly. With luck, the fear already instilled, and the sight of Pike's body, no one else would be unwise enough to try his arm any more this day.

As a restless calm filled him, Gerard began searching the remaining chambers for others. Each room proved dark and empty, save the last.

His eyes adjusted to the dim light provided by the wall candles. Gerard entered the sleeping chamber cautiously and demanded, "Show yourself." When he received no answer he proceeded around the perimeter of the room. "The keep is lost. You have no choice but to surrender."

Shredded white and pale blue curtains surrounded a bed across the room. Gowns were carelessly discarded, lying half out of the chest against the wall. A light scent, spicy and floral, wafted up from the rush-and-herb-covered floor.

Gerard clenched his jaw. No one, not one of the many spies had said anything about a female, not a wife, nor even a daughter. But then, he had to admit to himself that he'd never cared enough to ask.

He slapped his leg impatiently; he didn't have time for games. He used his sword to part the frayed curtains hiding the occupant on the bed. A light snore met his ears. Not sure if he should laugh or roar, Gerard simply stared, dumbfounded. *This couldn't be happening. Sleeping? A battle takes place outside the door, and she sleeps?*

The unsteady glow from the candles fell across the figure lying on the bed. Somehow, this girl—he took a closer look—this woman had not escaped her own battle.

A gut wrenching pain twisted his innards. As a warrior for his king he'd killed many men. He'd destroyed keeps and manors without second thought. The sounds and sights of blood and death were familiar to him.

Even as battle-weary as he was, Gerard knew he would never be enough of a coward to beat a woman in such a manner. It would take a vile miscreant, much like the one he'd just dispatched to hell.

Gerard grasped the hilt of his sword more tightly and stepped away from the bed. Had it been Pike? Or had the spineless cur been the other black-hearted knave he still sought?

Only one person could provide the answers.

He leaned over the form on the bed and lightly shook her shoulder.

Chapter Two

Catheryn sought frantically for a way to escape the advancing terror. But she stood in the open, outside the walls of Brezden. There was no place for her to hide, no where to run as Lucifer's horsemen charged forward. They were so close now she saw the gleaming whites of the riders' eyes.

The metal nose plates of their helmets glittered with each crack of lightning. Puffs of steam plumed from the over-taxed horses' nostrils. She felt the animals' warm breath on her bare flesh.

Would death claim her this night?

Catheryn fought to calm her racing heart, forced her trembling limbs to still. She would not cower before her enemies, nor would she kneel in the cold mud and beg for mercy. With a hushed voice, she prayed, "Lord, give me strength."

The leader of the pack of death-hungry wolves stopped before her as the remaining warriors raced past. A thunderbolt lit the sky. Raindrops rolled down the mailed arm reaching for her. These tears from heaven shimmered over an emerald and gold ring on the hand that grasped her shoulder.

Slowly, the fog began to clear. Her breath caught in her throat. She felt the grasp on her shoulder and realized she was not dreaming. Catheryn warily opened her eyes and stared into the burning gaze of her nightmare come to life.

Her heart stopped. Reality crashed around her. The events of this day flooded her with fear. Fear, as cold as a mountain stream, flowed up her body and clouded her mind with its icy grip. Unable to form any coherent thoughts or words, Catheryn remained still.

The man released his hold and backed away from the bed. His instant retreat helped to ease her fear and prompt her into action. Keeping a close watch on him, she moved to sit up.

Bruised muscles cried with pain. The cool night air brushed against her breasts. She lifted a hand to her now-throbbing face, groaning with the rush of recent memories.

Sir Raymond de Brye. Had he fulfilled his threat? There had been no one here to prevent him from doing so. Catheryn swallowed a sob. How would she know if he—she stopped the horrifying query before it reached completion. It mattered little either way. Surely Raymond de Brye had perished in the battle.

Her gaze flew to the man in her chamber. It was obvious he was trying hard to avoid staring at her exposed flesh. She thought it odd that a stranger, an enemy in truth, would show such restraint. *Ah, but he is no stranger, is he?*

Unable to hold the torn remnants of her gown together, Catheryn gingerly reached for a blanket. She flinched when pain accompanied her movements.

The intruder stepped back toward the bed. "Here, let me." He made quick work of covering her and then lightly touched her swollen face. Before moving away again, he asked, "Who did this?"

Catheryn looked up at him. After asking his barely audible question, he'd removed his helmet and pushed back the mailed coif from his head. Damp hair fell just above immense shoulders. The unruly, raven locks matched the color of his eyes.

Etched cheekbones, straight nose and squared jaw looked as if they had been carved in marble. But the artist's hand must have slipped with the chisel, leaving a small jagged scar running crosswise over his temple.

While he didn't appear as frightening in flesh as he had in her nightmares, he still caused terror to lift the hairs on the back of her neck.

This could not possibly be the love promised her.

When he stopped talking and glared at her with his piercing eyes, she realized he must have asked her a question. She apologized, "Pray, forgive me. I did not hear you."

"Who did this? Where is the vile knave?" he repeated in a clipped tone. He didn't sound as if he was used to repeating himself. Catheryn studied his arrogant face. No, this was a man who expected to be in complete control of every situation.

Her first impulse was to throw herself on his mercy. Except he did not have the look of a man who knew what mercy was. In the past she had taken many foolish chances to defend herself against any threat directed toward her.

If her nightmares were an indication of the truth, any fight offered against him would be lost before it even began.

She took a deep breath and clutched the cover tighter to her neck before whispering the name. "De Brye. Sir Raymond de Brye." It was all she could do not to gag as the words left her lips.

Pity and disgust flitted across his features. Catheryn would accept neither from him. Nor did she wish to discuss the man who had made her life little more than a living hell.

She ignored the pain flooding through her and sat up straighter on the bed. She squared her shoulders, lifted her chin and asked, "What have you done with my people?"

He stepped closer to the bed. "What few traitors we found have been dispatched."

"I care little what happened to Pike's men. What about Brezden's people?" She ignored the burning of her throat when she tilted her head back to look up at him.

"Brezden's people? What difference between Pike's or Brezden's? Was not Pike the lord here?"

Catheryn choked out a short, bitter laugh. "Pike? The

lord?" Shaking her head she fought the unladylike urge to spit on the floor. "Usurper Pike was only here due to Earl William's good, albeit misguided grace."

"You lie."

Her head snapped back up. "No. I would never lie about my keep, nor about my people."

She watched the emotions of disbelief and confusion cross his face before a look of bland unconcern settled there.

"So, you are the Lady of Brezden?"

If it'd been possible, she'd have torn out her own tongue for giving away even that little bit of information. Catheryn knew she'd have to guard her words more closely. But on this, the error was completed. "Yes. Since my mother's murder a year ago."

"Murder?" A frown creased his brows. "I was told of no murder. Only of a grieving lady whose desire to join her husband led her down the wrong path."

Every muscle, every bone in her body stiffened. Catheryn clenched and unclenched her jaw. "That is untrue."

Unwilling to permit this conversation to continue any further, she tightened her grasp on her cover and asked, "What do you want of me and Brezden?"

Gerard shook his head. This was not happening exactly as it should. "I want nothing of you. I already have Brezden."

She lifted her chin higher. Aqua eyes, while still wary, were rapidly changing to a darker green. He could only assume the darker color foretold of the coming anger.

"Nothing? Then go. This is my chamber. My keep." She motioned toward the door. "Leave."

He shook his head again. Aye, he was right. But along with the anger, there was arrogance, and a willfulness uncommon in most females.

Gerard leaned down, so they were eye to eye, and spoke

slowly, deliberately. "You must not have heard me. I have taken this keep. If it belongs to anyone save King Stephen, it belongs to Earl William. And I will hold it for him until his arrival."

He waited until he was certain that simple fact had taken hold in her mind. "Now, you can either help me control the defeated people of Brezden and assist me in finding any remaining traitors, or you can relegate yourself to a tower cell."

The lady paled, but said nothing.

Gerard backed away and stared at her. Something was not quite right here. While she called herself the lady of this keep, she appeared to have been most ill-treated.

He briefly studied the bruises and scratches. Between the purplish imprints of fingers on her throat, he saw the blood. Drops of blood, recently drawn, had hardened in their path toward her chest.

His stomach churned. He'd seen marks like that on a woman before. And she'd lived barely long enough to name one of her attackers. He'd never heard the other's name—until today. There was little doubt in his mind that the man who'd marked this lady so had also maimed and killed Edyth.

Rage, unbidden and nearly uncontrolled, boiled forth. To hold back his wrath he clenched his hands into fists at his side.

The Lady of Brezden had been left alive for a reason. What? If the man was not already dead, would he be back to finish what he'd started?

Earl William would not be pleased to lose something as precious as an heiress. Gerard had to do something to protect this woman from the same type of death Edyth had faced. Even if she refused his help.

Lightly touching her cheek, he promised, "He will pay for this."

The lady jerked her head away. In a trembling voice, she asked, "*Will* pay?"

The pleading gaze she then turned upon him almost made Gerard's heart cease beating.

"But you saw to his death, did you not?"

He was momentarily taken aback by the hopefulness in her tone. Had hers been the piercing gaze he'd felt just before he'd attacked Brezden? Had her fate, here in this chamber, been worse than the threat of death he and his men offered?

As much as he wanted to tell her that her tormentor had been dispatched to his maker, Gerard could not lie. "No."

Other than a startled gasp, silence filled the room.

"Milady, it is obvious who ever did this deserves to pay for his crimes against you. I am more than willing to find the knave."

A cold, bitter look of resignation replaced the hope on her face. He watched as tears welled in her eyes before she turned her head away. "Nay. If he is not already dead, then the dream was a lie."

Dream? Of what was she speaking? Gerard ran a hand through his hair before asking, "Can you not see that I am willing to try to help you?"

Catheryn resisted the need to laugh. *He offered help?* She rose from the bed, dragging the cover with her. Her movements were stiff. It took all of her rapidly draining control not to flinch with each step. "Help me? How? For what reason? So that I and Brezden may fill the king's coffers with sorely needed gold?"

The yarrow's promise had been naught but a lie. She knew that now King Stephen would sell her to the highest bidder without second thought. All knew how badly he'd drained his treasury for his unending war with Empress Matilda.

As far as Catheryn was concerned it didn't matter who

sat on the throne. Stephen with his meek, undecided niceness or Matilda with her cold, hateful disposition against anything English or Norman. One would be as bad as the other.

Suddenly, the quiet caught her attention. The storm had passed. Yet hardly any sounds came from inside the keep, or through the window from the courtyard below. No shouts from the men-at-arms or grumbles from the servants broke the eerie quiet.

Surely by now some sort of activity would have resumed in the keep.

The sick feeling of dread oozed into her limbs. A slight breeze blew the skin covering slightly away from the window opening. The acrid scent of smoke, burnt wood and straw drifted into the chamber.

Catheryn felt the blood drain from her face. She clutched her stomach tightly with one arm and bolted toward the window. Before pulling back the stretched hide that covered the opening, she whispered, "Dear Lord, be merciful."

The pre-dawn sky provided enough light for her to clearly see the destruction below. Tears ran unchecked down her face as her gaze briefly rested on each dead, or dying, body that came within her view.

Among the bodies of armed guards, were those of servants or freemen that had been foolish enough to get in the way of a swinging ax or sword. They should have followed her orders. They should have hidden themselves away. But she knew they had only done their best to protect their homes, to protect their families, to protect Brezden and its undeserving lady.

Catheryn saw that beyond the curtain wall the outer bailey had not fared any better. Huts, storage sheds, a stable and sections of the wall were completely destroyed by fire. The thatched roofs of a few cottages were damaged beyond repair.

Women and children knelt alongside the lifeless bodies of husbands, fathers, or sons. Livestock that had been frightened by the force that swept through their pens and stables were either wandering aimlessly, or lying dead in the trampled, bloody dirt.

Part of the nightmare had come true. And she'd not been there to stop it from playing out against innocent people. Catheryn did not attempt to hide from the misery that sought her.

She had only wanted to dream of her true love, hoping to dream of a fine, happy future. She'd trusted in the ancient lore of the yarrow and she'd ignored the teachings of the church. While she'd longed for a bit of peace, a bit of love, her people had faced terror and death. The shame and guilt she bore would never compensate for what the others lost this night.

Her feet carried her back across the room without conscious thought. Catheryn beat on the black covered chest with her fists. "What have you done?"

"Lady, I did nothing but my duty."

"Duty!" Catheryn pointed at the window. "It was your duty to destroy innocent people?"

She looped her fingers into one of the ties holding the arm of his hauberk together, then she pulled the unresisting man to the window.

"You have killed animals we needed for food. How will I feed those dependent upon me? Where will I lodge those without a home? The vegetable and herb gardens have been trampled." Catheryn stuck her arm out the window and pointed at a woman lying prostrate over the body of a loved one. "How do I offer to replace what she has lost?"

He stood silent during her tirade. Hands braced on either side of the window the man looked out over the courtyard and bailey. "Buildings will be rebuilt. Livestock can be purchased. It is just the beginning of spring; gardens can be replanted." He glanced at the floor. "All people die."

Catheryn lost all reason at the lack of concern in his simple answer. She swung her open hand toward his face.

Gerard caught her arm before the palm made contact with his flesh. He pinned her arms to her sides and leaned her against the wall. "No harm was done to this keep that cannot be fixed. I am sorry for any who died without reason, but I can do nothing for them."

Why was he explaining anything to her? She was lodged in the enemy's keep. He owed her nothing.

The lady's flushed face and full lips beckoned for more than just explanations. He felt a sudden, intense urge to gather her into his arms and promise that all would be well. His hands itched to stroke her hair and beg her not to worry.

"This is insanity!" He lifted her in his arms, carried her across the room and placed her on the bed. "Stay there."

Gerard walked to the chamber's doorway and shouted for his captain before grabbing a gown off the floor and taking it to her.

Guilt assailed him when he caught sight of her trembling lips and misty eyes. She'd brought this on herself.

Wearily handing her the gown, he gently ordered, "Put this on."

"Sir? Milord?"

Gerard turned from the bed and motioned Walter into the chamber. "I want all of the lady's things moved into the lord's chamber. Now."

He ignored her outraged gasp. Her injuries made it obvious that this chamber was not safe. Whether she wanted his help and protection or not, she was going to get it. "Get a few of Brezden's servants to help you."

Walter scratched his head. "A few? That is all we can find, and those are old men, women or children."

That made little sense. His spies had reported numerous servants and men at Brezden. He'd find a way to protect

Brezden's lady without moving her, but how had his spies been so wrong? Gerard swung back to face the lady. Her eyes were closed and her lips moved in what appeared to be a silent prayer.

He waited until Walter quit the chamber before returning to the bed.

"You had better be praying for divine intervention, milady. For I am bone weary of sparring with you." He knelt on the bed and grasped her shoulders, only to release her when she winced. "Damn you, look at me."

Had she not been so bruised and battered he would have shaken the glare off her face. Shame filled him at the thought. She'd had enough torment; he needn't add more.

Where had all of the keep's men gone? Why had they not been present to protect their lady? If not from the evil lodged within, then why not from the evil that threatened to take their keep?

He tipped his head to one side and looked at her through narrowed eyes. "You hid Brezden's men."

She didn't answer, but her gaze skittered away.

"Somehow you knew we were coming."

She bit the unswollen side of her bottom lip.

He didn't really expect an answer; nevertheless he had to ask. "How did you know Brezden was going to be attacked?"

A steady, unflinching gaze met his. One side of her mouth curved into a sad half-smile. Gerard had to lean closer to hear her odd, whispered reply. "Because I called you here. You had no choice but to answer the yarrow's call."

CHAPTER THREE

"I had no other choice?" He smirked and crossed his arms before him. "Do I look clay-brained to you? No one has ever thought me half-witted until now."

Catheryn couldn't stop her wandering gaze. The last thing she would expect from someone as well-formed as he would be half a wit. She had to admit that she'd expected her dream love to possess above average looks and strength, but she'd never expected the yarrow to call forth one so—she forced her wayward mind to cease its ramblings.

What difference did his appearance make? Had she suddenly lost the ability to reason?

She reached beneath her pillow and tossed the yarrow sachet to the floor at his feet. "This is what called you to Brezden."

Gerard retrieved the herb-filled bag from the floor and shook his head. When his sister was young she'd kept charms close to her person also—but that was years ago. "Are you not a little old to still believe in childhood tales?"

"Tales?" Her eyes narrowed. "You are here, are you not?"

"Coincidence and nothing more."

"I think not."

"Dreams and wishes are for little girls."

She shook her head and stated, "You are only half right. Wishes are for children. But dreams, with enough faith, come true."

"Lady," he paused a moment to swallow his impatience, "is there something else I might call you?"

"Nay, lady is just fine."

Gerard raised his hands in mock surrender. "I have tarried overlong in your chamber. There is work to be done below." He ignored her frown. "Get dressed. The sooner the dead are identified and buried, the sooner your people will be able to move on."

"Move on? 'Tis that simple, is it? Cover them with dirt, turn around and continue on." Her soft laugh grated on his nerves.

"There is nothing else anyone can do. I cannot bring them back." He took the gown from her hands and pulled it down over her head. "Would you rather have Baron Pike attending to them?"

Gerard regretted the words the moment they left his lips. She jerked away from him and finished dressing. "Leave me be."

"As much as that would please me, I cannot leave you be. Your presence is required in the hall."

"Oh, aye. To identify the dead."

"Yes."

A looked of pained defeat filled her eyes. "There is only one dead body I wish to view. And you have already said Sir Raymond de Brye is not dead."

For reasons he could not name, he wanted to give her hope. More than anything else, he wanted to take away the hunted look from her face. "By my hand, no. But who is to say he did not fall by another man's sword?"

Sadly, the lady stared down at her entwined fingers. "No. In the dream—"

"Cease!" His shout effectively stopped the rest of her explanation. "This is no dream, no flight of fancy. This is real." Gerard took one of her hands in his own and placed it over his heart. "I am flesh and blood. I am no one's dream."

Catheryn felt his heart beat beneath her palm. It drummed a constant tattoo. Strong. Steady. Reassuring. She lifted her head and gazed into his eyes.

The pulse tapping against her hand faltered, then jumped back to life.

A confused, almost questioning expression marred his forehead for a brief instant before he pulled away from her touch.

He nodded toward the corridor and said, "Come, enough time has been wasted."

~*~

Catheryn stared at the chaos before her. A little more than half of the keep's serfs and freemen were gathered in the shambled remains of Brezden's hall. Women clutched their children protectively close. Men, too old to be of any danger, stood at the front of the group wringing their hands and muttering softly to themselves.

The others—the older boys and the guards loyal to Catheryn hadn't been found. She kept her smile of triumph to herself. It'd been a difficult task to order them to seek safety. But at last they'd heeded her threats and now they were alive, hiding somewhere along the banks.

When the time was right, Catheryn would call them back. Until then, she could do little but pray for their well-being.

"Milady?"

Her captor's prompting drew her away from her worries. He'd ordered her down here to request the people's cooperation with their new master.

The thought galled her. The previous Lady of Brezden had done the same thing when Pike had arrived to oversee the keep. Lady Margaret had spoken her piece as if the words were being torn from her lips. Too naive then to understand her mother's hesitancy, Catheryn fully understood it now.

Would history repeat itself? Would she, as her mother had done, hand her people's safety, their very lives, over to an unjust, cruel master? Could she do that?

A gentle nudge at her shoulder provided the answer. Her

choices were slim. In truth…there was no choice.

Catheryn swallowed the bile stuck in her dry throat, before slowly looked from one frightened face to the next. Her breaking heart shuddered with the task before her.

She sought the dearest face in the room. The sight of Agnes's pale gray gaze brought a sigh of pent-up relief to Catheryn's being. The woman who had been her nursemaid since birth, and who had filled the empty void left by Lady Margaret's murder, appeared unharmed.

Not taking her attention from the softly wrinkled face of her maid, Catheryn sought words to ease her people's fears.

She stepped closer to the gathering and motioned them nearer also. She touched first one familiar face, then another, reassuring herself, and them, that for this moment all was well.

"Hush, cry no more." She brushed the tears from old Ephram's cheeks and felt her own begin to well at his stuttering attempt to apologize for not doing his share of the fighting.

"How old?"

Catheryn nearly jumped out of her skin. She knew who the owner of that deep whisper was, but she'd not realized he'd been so close behind her the whole time. She turned her head. In hopes of shielding her answer, she whispered back, "He has seen over sixty summers."

Her captor's gasp of surprise amazed her. But when he stepped around her and placed his hand on Ephram's trembling shoulder, Catheryn wondered if she would swoon from the shock.

"Sir Ephram, you have protected your lady many times over, I am sure." His words seemed almost kind. "She cannot fault you for this one lapse."

She felt his stare upon her and followed his lead. "No. Of course not. Never." She took the old man's cold, bony hand between her own. "Oh, Ephram, you know how I value your opinion, your wisdom. How I have always appreciated your loyalty. Surely you can't think I'd doubt you now?"

Catheryn's gaze swept the entire assembly. "I value all of you, for you are dear to me as family." She directed her stare at the new protector of Brezden Keep. It provided her the time needed to seek courage before continuing. "The fighting is over. We must all work together to rebuild our home, and our lives. I am certain you will join me in securing the continued good blessing of Brezden's new commander?"

No one muttered. No one discounted her words. But every gaze fell on her for a moment before moving on to the man she'd just declared their new overlord.

Gerard refused to flinch under their scrutiny. He was well pleased with the lady's compliance and waited only to see if her people believed her words. He sincerely hoped, for their sake, they would follow her lead.

It didn't take too long before Sir Ephram sought to kneel before him and, as that ancient man stumbled about to find a steady position, the others followed suit.

Sir Ephram's action was understandable. After all, one could tell by the lady's words to the old man that he'd at one time served as a guard or a trusted advisor. So he would know that one knelt to swear loyalty. But the others were mere servants. Yet these people knelt in a manner that decried their position.

Confusion knitted his brows as he looked at Brezden's Lady. Then he understood the reaction of her people. She had also dropped to one knee and was still motioning a few of the now giggling children to do likewise.

While assisting Ephram to his feet, Gerard thanked the others for their show of faith. Then he turned and held out his hand. "Milady?"

As she came slowly to her feet, her eyes widened and her face paled. Gerard followed the line of her shocked stare and cursed himself.

Baron Pike's body lay in the middle of the hall. He vaguely remembered ordering his men to deposit the corpse where all could see.

After finding the nearest man, he shouted, "Get that traitor's body out of this hall!"

He felt a small jerk of guilt tighten in his chest. Compelled to defend himself, Gerard began to explain. "Lady, that was Pike's choice. He—"

But she cut him off with a wave of one hand. "I care not about Pike. The devil may take him with my blessing."

She grasped his arms, each word softer than the one before, she begged, "Please, please, I must know. Where are the rest?"

Gerard motioned for Walter to join them before he gently grasped the lady's elbow and led her toward the door.

What if this Sir de Brye was dead? What if he wasn't? Either way, he wondered about her reaction.

He stopped abruptly. When he turned to call for the lady's maid, Gerard bumped into a servant who had been following too close.

The older woman caught her balance and glared up at him. "Where are you taking Lady Catheryn?"

Gerard ignored the wench. He glanced around the hall and shouted, "Where is her maid?"

He looked down at the old woman plucking on his sleeve. "I am Catheryn's woman." She put her hands on her hips and repeated her question. "Where are you taking Lady Catheryn? If you harm one hair on her head, you will answer to me." Almost as an after thought, she added, "Milord."

If her insolent manner wasn't bad enough, her whining voice set his teeth on edge. With a low growl Gerard looked down at the other woman standing by his side. "Well, Lady Catheryn, shall we?"

She straightened her back, then nodded.

With Walter's assistance, Gerard led the two women out into the bailey. Picking their way carefully between the bodies of men and animals, he slowly led them from one end of the yard to the other.

Catheryn knew that if she had to look at one more face frozen in the agony of death, she would go mad. But she also knew that until she gazed upon the hardened features of her hated enemy, she would keep looking.

Some of the men who had died were no more than boys. Boys whose souls had already been tainted by Pike and de Brye's evil. She silently pleaded with God to forgive them their sins and to accept them with His loving grace. She could do no more.

No more than wonder how this vile exercise affected the man who had wrought this destruction.

Catheryn stopped beside the body of young Daniel, an orphan the baron had forced into his service. She knelt down and brushed a lock of hair from his stiff face.

"He was but eleven, milord."

"Then he had no business playing a man's game."

Catheryn stifled the threatening tears. She'd be damned if she'd allow this war-hardened beast to know how badly this duty hurt her.

She took a deep breath before gazing up at him. "Think you he had a choice?"

Not only did he not answer, he wouldn't even look down at her.

"He was but a babe with no home, no mother, no food except for the scraps Pike tossed to his servants each evening."

Catheryn detested the break in her voice. She turned her attention back to the body of the boy and continued, "He barely had a life, let alone a choice."

She was unprepared for the hands that grabbed the front

of her gown and hauled her to her feet. She was less prepared for the hard, angry visage before her, or for the harsh words that seemed torn from his clenched jaw.

"A life? What care had Pike or his henchmen for life when they tortured, raped and killed other innocent victims?"

As if suddenly burned, he released her. "You dare speak to me of life, or of death. What do you know of either?"

A look of agony briefly washed over his features before he stepped away. Filled with a sudden need to offer a measure of comfort, Catheryn reached out toward him.

He held up one hand before him as if to ward her away. She winced at the harsh rasp of his voice. "No. Do not."

It was as if living stopped. And for the space of a lifetime she could do nothing but stare at the constantly changing man before her. His emotions flitted from anger, to hatred, to pain in the space of a mere heartbeat.

What had caused one so seemingly strong to behave in such a manner? Catheryn knew only what the dreams had shown her, and nothing of his past.

He seemed as changeable as the wind; Catheryn sensed he'd also be as dangerous.

She took a long, soft breath and sought to control the hard, rapid beating of her heart. The strong, acrid scent of smoke assailed her senses. But another breath carried the cleansing smell of a spring rain. Not another storm resembling God's wrath, but a gentle, steady rain.

She tipped her head back and stared up at the gathering clouds. A good downpour would help to wash away some of the terrors wrought on Brezden this day. She looked again to the man before her.

The gaze he turned on her had lost its anger-filled look. In its place was a look of complacency that she was certain was forced.

"Have you seen enough?" His voice sounded nearly as

flat and unemotional as his expression.

Catheryn nodded. "Aye. Yes, I have."

After motioning toward the keep, he opened his mouth. "Then why—"

A shriek cut off his words.

Her heart jumped at the sound. Catheryn and the others rushed toward the source of the scream.

A wooden pike had been purposely stuck in the ground near the postern gate. Catheryn felt the dirt beneath her feet shift and sway as her gaze rested on the severed head perched atop the gruesome pole.

"Oh, God, no. No."

Someone else screamed. Catheryn covered her ears to drown out the sound. But they wouldn't stop. Over and over the scream blasted in her ears.

She closed her eyes, but she still saw the remains of Martin, her most trusted archer. Nothing would ever wipe that sight from her mind.

Why couldn't someone stop the screaming?

"Catheryn! Catheryn, stop."

She heard a loud curse before strong arms closed tightly around her. "Lady Catheryn, hush."

She twisted and turned, trying to break free of the flesh and blood prison that held her. But her struggles were of no avail.

As if through a tunnel, she heard her name called once more, before a solid object made contact with her chin.

Within a heartbeat the screams ceased and Catheryn felt a dark, cold fog settle over her.

Chapter Four

Red-hued rays from the setting sun cast a pale glow across the room. Catheryn watched the shadows lengthen and overtake the pink evening light.

Subdued sounds from the bailey drifted up and through the window. While the noise was not at its usual boisterous level, its mere existence let her know that life in the keep continued. Brezden would never allow shadows to suppress its vigor.

Catheryn pressed unsteady hands against her throbbing temples. *Why was she abed at this time of day?* Thoughts swirled wildly back and forth. The effort to sort them out proved too much. As soon as one image appeared in her mind another one rushed to take its place. One more gruesome than the next.

She knew the keep had been taken. That much she remembered clearly. There had been screams—and blood. Whose? She also had some vague memory of Agnes coercing her to drink a foul tasting wine. Why?

Certain she'd not find the answers in bed, Catheryn tried to get up. Each time she struggled to rise, the room swam before her.

"My lady? You are awake."

Catheryn watched her maid approach. The woman's brisk movements nauseated her. "Agnes, please walk slower." Her mouth would not form the words correctly. She sounded more like a sodden soldier than the lady of the keep. "I feel like a boat being tossed about on a stormy sea."

"Do not fret, child, the dizziness will pass."

A blur of chestnut hair appeared before her. Catheryn willed herself to focus on Agnes's ready smile. She groaned, then asked, "When?"

"You have consumed a large quantity of spiced wine. Maybe in one more night you will feel more like yourself." Agnes pulled back the covers, permitting the cool air to rush across Catheryn's skin, and insisted, "But right now you should move about some. Come below and eat."

Catheryn shivered, then she scraped her teeth across her tongue. During her sleep fur had found its way into her mouth. She hoped the scraping would remove the irritation. "Spiced wine? Agnes, I do not know what you used as the spice, but I would prefer…"

She paused as her slower concentration caught up with her mind. Squinting to better see the other woman, Catheryn asked, "One *more* night? How long have I been in this bed?"

Agnes's smile faded. Her mumbled response was lost as she walked to the other side of the room and pulled gowns out of the wooden chest standing against the wall.

Catheryn sat up in the bed, only to fall back down onto its secure softness when the room spun with the swiftness of a child's wooden top.

"Agnes!"

Immediately, the maid came back to the bedside. She took Catheryn's hand. "My lady, you were distraught. After the episode with Martin," the maid's voice caught, but she regained her composure, "you spoke nonsense about finding and killing de Brye yourself. How would you do that? Where would you start? Who would help you?"

Martin. All of the memories that had swirled before now took form. Catheryn closed her eyes against the images in her mind. But it did not help. What de Brye had done to her archer was unforgivable. He would pay. Raymond de Brye would suffer the agonies of hell one day soon.

She pried her hand from the maid's grasp and pressed it back to her temples. "You know I never would have acted upon those words." Looking at the downcast face of the woman next to her, Catheryn asked again, "How long have I been abed?"

"You have slept through two sunrises." The maid added, "I did not know the drink would have this effect on you. Catheryn, child, you know I would not have intentionally harmed you."

She smiled weakly and wondered what good it would do to upset Agnes any more. After what had taken place at Brezden, none of them needed any further distress. She touched the woman's arm. "The last few days have been unsettling to all of us. Just promise you will give me no more of your witch's brew." Catheryn's heart lurched. "It was *your* brew, wasn't it?"

Agnes's laugh filled the chamber. "Oh, yes, milady. I did not obtain any concoction from Mistress Margaret."

"That is a relief to hear. But, no more of the drink, Agnes."

"Nay, Lady Catheryn. His lordship has already bid me to withhold it from you. He has been most worried, not to mention angry with me."

"His lordship?" Catheryn frowned, trying to pinpoint who her maid called his lordship. "Which lord?"

"Lord Gerard."

Her frown deepened. "Gerard?"

"My lady, you do remember that Brezden was—that Lord Pike is no longer the master here?"

"I am dizzy, Agnes, not addled."

"Then how can you not remember Lord Gerard?"

To regain what little patience she had at the moment, Catheryn took a deep, steadying breath. "Are you telling me that the tall, dark man's name is Gerard?"

"Aye. How did you not know that?"

She was beginning to think that patience required more strength than any amount of physical labor. "Simple. We were never introduced."

"But you were alone in this chamber…"

Catheryn sprang upright and fought to ignore the spinning room. "What are you saying?"

Agnes waved her hands in the air, as if trying to wipe away any misconstrued words. "Nothing, milady. I would only have assumed that if you saw a strange man in your chamber you might have asked him his name."

Indignant, Catheryn kept her sarcasm in check. "Oh, and you would probably also assume that if I asked this stranger his name, he would tell me? It would require manners and breeding to extend that much courtesy."

The maid glanced nervously at the door. "Lady Catheryn, you should not speak badly about Count Reveur. He has treated your people well."

Catheryn's shout of laughter sent a blinding stab of pain through her head. "Reveur? Surely you jest?"

Agnes's expression of confusion almost forced another unwelcome burst of laughter from Catheryn's lips. She felt around under her pillow, pulled out the nearly forgotten yarrow bag and handed it to her maid. "What is this?"

The woman shrugged. "'Tis a dream charm."

"Yes and instead of a dream it brought my nightmare to life." Unwilling to continue in this manner, she explained, "Agnes, *reveur* means *dreamer*. Do you not see the humor in that?"

Agnes's eyes widened before narrowing into an unforgiving squint. Firmly planting her hands on her hips, she scolded, "You should find no humor in the connection. 'Tis an omen to heed."

The maid's haughty position made Catheryn nervous. When Agnes took that stance, she was prepared for a siege of any magnitude.

"I tell you, Lady Catheryn, he has brought good to our people. Count Reveur has helped to rebuild the damage done here. Why he has even been in this chamber on a regular basis, to see how you fared."

Holy Mother of God! Catheryn silently asked forgiveness for the blasphemy, and then thought the curse again. Somehow the demon lord had won a champion in *her* maid. She felt as if someone had knocked the wind out of her. This just would not do.

Shock changed to outrage. "How dare you defend that…that murdering thief to me! How dare you allow him into my chamber? What has come over you to act like this?"

Agnes was adamant. "He did what any knight would do. He followed his lord's orders. You cannot fault him for that."

The woman was completely under this devil's spell. "His lord's orders may very well have cost us our keep. Agnes, what are you thinking?"

"I am thinking that this may not be such a terrible thing." She shook her finger under Catheryn's nose. "Even you must admit that Baron Pike's demise is not a bad thing. Catheryn, I tell you true. Count Gerard has more than made amends for his deeds. Already he has shown more concern for Brezden than Pike ever did."

"True, Pike may be dead and can harm me no further, but de Brye still lives and he is the worse threat." Catheryn's stomach rebelled at this exchange. The hammering in her head threatened to overwhelm her. "Agnes, I can argue with you no longer this day. You will never convince me that this man cares for anyone here at Brezden."

The maid relented enough to rub Catheryn's forehead. "I am sorry, milady. I know how poorly you feel. But if you would allow it, I am certain Count Reveur could assist you in dealing with Sir de Brye."

Catheryn cringed at the mere mention of the man's name. "I refuse to discuss de Brye with anyone."

One way or another she would think of a plan to take care of that man herself.

"Child, you are in no condition to discuss anything rationally at this moment." Agnes held up a gown. "Come, get out of that bed and I will help you dress. They will be glad to see you up and about in the hall."

The simple act of sitting on the edge of the bed drained Catheryn of any small amount of strength she possessed. "Please, just have something brought up here."

She didn't feel up to the task of dressing, or descending the stairs. She did not want anyone's company. All she required was time alone. Some quiet moments to think and decide what to do next.

Agnes's stiff movements and furious arm gestures made her agitation apparent as she headed for the door. "He is going to be quite angry if he finds out you are awake and refuse to come below." After pausing to turn and frown at Catheryn, the maid's expression softened. "But, I suppose I could make an excuse and bring you something to eat."

Catheryn wanted to scream. What difference did it make if *he* was angry or not? Instead, she nodded. "Thank you."

After her maid left, Catheryn grabbed a cover from the bed, wrapped it around her and moved to a bench by the fire.

What was she to do about this tender attachment Agnes had already formed for the new holder of this keep? She supposed that, as far as her maid was concerned, this Count Reveur was better than Pike.

Catheryn rested her elbows on her knees and leaned her chin into her hands. The woman simply would not admit that a goat would be a better master than Pike.

The heat from the fire felt good on her face; but the warmth would soon lull her back to sleep. She rose; holding the blanket securely, she began to pace the room. The cover softly swept the floor, leaving a trail in the rushes behind her.

Catheryn glanced out the window. She was pleased to

see that some of the repairs had been started on Brezden. Not only would that help to refortify the keep, but the people would be too busy to worry about anything else.

She walked back across the room. What was going to happen to her? "If they considered Pike a traitor, what do they consider his ward?" Catheryn sighed as she turned to cross back to the window. "I am nothing but a woman. They consider me not at all."

"You are mistaken. They consider you quite often."

Catheryn jumped when the deep voice answered her. She looked over her shoulder to see the speaker and gasped when she saw it was Gerard. "What are you doing in here?"

She'd been so lost in thought that she hadn't heard the door open. While twisting around to face him, her cover caught on the bottom corner of a chest.

Gerard enjoyed her struggle. Her fight to free her blanket provided him a glimpse of a long, shapely leg. The sight provided a welcome change for someone accustomed to seeing men dressed in armor.

Her creamy, unblemished skin was a feast to his eyes. By the time his intense perusal had roamed up the trim ankle, shapely calve and slender thigh, his own body screamed that he do more than just view the feast.

Gerard gritted his teeth at the uncomfortable demands of his body. He was not a saint. His will was not immune to penetration.

After clearing his throat, he said, "I only came to see if your maid was correct in her belief that you were too ill to leave this chamber yet."

She caught the line of his attention and gasped. He wanted to laugh at the shocked expression on her face when she realized he was looking at her legs. Finally freeing the cover, she jerked it tighter about her body. "I demand you leave my chamber immediately!"

Orders from her? Gerard stood in front of the window

opening and pretended to survey the sights outside. "Do you not think you have left your people unsupervised long enough?"

"Are you going to stand there and tell me that you have not taken care of everything?"

True, he had seen to all within his power, but he was not the lord here. These were not his people. "It isn't quite the same. They need to see you. After all, are you not their lady?" Turning to look at her, he asked, "Are you not the one responsible for them and their welfare?"

Her voice rose slightly. "Do not dare to tell me of my responsibilities. I know them well. You are the one who killed their kin and destroyed their homes."

Gerard crossed the room and grabbed her hands. "I killed no one but the traitor and his men. I destroyed nothing of value and that includes hardworking peasants or serfs. I am not the one who has left them to their own devices for the last two days."

She tried unsuccessfully to break free of his grasp. Angry eyes flashed up at him. "Get your hands off me! Leave me alone!"

"You have been left alone long enough." Dragging her behind him, Gerard walked toward an open clothing chest.

He stopped abruptly and pulled her to him. Catheryn's expression wavered from anger to fear and back to anger. She struggled to free her wrists from his hold. She stamped her foot and yelled, "Filthy monster, get out of here. Agnes!"

He'd thought about this woman night and day since he'd taken this keep. She'd not be free of him that easily. "Your maid has orders not to enter this room under any circumstances. My man guards the stairs to ensure those orders are carried out." He stared with appreciation at the fury he held. He released her wrists, wrapped one arm about her and grasped her chin with his other hand.

Catheryn tried to push him away. Gerard marveled at the fighting spirit of this woman. Even if her arms had not been securely pinned between their bodies, she had not the strength to force him away.

Holding her in his arms made his entire being spring to life. As he stared into a pair of aqua eyes, Gerard felt drawn into their dangerous depths. He could feel his blood run tempestuously through his veins. His mind heard her cry out to be tasted. A kiss. Just a kiss.

The need to answer that cry was urgent. "Spitfire, do you not realize your danger?" As his lips claimed hers, Gerard felt Catheryn stiffen for an instant before she relaxed against him and returned his kiss.

Flames singed his lips. He jerked back from the fire. Gerard watched desire, humiliation and anger flicker across her face and wondered which he preferred more. He frowned at his own rising passion, released her and sharply ordered, "Get dressed; and if you are not quick about it, I will return to see that it is done."

He stared at her. There was no chance she could mistake the hungry look he raked over her body. Gerard stamped out, slammed the door of the chamber, leaned against the wall outside and lifted a shaky hand to his brow. He had come up here intentionally to goad her into throwing a fit of temper. He'd hoped the rise in emotion would help to dispel any lingering effects of the wine she'd been given.

So, why was he the one whose emotions now ran wild? It made no sense. He knew he possessed more control than he showed around this woman. How many times in the last two days had he caught himself worrying when she would not wake up?

This odd concern for her plagued him. Gerard knew it would be unwise to care about someone who could prove to be as traitorous as Pike, or de Brye. His hand froze in midair when he heard her screech.

"Oh! Of all the arrogant, rude, insufferable filthy monsters!"

Monster? She thought him a monster? This lady had no idea what a true monster was. Gerard flung the door open so violently that it bounced against her chamber wall. He closed the distance between them in three long strides and stopped Catheryn's hasty retreat. "That is not the first time you have called me a monster. But it will be the last."

She stared up at him. When she opened her mouth, he glared down at her, daring her to speak. He drew her tightly against his chest and asked, "What do you think a filthy monster would do with you now?" He laughed at her fear-widened eyes. "Aye, Lady Catheryn, you would do well to remember your place."

Certain now that she understood the unspoken threat, Gerard released her and left the chamber.

He shook his head when he heard a solid object bounce off the closed door. If nothing else, she had spit and fire. In a way, he was heartened to know that her spirit had not been beaten by Pike or de Brye. Nor had it been diminished by what he had wrought upon her keep.

Mindless of the broken objects lying about, Catheryn raced across the floor.

"Dreams? Bah."

She grabbed the yarrow sachet and tossed it into the lit brazier.

"True love?"

Tiny sparks flew from the hot coals.

"Ha!"

She watched as a corner of the bag caught fire. "Mistress Margaret can keep her spells." Smoke rose from the smoldering herbs.

"Help? I ask for help and love and this is what I receive? What sort of help is he?"

An image of Gerard's smirk flitted before her. "I'd get

more help from a pig."

Catheryn turned away from the brazier. "A dog could provide more love than anything I might expect from that demon."

Her lips tingled remembering his kiss.

"Blast!"

Catheryn spun around and snatched the bag from its ultimate destruction. She cursed again, then smacked the sachet against the stone wall. Clumps of scorched yarrow fell to the floor.

Once certain the bag would burn no more, she tucked it back amongst the bed clothes. "What am I going to do?" There had to be a way to turn all that had happened to some advantage for Brezden and her.

Agnes had been correct. Pike was gone and no one could ever be as wicked or uncaring as he had been. *No one—except Raymond de Brye.*

Remembering his lordship's orders and his threat to come back up and help, Catheryn dressed. All the while her mind raced; de Brye. Before she could determine what to do about Count Reveur, she needed to find and deal with de Brye.

"Where are you hiding, de Brye?"

"I do not hide. I am right here." The answer to her question shot from across her chamber.

Catheryn froze. Surely that voice was a residue of the herbs Agnes had given her?

"Sweeting, I had no idea you'd desire me this soon."

Her heart resumed beating with a heavy thud. The hairs on the back of her neck rose. Slowly, she turned to face the owner of that sickening, false honey-dripped voice. The sight that met her nearly became her undoing.

Sir de Brye stood in her alcove. But he wasn't alone. Before the vile cur stood one of her guards—with a knife to his throat. Rolfe stood no chance against de Brye. Not only did her man have a knife pressed against his throat, he had a gag in his mouth and was trussed like a hog being prepared for slaughter. A thick rope secured his arms and legs, making escape impossible.

Now she knew exactly how de Brye had avoided capture—by using the same tunnel she'd foolishly sent her own men through. Catheryn fought desperately not to cry out. Had she sent Brezden's faithful few to certain death?

Without thought she took a step toward the men. Raymond de Brye smiled wickedly. She stopped, realizing her mistake too late.

"No, milady. It would be wise to stay there and not to scream." de Brye twisted the blade against his victim's throat. A small trickle of blood ran down Rolfe's neck.

Catheryn swallowed hard and prayed that her voice would not give away her fear and anger. "What do you seek here? Brezden is lost."

"Lost? You give up far too easily. Brezden still stands." De Brye's smile widened to a maniacal grin. "And I live to fight yet again."

"Again?" She couldn't help pointing out the obvious. "Instead of defending this keep, you ran."

"Why should I fight an enemy face to face? I seek revenge and it is far easier to attack him from inside."

"You are but one man."

"Nay, sweeting, you are wrong. Not all of my men were within Brezden's walls."

She tried to remember how many bodies she had seen in the bailey. While there weren't dozens, surely the majority of Pike and de Brye's men had fallen. He could have no more than a few with him. "Unless you have an army at your command, I do not see how you hope to regain possession of Brezden."

His laugh filled the room with ice. "A small force. More than enough to guard your men and to do my bidding."

Razor sharp terror cut past her flesh and heart. With the precision of an attacking falcon it sought her soul. Before the talons could strike, Catheryn held the horror at bay by grasping onto one small thread of hope. While de Brye was evil incarnate, he was, at heart, a coward. A lying coward.

To bolster her tenuous hold on sanity, she challenged, "You will lead your force to attack Brezden?" Never had the man chosen anyone bigger or stronger than himself as a victim.

"Beloved, you misunderstand." He reverted to using the oily voice Catheryn had come to despise—and fear. "I said nothing about attacking the keep, or even of doing the deed myself."

"Then who? I can think of no one inside who would do your work for you."

De Brye's expression settled into a mask of pure evil. "You."

"Me?" A surprised gasp burst from her lips. "There is nothing in the world that could convince me to do anything for you."

"You are wrong."

Catheryn stared in shock and horror as de Brye ran his knife down Rolfe's arm. The metal easily cut through the thin fabric of his tunic. Blood gushed from the long wound that laid his flesh and muscle open.

But it was the look in Rolfe's eyes that she would never forget. Beneath the pain and the hatred, she saw a desperate plea for help. A plea she could in no way answer.

At least not now.

De Brye pointed the blood drenched knife in her direction. "I will not hesitate to maim and kill every one of your men, Catheryn." He motioned toward the opening behind him. "You will find them, one by one, there."

"But—"

He cut off her words with a flourish of the grisly weapon.

"And when I am finished with them, I will move on to those you think are safe here. Including your harpy of a nursemaid."

Catheryn's heart constricted with the thought of any harm befalling Agnes. She would be lost without her maid's support and he knew that.

De Brye slapped his weapon against his leg and frowned as if contemplating his next words. He then lifted one eyebrow and looked at her. "Before you decide to spend any more time alone with Count Reveur, you might want to consider one thing."

Her mind leapt. Raymond had left the keep before it was attacked. She hadn't spoken Gerard's name, so how did de Brye come to know who had captured Brezden?

"Ah, yes, sweeting, I see your mind working. I'll answer your questions for you. Count Reveur and I are old friends. I have a great debt to repay him. You see, we've shared a few things in this life. So you might want to keep that in mind when you decide to keep his company." His voice lowered and with a raspy near-growl, he added, "I'll not share you."

They were friends? Acquaintances? He owed Reveur a debt? Had she traded one hell for another? Catheryn didn't know what to believe. De Brye was a cheat, a coward and a liar. He thought nothing of bending the truth to suit his needs.

But what did she know of Gerard?

Her attention was diverted when de Brye backed toward the tunnel entrance, dragging a near unconscious Rolfe with him.

"You will tell no one of this visit. Do not think for a heartbeat, Catheryn, that I do not have people already inside these walls. Gold and pain talk loudly when either is offered in the correct manner." He paused to place the knife back against the other man's throat. Looking at her intently, he added, "Soon I will return and you will do as you are told."

Catheryn remained still until the well-oiled hidden panel slid almost silently back into place. Once she heard the latch on the other side click softly, she stumbled to a bench.

Her limbs shook—from anger and fear. De Brye did not make idle threats.

Hopelessness, strong and foreboding washed over her. Its intensity took her breath away. Who could help her? She'd foolishly sent her men into de Brye's arms. What was she to do? She forced air between her clenched teeth, willing herself not to cry. Not to give up.

Somehow, some way she'd defeat de Brye—or she'd die trying. The thought of her death bothered a little, but she knew others would suffer too. That knowledge rested heavily on her soul.

Outside a man laughed. A loud, strong laugh. The sound floated up, through her window and brushed against her ears. The noise beckoned her to the opening and on still shaking legs she followed.

Catheryn leaned against the wall for support and gazed down into the courtyard. So, he could laugh. He could joke with the other men. He was the man she'd been sent in the dream. How could the dream have been so wrong? How could she have placed her people and herself at peril by blindly accepting what she'd seen in a vision of the night?

As if sensing her presence, he looked up. When he caught sight of her, his smile disappeared. In its place was an expression she could not decipher. While he did not appear angry, she did not doubt that emotion lay too far beneath the surface.

Catheryn's straightened her shoulders and held his stare until he nodded toward the keep. She stepped away from the window. It was time. Time to join him in the hall. Time to discover his reason for being here at Brezden.

And it was time to take control of her own destiny and that of her people. Time to stop trusting in childish dreams.

CHAPTER FIVE

"And then the harlot…"

Gerard ignored the jesting of the men. He didn't care what the harlot said to the king, or what the king did about it. Nor at this moment did he care about the men gathered around him. His attention was focused on the woman who'd just turned away from the chamber's window.

"Milord! Count Reveur!"

It was all Gerard could do to tear his gaze away from where Catheryn had stood. Even though he couldn't see her face from this distance, he knew something was wrong. He felt it somehow.

Maybe by her curt nod of acknowledgment when he'd first spotted her in the window, or maybe by the rigid way she'd held herself. He couldn't place his finger on it, but he knew. And the simple knowing she was upset bothered him more than words could describe.

"Count Reveur?"

"What?" Impatient to meet Catheryn in the hall, Gerard glared at his pestering squire.

The men in the small gathering ceased talking and backed slightly away from him. It amused him that these grown men could be intimidated with just a look, yet the lad did not flinch or cower before his scowl. Gerard recognized his squire's air of excitement and bid him to continue.

"Milord, Earl William approaches."

His curiosity over Catheryn's apparent mood evaporated. "Of all the snook-backed luck." He headed for the main gate. "What in the name of God brings William here so swiftly?"

He'd fully expected the earl to arrive. After all, Gerard had taken on this mission in William's name. Brezden did owe fealty to the Earl of York. But he hadn't expected William to leave the comforts of his own castle quite this suddenly.

"Were there any front riders? Any messengers?" He asked the breathless squire following behind him.

"Nay, milord."

Gerard stopped, turned and stared at the lad. "Then how can you be certain 'tis William?"

Unbelievably, the squire's already red face darkened further. He shuffled his feet in the dirt. "Well, um, milord..." The lad paused and looked up at the sky. "The, um, he is, um..." Stopping to take a deep breath, the flustered boy then finished in a rush. "There is no mistaking, milord. It is, with a doubt, Earl William. No one else could be as—"

Gerard cut him off with a laugh. "Enough." He didn't need the boy to tell him that no one else could possibly be as big as William. Big not in height, but in width. William had earned the nickname 'le Gros' for more than one reason.

While mounting the ladder to the wall, Gerard realized the squire wasn't the least bit mistaken. William was one of the few who traveled with over fifty men on horseback and just as many on foot. And if the line of wagons trailing behind the coming visitors was any indication, they were planning to stay more than a few days.

He wondered how the people of Brezden would react to this sudden arrival. And he prayed they would be up to the rather daunting task.

After motioning the men on the walls to lower the drawbridge and raise the portcullis, he descended to the bailey.

When Earl William entered the yard, Gerard realized his earlier fears were needless. Brezden's men paused at their work, doffed their caps and bowed. The women and children scrambled for a glimpse of their overlord.

Gerard simply stood with his arms crossed before him and shook his head as William dismounted. Now it took two men to assist the earl in that task and Gerard couldn't help but wonder how long it would be before William was unable to ride a horse; let alone mount and dismount.

William turned and glared at Gerard.

"This is how you welcome your overlord to your keep?"

Gerard laughed and found himself suddenly clasped in a bruising embrace. He tried to extricate himself from the bear hug, mentally noting not to underestimate William. Despite his size the man could still move, and there was no doubting his strength.

Free from the hold, he tapped William on the shoulder with one fist. "No, you fool, this is how I bid a friend welcome to his own keep."

"That remains to be seen."

Gerard's humor left him. "Pardon me?"

"Come," William motioned toward the keep, "let us speak inside."

~*~

Catheryn descended the stairs with trepidation. When the fresh scents of lavender and spice floated across her nose, her anxiety increased. She paused.

After her mother died she'd become used to the filth Pike had allowed to accumulate in Brezden's great hall. The few times she'd tried to remedy the situation she'd tasted his brand of discipline. She'd soon decided that sweet smells and a clean hall weren't worth the taste of her own blood.

Another scent caught her attention. Paint. Newly applied. The strength of the aroma brought tears to her eyes. The memory of the last time the walls had been painted brought tears to her heart.

These walls had regularly been refreshed in her mother's

day. But, as with the hall itself, Pike had not seen fit to wipe away the filth, nor the soot coating the walls.

It took no amount of thought to determine who had been responsible for these changes. But one question did plague her—why?

How long did Count Reveur plan to remain at Brezden? Would he be here long enough for her to determine his trustworthiness? If she could not thwart de Brye alone she would be forced to seek assistance somewhere. Should she, as Agnes had prodded, seek help from Gerard?

No. If she sought help from Count Reveur, de Brye would find out. She would not risk her men's lives in such a manner.

"Milady!"

She glanced at her obviously flustered maid before descending the remaining few stairs. "Yes, Agnes, what is it?"

"'Tis Earl William. He has arrived."

Catheryn knew that, if it was possible, her heart would now be lying on the floor amongst the clean, sweet-smelling rushes.

What was the Earl of York doing at Brezden? He'd not bothered to make an appearance when either of her parents had died. He'd not bothered himself with the only child of those loyal to him. Instead, he'd seen fit to appoint Pike guardian and to leave her to her own defenses.

Then he'd sent someone else to dispatch Pike when the Baron proved to be a traitor. He'd sent the man of her dreams to commit murder and mayhem in her keep.

Nay, she had no interest in meeting this overlord of Brezden. As far as she was concerned he could go straight to the devil and spend time there with Pike.

She bit her tongue and tried hard to force a smile to her lips, but realized she failed miserably. "When can we expect his lordship's presence, Agnes?"

"Now."

The answer came from two places at once. One came from Agnes, who was backing away as rapidly as possible.

The other response came from Gerard.

She bit back a gasp and looked toward him. Even though he was the taller of the two, the man standing beside him dwarfed Gerard. She had heard that William le Gros lived up to his name, but she'd never imagined just how massive he was.

She approached the men, ignoring the swimming of her head and the pounding of her heart. Regardless of whether she wanted to meet the overlord of Brezden or not, he was here. She had little choice but to greet him appropriately.

Catheryn drew in a breath and knelt low before him, silently praying that the earl would not suddenly decide she should share Pike's fate.

"Welcome to Brezden, milord. I hope everything has met with your satisfaction." She had the strange sensation that Gerard breathed a sigh of relief at her words. But she was too afraid of the broadsword hanging at the earl's side to chance a glance at Count Reveur.

"My, my. What have we here?" William asked as he reached down, grasped her hand and assisted Catheryn from the floor. "I knew Pike was guardian to a girl, but never did I guess how fine a woman he had wardship to."

While he turned her around to look at her, Catheryn felt like a horse on the auction block. She forced her humiliation and terror down. "Thank you, milord." The words tasted bitter as they left her lips.

"Yes, yes, fine indeed." The earl's voice was as smooth as cream.

"My lord, is there anything I can get for you? Have you eaten? Would you like to rest a while first? Could I have a bath brought for you?" Catheryn tried not to ramble, but the words just kept coming. Anything to make him stop staring at her.

"Nay, nothing this moment," he replied. "I would like to sit and just visit for a while."

She glanced at Gerard. He did nothing but shrug and motion toward the fire.

After the earl was comfortably situated in the only high back chair, Catheryn took a seat on a stool while Gerard leaned against the wall.

Without any formalities the earl bluntly asked, "You are still a maiden?"

She felt the heat of embarrassment and anger rise. Right behind the anger came fear. She truly didn't know the answer. Had de Brye succeeded in raping her? She'd felt so battered and abused after his attack that it was hard for her tell. Aware the earl was still waiting, she answered, "Aye, sir." She could only hope she was right.

"How is it you have remained unclaimed this long?" he inquired. "Are there no betrothals?"

Was this question a trick? Did he truly not know that Pike had repeatedly tried to force de Brye upon her? "Not that I am aware of, milord."

"We need to take care of that immediately." The earl must have seen the blood leave her face. He leaned forward and patted her hand. "Now, now, not to worry. As your guardian, I will make sure you are taken care of properly."

His hot and sweaty hand nauseated her. Catheryn was not certain how to respond without letting him know how ungrateful and disgusted she felt. So she remained silent.

With a firmer tone William asked, "Surely you see the need? I must have a strong arm in this part of the shire. You cannot hold Brezden from King David in Scotland and from Stephen's enemies too."

Catheryn's heart missed a beat; he did not appear to know of Pike's plans for her. Did he know anything about Raymond de Brye? Perhaps it would not be wise to anger this man just yet. He held her life, and that of Brezden, in his hands.

After brightening her face, she looked at the earl and smiled. "Oh, I see it now, milord. Forgive me for being so silly. Yes, of course you will see to it all. I know I may trust you to do what is best." She wanted to gag on her own words.

A big smile from William rewarded Catheryn. A smile so false that it never reached his eyes.

She stiffened with fear and renewed anger when the earl reached out to smooth a braid that hung over her breast. Catheryn forced herself to give him a bland look of resignation, and willed her rapid breathing to slow. The earl leaned back in his chair and called for wine before he dismissed the men and servants from the hall.

A shiver ran up her spine. She felt as though she'd just been threatened. But what could she do? Other than try to remain calm and hope the man drank himself into a stupor tonight. Or that he was so tired from traveling that he would seek his bed early.

She sought Gerard's gaze. She found it slightly amusing that now she was looking for protection from the man she considered little more than her enemy.

Gerard met her pointed regard. She was looking to him for help? Inwardly he sighed. Who else was there? He noted her white face and pale eyes and wondered what William was truly up to this time.

If the earl looked to Catheryn as the vessel for his third bastard, he could look elsewhere. Gerard moved away from the wall. "So, tell me, Lord William, how was your journey?" He flashed a small smile at Catheryn and watched some color return to her face.

"Fine. Thankfully, we encountered no delays."

Gerard knew better. William liked nothing more than a good battle. If there had been no delays then the earl was, in all likelihood, bored. "How did you find the king and his family?" He took the stool Walter brought him and positioned himself between William and Catheryn.

"They are as well as can be expected. Stephen is now physically in possession of the crown, with the church's blessing." William shrugged. "But my cousin is, mentally, still recovering from his long ordeal."

"He was not injured?"

"Nay. Matilda's men may have captured and held Stephen, but they would not have dared harm him."

"How is the queen?"

William raised his hands, palms up and laughed. "Maud is—Maud. What else can I tell you? She is in control and mothering everyone, especially her husband."

After shouting for one of his squires, William asked, "How have you found Brezden, Gerard? Has all been well?" He sorted through a packet the squire handed to him.

"Fine." Gerard hesitated while he formed his answer.

"There have been no difficulties of note." He glanced down and added, "Nothing I could not handle."

William smirked at him. "I see."

Catheryn felt the undercurrent between these two and wished she knew what was coming. She had the impression that Gerard did not quite trust the earl.

"Ah, here it is." He pulled a folded parchment from the packet, then handed it to Gerard.

"What is this?"

"'Tis from Stephen."

Gerard barely noted the wax seal that held the cords wrapped around the letter. After flicking the seal and cords to the floor he unfolded the parchment. Catheryn was surprised at the anger that leapt to his face as he read the missive.

He crushed the document in his hand, then turned on William and asked, "How long did the two of you conspire before you agreed upon this?"

Catheryn stared at Gerard's clenched jaw and blazing eyes as the earl laughed. "Not long. 'Tis the only thing that made sense."

She could not stand the suspense any longer. "What? What is amiss?"

Gerard's tightly reined ire exploded. He threw the crumpled letter at Catheryn, then stood and yelled at William. "This is absurd. You have both lost all powers of reason!"

Catheryn barely heard the earl laugh again in the background as she retrieved the balled up parchment from the floor. After smoothing out the wrinkles, she scanned the cause of Gerard's outburst. The room spun. "Nay." She dropped the note to the floor. "Oh, no," she repeated hoarsely.

Gerard replied with a snarl in his tone. "I see the lady agrees with me."

Tears of laughter formed in William's eyes as he rose and slapped Gerard on his shoulder. "Come, Gerard, you deserved something for your work here."

Gerard jerked away from the earl. "You know why I accepted this mission. Yet you think to repay me with a wife from Brezden?" He glared at Catheryn. "A wife I do not need, or want?"

She stepped back from the anger on his face. "Do not look at me. It was none of my doing."

William wiped the tears from his face. "Was there something else you expected?"

"Nay. Nothing. I wanted only Pike's head. I wanted revenge for what was done to Edyth."

Catheryn could not help but wonder what had happened to this Edyth. Who was she to Gerard? The way he'd attacked Brezden, she assumed it had been his wife. And if the earl was now offering her hand to Gerard in marriage, then his wife must have died.

At Pike's hands? Or at de Brye's? It mattered little. Either way the death would not have been pleasant. And now he was being offered Pike's ward as a replacement? She shuddered. A lifetime with this dream knight of hers could become a worse nightmare than Pike had been.

Or de Brye still was.

She watched Gerard's fingers curl around the grip of his sword. She looked at William, who was no longer laughing, then briefly back to Gerard, before asking the earl, "Why me?"

William answered matter-of-factly. "I need this keep. Stephen needs this keep. It must remain in trusted hands. We know of no one better suited to the task than Gerard." He sighed. "To be honest, the idea was Maud's."

"Maud's idea?" Gerard wiped one hand across his face. "Who did you say wears the crown?"

"I believe you hold land from the queen, do you not?"

Gerard conceded. "Yes. I hold land in Boulogne, directly from Maud. You know of my land in France. Why would I want more property to care for in England too?"

"That is not a consideration. Many men have holdings here and elsewhere." William cocked his head. "I love you like a brother, Gerard, you know that. But if you refuse the king you will share Pike's fate. I will be able to do little to save you."

Catheryn did not want the men's conversation to continue in the same manner. She looked at Gerard. "Marrying me would not be pleasant for you, I am certain. But you would gain a keep and its wealth."

Gerard whipped around. "Get out of this hall!" He issued the order through clenched teeth.

She wasn't going to argue with him now. Catheryn knew by the tone of his voice that she'd not win this one. Just as she turned toward the stairs she heard William thunder.

"Nay! The girl stays. This concerns her also."

Oh, Lord, now what? If she stayed, Gerard would flay her. If she left, William would do the job. Gerard lightly touched her shoulder. "Stay."

As they all sat back down, the earl let out an exaggerated sigh. "Good, that is better. Gerard, you have done an excellent job here. I cannot find an appropriate way to thank you."

He looked at Catheryn. "You cannot defend this keep yourself. As much as you may dislike the idea, you must have a strong man here and Brezden's people already know Count Reveur."

Gerard came to the edge of the stool. "William," he paused to look at Catheryn briefly before continuing, "There is another option no one has taken into consideration."

Catheryn did not like the sound of this. The gleam in his eyes looked more unholy than good.

The earl prompted Gerard. "You will not rest until you tell me. What else can we do?"

"You already have this keep. You could add to your profits by keeping Brezden and offering the lady's hand in exchange for gold."

William intently studied the idea. "To the highest bidder?" He looked from Gerard to Catheryn. "She would bring a tidy sum to my coffers."

Catheryn was speechless. A cold sweat broke out on her face as a bone-chilling surge ran up her spine and neck. She knew who the highest bidder would be. Somehow, in some devious way, de Brye would win the bid.

Unsure of anything else except the desperate need to sway them from this idea, Catheryn leapt from the stool crying, "No, my lord, no!"

Oblivious to the cold, hard, rush-strewn floor, Catheryn fell to her knees before the earl. She grasped his leg with a trembling hand and forced herself to meet his startled gaze.

"Please, my lord William, I will do whatever you ask of me. Just do not do this."

"Jesu, Catheryn, what are you doing?" Gerard was instantly at her side, his hand on her arm.

William brushed him away. The earl's keen stare held her still. "What are you afraid of, lady? What are you not saying?"

Catheryn's eyes darted away and back to his. What could she tell him? That she would rather marry her enemy than the cruel man who was her guardian's choice?

No matter what it cost her, she refused to lose the chance to keep herself free from de Brye. Leaning closer to him, she steadied her voice and began. "Sire, I wish to marry no one. But I am not foolish enough to think I will be allowed that freedom. But if..."

William's strong hand caught her hand. "Keep your secrets. I will not force them from you." As William lifted her head higher, Catheryn felt a moment of panic. Was he going to snap her neck? "Anything I ask of you?"

Catheryn heard Gerard's hiss. She stiffened her spine, drew a quick breath, then whispered, "Aye"

The earl held on to her for a few agonizingly long heartbeats. His bruising grip brought tears of pain to her eyes. A slow smile spread across his face. "You will agree to this marriage with no further arguments?"

"Yes."

His hand fell from her chin to her arm and he helped her to her feet. Catheryn hung her head. She was too afraid to discover what else William would ask of her. She turned and bumped into Gerard. The look on his stark white face was one of pure anger. Her insides quaked as she stood still and met his glare without flinching.

His brows formed one line over his fiery eyes. The square jaw was clenched so tight Catheryn wondered if his teeth would break. A half step closer brought him tight against her. Catheryn was sure he could feel her shake. He stared down at her, shaking with rage. "Get up to your chamber, woman and stay there until I tell you to come down!"

Without hesitation, Catheryn lifted her skirts and ran for the stairs. She heard the earl's booming laughter follow her up to the safety of her room.

Chapter Six

Livid, Gerard asked, "What has taken hold of your mind, William? We have been friends a long time. You have never done anything this high-handed before."

Still laughing, William answered, "Look at you, Gerard. You are not getting any younger. Your wife is dead and you remain alone."

"What does Edyth's death have to do with my marrying Catheryn?" He itched to grab his sword and finish the job William's many enemies could not. "Since when did my state of marriage become your concern?"

"Gerard, be still." After pushing him down onto the stool, William shoved a mug of ale into his hand. "What is wrong with the girl?"

There were many answers to that question. But Gerard chose the simplest. "She is not for me."

"That is not an answer. What is wrong with the girl?"

Gerard ran a hand through his hair and shrugged. "She is not capable of running a keep."

The earl scanned the hall. "Everything looks in order to me."

"No thanks to her. My dogs would have turned up their noses at the filth that used to occupy this keep." He knew that lame answer was unfair. The condition of Brezden had nothing to do with Catheryn.

William studied his fingernails. "I understand that your contacts with the lady have been, ah, somewhat heated."

There was only one way William could possibly know what had taken place here before his arrival. Gerard searched the hall and located his errant captain. Walter stood in the far corner of the room, trying desperately to disappear into the wall.

"Do not flay your man with your hot looks. He escorted me into this keep and only answered my direct questions."

Gerard groaned. He could just imagine William's questions. An excellent captain for the guard, Walter was not equipped to play the games the earl liked so well. "What else did you glean from my man?"

"I know that there is a part of you that would be eager to have this girl as wife."

"Any whore could satisfy that hunger. I do not need a wife for that."

"Oh, aye, now there is an excellent argument."

William's flippancy angered him even more. Gerard grasped for excuses. "She has no respect for authority. I could never be certain she was following orders."

He was not prepared for the earl's laughing reply. "Respect for authority? We are speaking of a wife, a woman, not a steward for one of your keeps."

"I would expect a wife to do as she was told."

William shook his head. His attention roamed from Gerard's feet up to his head. "I do not see where you would have much difficulty convincing anyone to follow an order if it were truly your wish. How could you expect this girl to meekly do as you bid? Were you not the one who had her men killed, damaged her keep and from what I understand were near to seducing her? Gerard, if you were my son I would beat you black and blue for your stupidity."

Gerard threw his drinking vessel to the floor and rose. He'd had enough of William's senseless banter. "Stupidity? You think it wise to marry into a nest of vipers? It is wise to marry one closely associated with those who—"

The vivid memories of what he'd witnessed the day of Edyth's death closed his throat. He could not speak of the atrocities done to his wife and child. Not even to save himself from this marriage could he voice his nightmares. But that didn't stop the horrors from filling his mind. He swayed on his feet, unsteady from the force of the visions haunting him.

Walter sprinted across the hall. "Milord, do not."

Gerard heard the concern in his captain's voice, but he waved the man away. He knew he looked and sounded crazed. No one but he and Walter had seen the destruction; the atrocities wrought in his keep that day. He'd permitted no other hands but his own to tend to the dying Edyth. No one else had been allowed to touch the already dead babe she'd clutched to her breast.

He'd told no one of the horrors of that day. And he'd sworn Walter to silence. Pike had been dispatched. He had to find the other man responsible.

Other than Catheryn and Walter, no one else knew about de Brye. Gerard kept the devil a secret from William for a reason—vengeance would be his. And his alone.

His breath, ragged and painful, tore from his chest. He gritted his teeth, forcing the rapid pounding of his heart and head to slow.

Gerard grabbed a slender thread of control before he looked down at the earl. "Yes, it is true. I do desire the lady. But I cannot take her. I would never know if the act were out of desire, or revenge. I cannot marry her. Whose face would I see? Catheryn's lovely, living countenance or Edyth's mask of death? Find someone else to marry the lady."

William slowly rose. Gone was the trusted friend and confidant. In his place was William, the Count of Aumale, the Earl of York, the Lord of Holderness. The man's many titles enveloped him like a cloak.

One look at the earl's reddening, angry face made Gerard aware that nothing he said would change anything. He had lost this argument.

"Enough. I am truly sorry for your loss. But it is over and done; you cannot change what happened. You are here. You are free. You have a title. You have the money and men it will take to hold this keep. Your king has ordered it. You have no acceptable reason to refuse me. You are going to marry Lady Catheryn of Brezden if I have to beat you to do it. I will do whatever it takes to ensure Stephen's order is followed." William paused for a breath before asking, "Do you understand me?"

Gerard tasted the bile in his throat. By refusing to marry her, he would lose everything his family had fought so hard to acquire.

Agreeing to the marriage would cost him only his soul. "Aye."

The earl gripped Gerard's shoulder and asked, "Do you seriously think Lady Catheryn had any responsibility in Edyth's unfortunate end? Nay, even you know better than that. Have you not quenched your thirst for revenge yet, Gerard? Must you destroy yourself for something that was not your fault?"

"Not my fault? Are you mad? I should have been there."

"Just as I should have been there when Stephen was taken. I cannot undo what happened and neither can you."

Gerard was silent as he stared down at the floor. Life with Edyth had been calm and steady. He didn't want a life of unending fighting and arguing. He just wanted to be left alone. But Gerard knew his fate had been sealed long before William had ridden through Brezden's gates. "When?"

"On the morrow. There are no impediments. The banns have been waved. Any monetary or property disputes can be settled later." William pulled him into an embrace of friendship. "Come, it will not be as bad as you think."

Gerard pulled himself from the earl's unwelcome hold. After bowing he turned on his heel and left the hall.

~*~

Ever since she had heard the heavy door to the hall open and close hours ago, she had gone over and over fragments of the men's conversation. Catheryn wondered if either of them realized she could hear bits and pieces of what they'd said. And if she could hear them, she was certain de Brye could also. Shivering, she pushed that thought from her mind.

Instead, she focused on what she'd heard. Even with the missing pieces, Catheryn garnered that Gerard's wife had died. And she had a pretty good idea that Pike and de Brye were involved. The dismal tone of Gerard's voice told her that she really didn't want to know what had happened.

She could think of no way to spare Gerard or herself from this marriage. He was not going to be an easy husband for anyone. If her inklings were correct, she was the worst possible choice for him.

How could the earl or the king expect Gerard to take her as his wife? And to think she had called him here to Brezden. It was little wonder that he'd torn through this keep like a storm gone wild.

It was amazing that in his rage and grief he'd not meted out more punishment. Only an iron will, grasping tightly to his control, could have kept his revenge targeted on Pike and de Brye.

Even though she sympathized greatly with his plight, Catheryn could not help wondering about herself. She rolled over onto her side, closed her eyes and tried to think. How could she have agreed to this so easily?

Catheryn opened her eyes. How could she not? Saying no to William would have gained her nothing except her own head detached from her neck. Or worse than that, she could have been given to Raymond de Brye. Either way, she would gain nothing but death.

Familiar, heavy footsteps stopped outside her door. Catheryn knew it was Gerard. Her stomach tightened. Why was he here now?

At the same time she heard the distinct click of the hidden panel in her alcove. As easy as it would be for her to call for help, one thought kept the words in her throat. Her men. De Brye's force held her men. She would do nothing to bring harm to them.

The footsteps did not move away from her chamber door. From the alcove the panel hissed slowly open. Catheryn bolted from the bed and ran toward the alcove. "Go. Get away from here." She knew that if anyone heard her warning to de Brye it would look as if she were protecting the man. But that couldn't be helped. Again, she whispered urgently to the slightly opened panel, "Get out!"

The door to her chamber banged against the wall. Gerard barged into the room. "What is wrong?"

A vile oath issued from behind the panel was meant for her ears alone and she hoped the curse had carried no further. Catheryn spun around to face Gerard. She approached him, asking loudly, "What are you doing in here?"

With luck, her voice covered even the slight sound of the panel door sliding closed.

Though his searching gaze shot from one corner of the chamber to another, Gerard appeared not to have noticed. "Someone was in here. I heard you. Is all well?"

Her heart tripped over itself. She had to remind herself that this was not the time to be impressed with his show of concern. "There's no one in here. See for yourself, milord."

His search completed, he stood before her. "I was not hearing things."

Catheryn knew by the smell of wine on his breath what he'd been doing while she contemplated their future—or lack of a future. "Are you sure?" She shrugged and glanced around the room. "I see no one here but you and me."

He frowned, but made no comment. Her sigh of relief caught in her throat when she looked up at him. Catheryn fought the sudden urge to brush away the dark lock of hair that had fallen across his face.

He looked tired and sad. The impression of a child, lost

and unsure of what to do next, flitted briefly across her mind. Her perusal dropped to his shoulders and chest, erasing the image of a child.

She took a step back. "What are you doing in here?"

He closed the distance between them. "I heard you tell someone to go away."

Heat emanated from him. It curled around her, inviting her to share the warmth. To keep herself from placing her hands on his chest, Catheryn clasped her hands behind her. "Before that. You were outside my door. What did you want?"

"To talk. To explain." He brushed a strand of hair from her face.

Catheryn took another step back and nearly groaned when he moved with her. "There's nothing to explain. You made it quite clear what you thought about our marriage." She tried to sound angry. Tried to keep her breathless voice under control. But knew she failed miserably.

"My thoughts matter little. We have no choice."

His fingers lingered behind her ear. The tiny shivers running down her neck made it harder and harder to think. "So, what is there to talk about then?"

"Would it not be easier if we could find some common ground?"

Catheryn gasped as his touch trailed down her neck. "There is nothing we have in common, milord. Nothing we share." She closed her eyes against the sensations his gentle caress inflamed.

Gerard had spent the evening and part of this night arguing with himself and railing against the injustice of William's order. One thought had kept coming back to him over and over. None of this was Catheryn's fault.

He knew he had to find a way to make some sort of peace with her before the morrow. He'd not take an unwilling and hate-filled woman as his wife.

At this moment, Gerard wanted nothing more than to hold

her. To bury his face in her hair. To breathe in the scent of her. He knew half of his wants were caused from the wine. But it was more than just drink.

"Then we shall have to find something." While she pondered that thought, he gently pulled her into his arms.

Within the space of a breath, Gerard felt her relax against him. Her breasts pressed against his chest. Their hearts beat in unison. He sent one message, one order to his suddenly errant mind. He would not take her to bed this night.

Strands of her hair tickled his nose. He smoothed the silken mass and let his hand come to rest on the side of her neck. While searching for words, he absently brushed her soft flesh with his thumb.

"I will not make a good husband for you."

"I know that."

He breathed in the scent of flowers, light and fragrant, and bent his head to rest his lips just below her ear. "But I will not beat you. I will not harm you. I will care for your keep and your people."

She moved slightly against him. A soft moan floated to his ears. The low, gentle sound ran warmly the length of his body, pausing to ignite small fires in his heart and groin.

"That is good to know, milord."

Just the sound of her voice, soft and breathless, threatened to make him forget his resolve not to move them to the bed.

Slowly moving his hand along her shoulder and back up to the side of her neck, he gently brushed his thumb along the soft flesh. A shiver rippled through her.

He found it interesting that such little contact could give this woman a reaction that no amount of wooing had brought to Edyth.

Catheryn made a sound deep in her throat and then gasped softly. "What are you doing to me?"

Gerard drew her forward and rested his forehead against hers. "Catheryn, it is called desire. It is fleeting and brief. Do not let it rule your head."

She tried to pull away, but he held her tightly. She placed one hand on his chest. "I know what it's called. Does it never carry you away, milord?"

It had been so long since he'd permitted any emotion to rule him besides anger that he had to search his memory. Gerard finally admitted, "Certainly. When I was a boy and desire was new. But when I grew up I learned that things like desire, passion and love had no place in a man's life."

Catheryn felt as if some demon imp had invaded her heart and soul. She wanted nothing more than to prove his words false.

One side of her mind said that he would think her a whore. A cheap strumpet. But the stronger side laughed and told her that it didn't matter. They'd be married on the morrow so what difference would it make?

She slid one hand around his neck. With the other she stroked his cheek, coaxing his lips to meet hers. Having only his hard, demanding kisses as experience, she imitated it. His lips parted easily under hers, but his tongue gentled her intensity. She found that soothing caress far more enjoyable.

Catheryn pressed her body tighter against his. Her softness melted against the hard planes of his chest.

Instead of thrusting her aside in disgust, Gerard wrapped his arms around her and with a groan moved both of them to the bed. Lying side by side, he slipped one leg between hers and ran one hand down her side. He stroked her from her breast to her thigh.

Slowly.

Thoroughly.

She felt her heartbeat increase and move. It tapped a steady, strong beat in her head, her throat, her chest, and her stomach. It thumped with an impatient ache between her parted legs.

No matter how she moved, or how hard she tried, Catheryn

couldn't get close enough to him to ease the throbbing.

He broke their mind-stealing kiss and laughed softly. "Catheryn, has no one ever told you not to play with fire?"

She heard the smugness in his voice and realized he knew what she'd been about. But at this moment it mattered little.

Catheryn drew his mouth back to hers. She admitted in a whisper, "No, they haven't. Show me why."

With a low moan, he covered her lips with his own and rolled on top of her. Gerard held her head between his hands; he kissed her eyes, her nose, her lips and her neck before moving to her ear.

As if having a will of its own, her body rose up harder against his. His breath burned like fire in her ear. "Shh, Catheryn, not tonight. But I admit I was wrong. It would be damned easy to forget myself with you."

Suddenly embarrassed and ashamed, she tightly closed her eyes and bit her lower lip.

Still nuzzling her ear and neck, Gerard whispered, "No, none of that. I issued a challenge you couldn't refuse."

His words did not ease her guilt. "I apologize. I acted like a, like a—"

He placed a finger over her lips. "Catheryn, look at me."

Warily, she met his gaze. Relief flooded her when she did not see disgust on his face.

He removed his hand and lowered it to her breast. Even through the layers of fabric separating his touch from her flesh, she felt him circling her nipple with his thumb.

His touch kneaded and teased, sending unfamiliar pangs all through her. Like small bolts of lightning, they streaked from her breasts to her toes. When his touch ran lightly over her hardened nipple, she gasped. She strained toward his hand and closed her eyes against the shivers and tingles shaking her.

He paused. "Look at me."

When she found the courage to do as he bid, he resumed his movements. Catheryn stared into his dark eyes and couldn't decide which burned more—her body, or her face.

A smile curved his lips. He brushed a kiss across her forehead. "Catheryn, no strumpet would ever be as embarrassed as you are now."

He trailed a path to her mouth with his tongue.

Catheryn grasped his shoulders. Unable to bear anymore, she cried out, "Stop, Gerard, please."

She felt bereft of his touch when he stopped his teasing torment and rolled onto his side. After what seemed a lifetime her breathing returned to normal. Her heart slowed. But the feel of his touch lingered on her breast. The taste of his kisses remained on her lips.

Gerard cupped her cheek and turned her head toward his. "So, I was wrong."

She wanted to laugh, but had not the strength. "That is not a normal occurrence, is it?"

His smile lit the now darkening room. "Oh, it has happened once or twice before."

Catheryn wondered if he knew how devastating his smile was to her. "Milord, I would say that if nothing else, we do have a common desire between us."

He agreed, but asked, "Do you think it is strong enough to carry us through a lifetime?"

A serious discussion was the last thing she wanted at this moment. Instead of debating the possibilities, she asked, "Is it not a place to start?"

"The church says no."

She turned away and said, "Think you I care what they say? The church refused to bury my mother in sacred ground, next to the man who loved her. I left the church and its teachings behind—in my mother's unhallowed resting place."

"Then I guess it will have to be a place to start."

A soft, almost soundless click took Catheryn's breath away. She'd foolishly forgotten about de Brye. Why had she not noticed earlier that while he'd closed the panel, he hadn't secured the latch? Panic assailed her. The madman could have killed them both.

Had Gerard heard? She glanced at him. He was now lying on his back with his hands behind his head. His eyes were closed and he didn't appear poised for any type of quick movements.

Catheryn swallowed a soft whoosh of relief before asking, "Are you hungry? Have you eaten?" She knew that soon she'd have to confide in Gerard. But not now. Not yet. Not until they were truly wed.

Only then could she be certain he would not leave her to fend for herself. No man in his right mind would walk away from Brezden if it belonged to him.

Especially not a man who still had a score to settle with de Brye.

Gerard stretched and sat up. "No, I am not hungry, but I need to seek my bed."

Catheryn's heart fluttered. Beads of sweat covered her face and back. She didn't want to be alone in this room tonight. There was little doubt that de Brye would not let what he'd surely heard and seen this day pass without seeking her out.

She patted the warm spot he'd just left. "Why don't you stay here? There's no need for you to leave."

Her heart plummeted at his frown. But she said nothing, waiting for him to work out whatever was running through his mind.

Finally, Gerard leaned over and ran a hand down her cheek. "You are afraid of something."

It wasn't a question, so she didn't answer.

"Catheryn, you might be permitted to keep your secrets from William, but someday you will have to share them with me."

She bit her lip. Her heart screamed: *Now. Tell him now.* But her mind cautioned her to wait.

Logic won out over feelings. "Please, Gerard. Stay."

She nearly cried with relief and gratitude when he grabbed a cover and a pillow from the bed and placed it on the floor. "I will not sleep in your bed this night, milady. But I will not leave you."

The room fell silent while he tussled with the cover and pillow. Catheryn climbed beneath her covers, certain de Brye would not be so foolish as to enter this room with Gerard here.

From the floor a voice whispered in the darkness. "Regardless of what has gone before, or what you think, I will always keep you safe, Catheryn. Trust me."

Chapter Seven

"Are you ready?" Agnes's voice reached through the quiet of sleep.

Catheryn stretched. The cool morning air convinced her to open her eyes; at least long enough to find the covers the maid had removed. Catheryn curled up beneath the warmth of the blankets she'd retrieved from the foot of the bed.

"Wake up, Lady Catheryn. 'Tis your wedding day and we have to get you ready."

"The sun is not even up yet. Go away."

What the maid had said sifted through the fog of sleep. Her wedding day? Catheryn sat up, instantly wide awake.

Both women turned their heads toward the man rising from the floor alongside the bed. Gerard leaned across the bed and placed a quick, chaste kiss on Catheryn's brow.

"What is the meaning of this?" Agnes's voice reached the level of a near shriek. The sound tore at Catheryn's ears.

"It means nothing. But I've other items to attend to." Gerard cast a guilty glance toward Catheryn before making a quick exist.

Leaving the explanations to her.

"Thank you, milord." The comment tossed at his retreating back did not slow his steps.

"Lady Catheryn?"

She covered her laugh with a hearty cough, gaining a moment to think. "Truly, it was nothing." She pulled the sheets from the bed. "Would there not be evidence if anything had happened?"

Agnes's thorough inspection of the bed covers seemed to satisfy the woman's fears. But not her questions. "Then what was his lordship doing in here? And why was he sleeping on the floor?"

Catheryn reasoned that a half-truth would work better than a lie. "He was sick with drink. I was frightened by a noise. The idea seemed rational at the moment."

Agnes did no more than scowl for a moment before pulling Catheryn from the bed to begin a furious whirl of dressing and grooming.

Catheryn paid little attention to the maid's fussing. Her gaze kept straying to the hidden panel. The door seemed well sealed at the moment. With luck de Brye was not sitting on the other side.

She doubted if he would have missed the chance provided him right now. With only her maid for protection, she was an easy target for the lunatic's wrath.

Her thoughts whirled round and round. Should she tell Gerard? Should she try to thwart de Brye on her own? Should she confide in Earl William? Should she keep her fears and plans to herself? She had no answers. Only more questions.

"Agnes," Catheryn's fingers brushed the thin under gown the maid had slipped over her head. "Why am I doing this?"

"Do you not want to look presentable for your own wedding?" Deftly lacing one side of the gown, she moved to the opposite side. "You are the lady of this keep. It would not be proper for you to appear unworthy of your position." Her hand moved down to smooth out the long skirt. Sighing, the woman shook her head sadly. "If only your dear mother could be here."

The sudden urge to scream was overwhelming. Catheryn yanked the gown from Agnes's preening fingers. "Quit blathering. You know I wasn't referring to the clothes." She turned away from the older woman's slumped shoulders and downcast face.

"I'm sorry, Agnes. I did not mean to snap at you. It must be thoughts of what will happen this day."

Her guilt was relieved a little when the maid patted her

arm. "I know, sweeting. That is only natural."

Catheryn looked at the ceiling, then asked again, softer this time. "Why me? Why must I marry him?"

The frown on Agnes's face warned Catheryn that she wasn't going to like the answer. "Why not you? Why should you have a choice in your marriage partner? Even if your parents were alive the choice would not be yours. And you know what decision Pike would have made. You know this, child. You know you can do nothing to change your fate."

"But I cannot help wishing that my husband would be my true love." She found it impossible to keep the tremble from her voice.

Agnes snorted before asking, "How do you know he won't be? Even if he is not, you are not in a position to dwell on dreams of love."

The maid smoothed Catheryn's hair. "For right now, what you need to face is that you and Brezden were taken by this man. It seems to me that your only choice is to marry, or join your father and his men." Agnes's tone grew sterner with each sentence. "Is that what you want?"

"No." Catheryn's answer was mumbled.

"If you refuse him now you would risk the lives of all of us." Agnes grasped Catheryn's shoulders. "Will it be so terrible? Can you not be happy that you are not being given to someone as evil as Raymond de Brye?"

That much was true; she could be marrying someone as repulsive as that lout. At least Gerard was young and far from repulsive. Lifting her head, she agreed, "You are right, Agnes."

"Catheryn, you cannot be certain that love will always be denied to you. Count Gerard is not a bad man; he may come to be what you are seeking."

She doubted if that would ever happen. Catheryn kept her thoughts to herself. She sat silent while Agnes finished.

At about the same heartbeat the maid's ministrations

were completed, Gerard reentered the chamber.

"Are you ready?"

After rising, she brushed the imaginary wrinkles from her gown before replying, "Yes, milord."

Catheryn found herself feeling a little sorry for the man. No one should be forced to marry against his will. This was his life, not William's. But she didn't know what she could do to take the sadness from his eyes. And even if she did, what would become of her?

She watched him force a smile on his face before he said, "Come, William will be waiting." The couple walked downstairs.

After relinquishing Catheryn to the earl, Gerard told her, "I will await you at the chapel door."

Catheryn watched him leave the hall and asked, "My lord William, is there no other way?"

"Nay, child. Do not worry about him." He sighed deeply, then tried to reassure her. "He will come around."

~*~

Gerard slowly walked toward the chapel door. Even though it was a fine spring day, his heart was as heavy as the plodding footsteps that carried him to his fate.

He reached into the *ausmoniere* hanging from his belt. Besides a few coins, the pouch held three rings. One was the plain gold band he had once given to Edyth. His fingers closed over the smooth green stones of the other two.

His mother had given him two emerald rings after his father had died. Except for size, they were identical. One had been his father's ring. His mother had made Gerard swear to bestow the smaller ring only on his true love when he found her.

The pieces of jewelry were cold from the many years they had spent in his pouch. He clenched the rings briefly, then released them and pulled out the plain band.

True love? He would never have what his parents shared. On rare occasions the knowledge hurt. At this moment, it cut like a knife into his chest.

Instead, he was being blessed with a wife he didn't want. A woman who held her secrets too close for his comfort. A woman who lied, rather than tell him who had tried to enter her chamber.

Did she think him a dolt? His life depended on his senses. Sometimes hearing was more important than seeing. Only a dead man would have missed the soft click of a latch being slid back in place. And the sound had not come from the chamber door.

If she refused to confide in him soon he would have that chamber dismantled piece by piece until he found the hidden door.

~*~

Apologizing, William patted Catheryn's hand as he led her across the bailey. "Lady, I am sorry that your wedding must be so hasty, but I cannot linger. There will be no betrothal ceremony and the feasting will not be large or long. I fear you may look back on this and find it lacking."

Lacking? She was amazed. "How kind you are to concern yourself." William looked at her in question. Catheryn smiled and continued, "Lord William, how many ladies of my standing can say that not only did the Earl of York attend her wedding, but he escorted her to the chapel door?"

"William," she paused to see if her use of his first name offended him. When she noticed that he wasn't, she began again, "William, I thank you for this. I am truly grateful." Catheryn knew that the man had no idea how grateful she was.

The earl stopped and smiled at her. "Nay, do not thank me yet. If I remember correctly, you vowed to do anything I asked."

Catheryn shuddered. What and how much would this man want from her?

William chuckled. "Catheryn, as much as I would surely enjoy myself, I do not want you in my bed."

She heard him snort at her sudden release of air. "Lady Catheryn, you are marrying a man dear to me as a friend and an ally. The fire I see in his eyes whenever you are around cannot be ignored. I would not let him escape from you no matter how desperately he wanted to."

"I do not understand."

"I know, and I am sorry there is no time for lengthy explanations." William stopped walking. "The Gerard you know is not the same man I know. The only emotions your Gerard knows are anger and indifference. He has become cold and remote."

Catheryn raised her hand; she wasn't sure they were talking about the same man, but the earl didn't need to finish his description.

"Walter tells me that you are the first person to fire Gerard's blood since Edyth died."

She felt herself blush. Aye, she fired his blood. And not always with anger.

If William noticed her heated face, he made no comment before continuing. "Gerard is of no use to me, to Stephen, or to his lands if he cares about nothing except his thirst for blood."

Catheryn could not stem her impatience any longer. "You still have not told me what it is you expect from me."

"What I expect from you will make you think me daft. But trust me; I am in full control of my mind. Do you think I do not recognize Gerard's sadness? Do you think I do not see him seeking self-destruction in his quest for revenge?

Catheryn, I do. But his Edyth is never coming back."

If this man recognized all those things in a man he called 'friend', why had he done nothing to help Gerard? She had lost both of her parents, yet had Agnes to help her wake each painful morning. Gerard had lost a wife and a son and who had helped him to face each day? Anyone?

The earl took a slow breath before finishing. "'Tis time Gerard faces a new life. If all I can give him is someone to fight and argue with, then that is what I will do. I want you to promise me that, regardless of your feelings for Gerard, you will not go soft on him. Do not permit love to smooth edges of your temper or tongue."

She swallowed her laugh. "Love him? Gerard? Lord William, I think you have little to fear in that."

William shook his head. "You misunderstand. I care not if you love him. I care only that you keep his fires burning."

Keep his fires burning? Gerard was looking for an escape from the pain he felt. Looking for vengeance. Would not anger add to his pain?

"Milady, I know the idea must seem cruel to you. But trust me. Gerard and I were raised in Henry's court. I know him well. The only way to direct his anger away from this revenge is to bring it to you."

When she didn't respond to his ludicrous suggestion, William added. "He will never harm you, Catheryn. Never. He will make it his mission to bend you to his will."

That statement only added to her confusion. "And how will this bending not hurt?"

The earl's smile could only be called seductive. "No. It will not hurt. He will find other means to convince you that his ways are the best."

Her understanding came more from the look on William's face than his words. She felt her own face burn hot. "Oh."

He laughed at her. "Good. I see you do not mistake my

meaning."

She wanted this conversation to stop. Now, before it went any further. Turning away from the earl, she said, "I will try, William."

"That is all I ask."

They resumed their approach to the church. Catheryn noticed that the yard in front of the chapel was filled with people from the keep. Beside Gerard, Walter had his arm around a crying Agnes.

Catheryn's feet slowed of their own accord. What was she doing? She stumbled slightly when the almost forgotten sound of Pike's cruel laughter sounded in her ears.

William's hold on her hand tightened. "Lady Catheryn?" His voice had reverted back to that of a lord—cold and questioning.

That laugh. Had it been her imagination? Or had it been Pike's ghost warning her not to go through with this marriage? *Escape.* The thought ripped through her mind. She looked left and right, and knew she'd not get through the line of men that stretched across both sides of the path.

It was too late. There would be no escape. She knew that. Catheryn squared her shoulders, then took a deep breath. "I am fine, William. I simply tripped."

His look of disbelief was brief, but the earl made no comment as he led her forward.

When they reached the foot of the steps, next to Gerard, the fat little priest asked, "What can I do for you, my children?"

The earl stepped forward. "Father, we come for your benediction. This couple willingly seeks your blessing on their vows of marriage." He stressed the word *willingly*.

The priest looked at Gerard. "Is this true?"

Gerard answered in a strong, steady voice, "Aye, Father."

"Are there any reasons this couple should not be joined?"

"Nay." William answered, loudly.

"Who gives this woman?"

"I, William Albemarla, Count of Aumale, Lord of Holderness and Earl of York." All present heard the earl's booming reply. None could doubt, or question, this powerful man's allegiance with this union.

William smiled down at her. He then placed Catheryn's hand on Gerard's arm, before stepping back.

Gerard turned toward her and tipped her chin up with one finger. "I, Gerard, Count of Reveur, dower you with the keep, farms and fields of Keene's Gate in Boulogne."

William gasped. "Gerard, it is not necessary..."

Gerard's steady gaze never left hers. "I would not dishonor myself, nor Catheryn, by offering any less than her fair third." He smiled slightly. "They are mine to give."

While slipping a heavy, plain gold band on her finger, Gerard continued, "From this moment on I take you as my wife, and offer this ring as a token of my pledge." He hesitated. "Do you accept me as your lawful husband, Catheryn of Brezden?"

Even though it was not the time, Catheryn wanted to laugh. Accept? With William and all of his men surrounding them, she could not see any other choice.

First taking a quick breath, Catheryn then forced the uncontestable words from her lips. "Yes, Count Reveur. I, Catheryn of Brezden, do accept you as my lawful husband from this moment on."

Catheryn wasn't sure, but she thought she heard a sigh of relief. Had it come from William, Walter or Agnes?

Gerard turned back to the priest. They followed the man into the church. As mass was said, she gazed around the small wooden building. The dark church was crowded as they all stood shoulder to shoulder. The slits for the windows were up high and they were too small to allow much light to pass through. Plain timber pillars formed the support for the roof.

Before she realized that the service was almost at an end, the priest called for her and Gerard to come up front. While holding her hand, Gerard pulled her down to kneel with him. They were covered with a white linen cloth and the priest chanted a blessing over them. When the ceremony was completed, they rose, turned and left the chapel.

She had not paid any attention on her walk to the ceremony, but now she could not help but notice how much of Brezden had been put back to rights. Gone were the charred remains of buildings. New patches had been overturned for small vegetable plots. Those waving and shouting their blessings did not have the appearance of a beaten people; they looked and sounded happy.

Gerard was quiet as he led her back to the hall. Catheryn wished there was a way to lift the clouds from him. All knew that he was not pleased with this marriage. Neither was she. But she had more to lose if it had not taken place.

Catheryn sighed. If nothing else, he had unknowingly saved her from death. She owed the rest of her days to this man.

"Catheryn? Where are you now?"

"I am sorry, Gerard, what?" Catheryn worried that he would be quick tempered and moody this day. She had hoped to spare him any further frustrations.

"It was nothing," he said, leading her up the stairs into the over-crowded hall.

"Please, Gerard, what did you say?"

He patiently repeated, "I wonder what kind of entertainment the earl has planned for us."

"What do you mean?" The earl hadn't been here long enough to plan anything.

"Do you really think William would have been able to plan our marriage and a celebration this large without help beforehand? Did you see the size of the baggage train he arrived with?"

She groaned. "So his questions and orders were a moot point?"

"Correct. There has never been a choice for either of us." Gerard pointed at the tables already set up and laden with food. He also directed her attention to the musicians milling around in one corner. "I would say that our marriage, the meal, and this evening's amusements were taken care of long before William crossed your borders."

Gerard shook his head. "The rest of this day and evening should prove interesting." He glanced down at her. "What did our crafty earl request of you?"

Catheryn sucked in a breath. What could she tell him? "Nothing."

His eyes widened in apparent disbelief. She wasn't the least bit surprised when he took her arm and dragged her into a private corner of the hall. "What did William ask of you?"

"Gerard, I, he..." She didn't know what to say. If she told him, he would take his tightly reined anger out on William. If she remained silent, she would be his target. Just as William had requested, Catheryn chose the latter. "Nothing that should concern you."

His face was confident—smug. "I will find out eventually. You know that. So why not just tell me now?"

"Gerard, he cares about you. He truly does."

"Oh, aye, that is obvious." He ran his finger along her jaw and up behind her ear. He cupped the side of her head and leaned forward. "What else did he say?"

Catheryn's heart thudded as he teased the side of her neck with his lips. He was going to seduce the answer from her? Even though the earl had warned her of this, it was a new tactic. "This is not fair, Gerard." She placed her hands on his chest to steady herself.

He trailed his lips up to her mouth. "Nothing is fair." He

kissed her once. "Life is not fair," he whispered before kissing her again. His tongue coaxed a quick and eager response from hers, lingering briefly before moving up to her ear.

Gerard's voice was soft and low. The deep timbre sent little shivers of pleasure down her back. "Tell me, Catheryn."

Her resolve was weakening, along with her knees. "He explained what I had to do for him."

Gerard stopped his assault. "And, pray tell, what could that be?"

She leaned toward him, running her hands up his chest, trying to draw him back.

He stepped back out of her reach. "What does the lout want from you?"

She looked up at him. "He wants nothing for himself."

Gerard laughed harshly. "William always wants something for himself. He does nothing from the goodness of his heart, my lady."

My lady? What did he think she was going to do? She narrowed her eyes. "Surely you do not believe that he requested anything immoral of me?"

"I would believe anything of William."

Catheryn's passion turned instantly to hot anger. "I appreciate your trust, my lord." Sarcasm dripped from her voice.

"Trust? What have you done to prove yourself trustworthy?"

She had listened to more than enough. Catheryn scooted away from the wall and stepped out from the shadows. "Stand here and snarl at yourself, my lord. I have other things to attend to."

Gerard pulled her back. "I can imagine." He ignored her gasp of outrage, leaned down and locked his mouth over hers.

She felt him laugh silently when she wrapped her arms around his neck to hold him to her. But this time he didn't break away. Instead, he artfully carried them away in a crashing wave of desire.

Chapter Eight

"My pardon, Lord Gerard?" A shuffle of feet behind them broke the pair apart.

"What?" Gerard nearly growled at the impertinent page.

The boy held his ground. "My lord, the earl sent me to find you."

Catheryn answered the child. "Tell him we will be there directly."

"We will continue this later." Gerard's lips were against her damp forehead.

"If that is a promise, I look forward to it."

He hadn't moved yet, except to take her head in his hands. "Catheryn, I will not calmly stand by while another man touches you. Not even if that man is William."

"You have no cause for worry."

Before releasing her, he warned, "Make certain that does not change."

Stunned, Catheryn realized that he was deadly serious. A sarcastic retort about ownership and possessions sprang to her throat, but she held it at bay. Instead, she merely nodded and stepped out of the alcove.

She surveyed the hall and noted that Gerard had not been mistaken. It was obvious someone had had a deft hand in arranging this banquet. Sideboards were laden with pork, fish and redressed peacocks. Snowy linen cloths covered each long table.

As they walked across the hall to the main table, those from Brezden and Reveur cheered for Gerard and his new wife. Catheryn was not surprised to find that Gerard had already gained the allegiance of Brezden's people.

At the table, Gerard sat to the right of the high backed chair and invited Catheryn to sit next to him. She wondered if Gerard was as angry with William as he acted.

Why would he leave the seat of honor for the earl if he was? She truly hoped the men's friendship would not be strained to the breaking point by this match, or by William's maneuvering.

"Welcome to the Lord and Lady of Reveur and Brezden." William said, as he sat down. "I hope you do not mind, but I took the liberty of ordering entertainment for the evening."

"How convenient, William." Gerard replied snidely.

"Gerard, what is a celebration without a fine meal and a little entertainment?"

"Some meal, my lord." Gerard snickered as he nodded his head at the overly laden tables. "An excellent feast for a man who has been here less than a full day."

Catheryn watched the steady pulsing in Gerard's temple and wished the earl had taken the Lenten season into consideration.

William waved away Gerard's comment. "I do not think any present will naysay my largess."

Gerard's low laugh rang a warning in her ears, but it did not affect the earl one whit. "My Lord William, is there any in York or even in all of England who would naysay you on anything?"

"Other than you? Nay."

"Gerard, please," Catheryn begged. Even though she agreed fully with Gerard, she did not wish a fight to ruin everyone's enjoyment. Brezden's people had been through much these last few years and deserved an excuse for merriment.

For a moment, Gerard glared at William in silence; then glancing at Catheryn, he bowed his head and relented. "William, I will let it pass for this night."

"Aye. Agreed. A truce for tonight and to seal that truce I will pray for God to forgive all those present for obeying my desires on this meal." He clapped his hands and ordered the meal to begin.

Gerard placed select bits of meat and vegetables in their shared trencher. After cutting up small pieces, he pushed some to Catheryn's side. Guiltily picking up her eating knife, Catheryn could not help but look forward to savoring the feast.

Course after course found its way to the tables. The pork had been cooked over a spit and was basted with a garlic sauce. A rich, thick wine and raisin sauce was spooned over the peacock.

The earl and Gerard discussed a hunting party planned for tomorrow. It seemed the earl wanted to take out a new falcon he had brought along and Gerard wanted to test the skill of Brezden's hounds.

Catheryn excused herself from the discussion with little notice from either man and made a hasty exit. The overcrowded hall was stifling. She needed air. Air and a moment or two alone.

After pausing to retrieve a cloak from her chamber, she raced up the curving tower stairs. Thankfully the door was no longer locked and she stepped out onto the battlements surrounding the keep.

It had been many months since she'd been permitted this escape. Pike had mistakenly thought she'd be desperate enough to throw herself from these high walls. More likely, she'd have tossed him over the edge, with never a twinge of guilt.

Dusk slowly overtook the land, casting the lengthening shadows into darkness. She liked this time of day. The hustle and bustle of the keep slowed to near silence.

Enough light to see without the benefit of a torch still surrounded her. The settling quiet gave her solitude to think. Springtime air, brisk and fresh, whipped her cloak around her. The quick chill was a welcome respite from the stuffiness of the hall.

Catheryn leaned against the crenellated wall. To hold this moment forever would be a blessing indeed.

"Are you satisfied, Lady Catheryn?"

The meal in her stomach churned. When would she remember to always be on guard against Raymond de Brye? She spun around and inched away from the wall. "Satisfied?"

"I was to be your husband and well you know it."

He was barely visible in the still deepening night. But his harsh voice rang clear. Catheryn knew he was close.

Too close.

"What choice had I? When has any woman ever had a choice?" She needed to distract him. Get him to move away from her only escape—the door.

"You could have declared a prior betrothal."

The hounds of hell would have to be at her heels for that to ever happen. "That would not have been true. Besides, the ploy would have been useless. Earl William already carried writs from the church for every consideration."

"You could have said you were not a virgin. Your lord would not have accepted sullied goods."

"Would not that have been easy enough to disprove?"

He was moving away from the door—toward her.

"Or easy enough to prove."

Catheryn gasped. "What are you saying?"

"Ah, my beauty, you break my heart." He moved closer. "How can you not remember?"

The memory of that night nearly made her retch. *No. Surely she would remember if he'd completed his dastardly act.* "You did nothing that night except knock me senseless."

"Are you certain?" His mouth slanted into a smirk. "How, Lady Catheryn, in your limited experience, can you be so sure?"

Her head spun. She'd be damned before letting him know exactly how uncertain she was. "I would know."

"Would you now?"

She kept her concentration locked on de Brye. "Of course I would know."

A snicker of a laugh preceded his next question. "How is that, milady?"

She'd not let his apparent amusement catch her off guard. Moving away, Catheryn shrugged. "There would be signs."

Inching along the wall with her, de Brye shook his head. "What kind of sign would that be?"

Grateful that the falling night hid her now burning cheeks she remained silent.

"Are you perhaps thinking of blood?" A cold, mirthless laugh filled the air around them. When he caught his breath, de Brye backed her against the wall. "Wipe that notion from your mind, sweeting. Not all virgins bleed."

Catheryn knew she was very near to panic. She had to remain in control of her senses. She had to. At this moment her life probably depended on it.

"But if you would like your blood spilled this time, I can make it possible. There are ways."

At first she didn't understand his statement. Slowly, his meaning dawned on her. Unfortunately, not quick enough. He grasped her arms before she had time to flee.

"Ah, yes, my beauty, there is plenty of time. Time to warm my cock in your blood, if that is your wish. Time to let the whole world know who first tasted your innocence and who will enjoy your favors again. Now. Here."

Her shock subsided in a heartbeat. She struggled against him, trying to push him away. Unable to break his hold, she tried to reason with him. "No, we cannot. Not here. Not like this."

His hands tightened on her. Catheryn knew she'd be

bruised and for a hair's breath wondered what Gerard would say when he saw the marks.

"Here and now is the perfect place. No one will hear your screams, nor my own groans of pleasure." His mouth came down over hers. Hard. His broken, jagged teeth tore at her lips. The stench of stale wine and ale attacked her nostrils. She could do nothing to stop from gagging.

In the space of one day she'd been ordered to marry by one man, yelled at by her then future husband, and now a third sought to assault her. Catheryn's mind screamed: *Enough! No more!* Had she not been the one who'd said it was time to take charge of her life?

The time was now.

When de Brye pulled her forward and pressed his groin against her belly she felt his erection. She also felt her cloak slide apart with the action.

Catheryn cocked her leg back and rammed her knee into his groin with all the force she could summon.

Thankfully it was enough. His hold fell away from her as he toppled to the floor.

Not pausing to see his reaction, she ran through the door and down the steps. She held her hand over her mouth to keep the bile intact, while she skirted the hall and ran for the kitchens.

There would be people there. People meant safety. Safety...and perhaps a chamber pot.

She was right on both counts. At least the servants had enough sense not to ask the lady of the keep why she was vomiting. All but one.

"Milady?"

"Oh, please," Catheryn groaned. "Agnes, go away. Leave me be."

"Lord Gerard sent me to find you."

Catheryn wanted to laugh. The last thing she needed at this exact moment was Gerard.

The maid unfastened the brooch on Catheryn's cloak and handed the garment to another servant. "Lady Catheryn, what has happened?"

Agnes passed a cool, wet rag over Catheryn's face and neck. "Come, child, sit down."

Not having the strength to argue, she allowed Agnes to lead her to a stool in a private corner. She wondered how she would calm herself enough to return to the hall.

Agnes knelt in front of her and brushed the stray hairs from Catheryn's damp forehead. She shook her head. "Your lip is bleeding." After wiping the blood away, she stared into Catheryn's eyes. "I know that look of fright well, child. What has happened?"

"Nothing. It is nothing." Catheryn wanted nothing more than to throw herself into Agnes's arms and cry. But the time for tears was past.

The maid plucked at Catheryn's gown. Smoothing and straightening. She brushed a hand down the sleeve. Catheryn flinched without thought.

Agnes paused. Then she laid a finger on Catheryn's upper arm and pressed lightly.

Catheryn jerked away and gasped in pain. "Oh, please. Don't, Agnes. Don't touch me." She bit her now swelling lip, fighting the tears that threatened to fall.

Agnes wrapped her arms around Catheryn's waist and cried out, "He is here. Oh, lord, he is here."

Catheryn patted her maid's head lightly. She kept her voice to a whisper and did not deny what Agnes had so accurately guessed. "Yes. He never left, Agnes."

"You must tell Lord Gerard, or the earl."

"No. I cannot. I cannot even explain to you."

She tugged at Agnes's arms, reluctantly pulling the safe embrace away from her. "Please, swear to me you'll tell no one. Agnes, my life, our lives depend on secrecy."

"Milady, your husband will see your bruises. Only

someone blind will not notice your lip. How will you explain?"

Catheryn shrugged. "Gerard will know nothing for a fact unless I tell him. He will rail. He will demand answers. He will get none."

"But—"

She looked at her maid and smiled sadly. "Agnes, what is the worst he can do? Kill me? Somehow I do not think it is within Count Reveur's nature to kill a woman. I can live with his anger." A bitter laugh escaped her. "Have I lived with anything but anger and pain since my mother died?"

"I do not agree, Catheryn. I think your safety depends on confiding in your husband. He will help you."

"I cannot."

Agnes patted Catheryn's leg. "You will see in time that I am right. Is there anything I can do for you now?"

Catheryn ran a hand over her disheveled hair. "Without going to my chamber, can you make me presentable?"

"Of course."

Agnes was as good as her word. In very little time Catheryn was ready to rejoin the men.

She took several deep breaths on her way back to the hall. It required every one of them to gain her composure. She convinced herself that all would be well. She'd worry about her lip when, or if, anyone questioned her. She'd worry about her other bruises—later.

"Ah, here she is. Please, Lady Reveur, join us." William patted the bench. "If you are finished eating we can have this cleared away and then begin the entertainment.

Food? Catheryn's stomach rolled at the thought. "I am done. Please, have it cleared away. What do you have planned for us?"

"Nothing grand. Not on such short notice." The earl signaled for the tables to be moved.

Catheryn snatched a large cushion to recline on and

placed it between Gerard and William. She had no desire to be alone with Gerard just yet. It was all she could do to avoid his searching glances. Agnes had arranged her hair so that it fell in ripples over her face and Catheryn took full advantage of the makeshift curtain to hide her lip.

Wine and ale flowed freely as musicians and jugglers performed for the party. She realized that just as soon as her goblet of wine ran low, Gerard had it refilled. Obviously he was trying to get her drunk.

Catheryn also noticed he was becoming successful at arriving in a like condition himself. Unused to the strong wine, she soon began to feel a little woozy and declined another refill. "No, Gerard, please. No more."

"You may want to allow your husband to decide your limit." William said as he presented her with a smug, indulgent smile.

Surely they must consider her a poor, witless dolt. Was she not even capable of deciding what, or how much, to drink? After a quick glance at two sets of narrowed eyes, she allowed Gerard to pour the wine.

"Wise choice, my dear wife."

Even though the heady beverage helped to set aside her fears and worries, it grated that she was always treated as a child—or a possession.

"'Tis what every woman needs. Plenty of men to tell her what to do and when to do it."

"Plenty of men? One would have thought that a father, guardian, or husband would be enough. How many have had the *pleasure* of ordering you about?" Gerard did not sound amused.

"First my father. Then Pike. Now you and de Brye." She'd spoken without thinking and now wished she could cut out her own tongue.

She felt Gerard's stare and knew she'd not be able to avoid him. Catheryn shifted slightly, away from the fire's light. She swung her hair over her face and met his stare for a moment.

The impulse to laugh nearly overwhelmed her. If the wine had been meant to help her relax, he'd succeeded beyond anything he could have hoped. How was she going to guard her wayward tongue when she could barely feel it?

Catheryn glanced down into her goblet. The deep red liquid bore a remarkable resemblance to blood. Her heart beat furiously. Blood? Whose? Hadn't she just been foolish enough to mention de Brye? The blood would be her own. She closed her eyes and fervently prayed for a miracle.

Upon opening her eyes, Catheryn was shocked to find Gerard leaning on her cushion. She stared up at him over the rim of her goblet and could not believe the wanton desire that overtook her mind and body.

Her pulse pounded madly in every part of her body. It required every ounce of willpower she possessed not to reach out and touch him. She wanted to feel his skin beneath her hands. To be consumed by him.

What was wrong with her? How could she detest and fear one man's touch and crave the touch of another? Maybe she was little more than a whore. These feelings couldn't be natural.

If the wine had brought about these unholy desires, maybe a little more would take them away. Tipping the goblet for another swallow, she was startled when he stayed her hand.

"No more."

He cupped the back of her head. As he leaned to kiss her, Catheryn forgot her retort. Her mind and her senses were focused on his coming kiss.

His lips tasted of wine. The heady scent of him was more intoxicating than any drink or perfume. She wanted to spend an eternity with his lips on hers. But his kiss was brief.

It ended the instant his tongue swept over her lip. "What

is this?"

"What?" She looked away from him, deciding what to say. But her mind clouded. With drink. With lingering desire. With guilt. She couldn't think.

His hold on the back of her head tightened. He forced her to look at him. Gerard brushed the hair from her face and demanded, "Catheryn, answer me. Now."

Suddenly frightened by the pronounced tick in his cheek and rigid jaw line, she answered with the only thing her muddled brain could think of. "I—I wasn't watching where I was going and I ran into a wall."

She tried to pull away, but he wouldn't permit it. His stare went cold and hard. A vein running from his eye to his hairline was prominent and pulsing. Catheryn wanted to run away and hide. His disbelief was obvious. This night was going to be a nightmare and she could think of no way to avoid it.

Gerard released her and ordered, "You have but a few moments to get yourself situated in my chamber." As he signaled for Agnes, he added, "I will have the truth this night, Catheryn. Do not doubt it."

A cold knot of fear grew in her stomach at an alarming rate. "Gerard, can this not wait? It is still early." Suddenly, Catheryn wanted to postpone the bedding for as long as possible.

"No." His tone left no opening for an argument. Yet, he didn't look like a man eager to get at his wedding bed.

"Come, milady." Agnes tugged gently at Catheryn's sleeve. She followed her maid like a compliant lamb. Catheryn wanted to scream. This was not how she had envisioned her wedding, or the night. She had never dreamed the bridegroom would come to their bed in anger.

"Your clothes have already been moved to the lord's room." Agnes opened the door to Gerard's chamber.

Catheryn vaguely noticed the elegance of the room. She

had little thought for the decor. It was all she could do to force a sense of calmness to her quaking limbs.

After undressing with Agnes's help, she climbed into the big, curtained bed. Agnes sat down alongside her and touched the bruises on Catheryn's arms.

"Catheryn, I know not how to ask this, but I must."

"No, Agnes. De Brye did no further damage than what you see." *At least not this night.*

The maid's audible sigh of relief would have been laughable at any other time. "There is still some hope then. If you can keep him from seeing these marks until you are well and truly wed, you may yet avert any complications."

"Some hope? Agnes, what you mean is a very tiny thread of hope. How will I manage to keep these hidden?"

Catheryn held out her arms. Candlelight flickered over the red and purple fingerprints evident on her pale flesh. "It has always been my curse to bruise this easily. Never could I hide a fall from a tree, or a dunk in the stone-bed creek. I'll not be lucky tonight either."

"Now think just a moment, Catheryn. We are not speaking about an anxious parent closely observing their child. We are talking about a man coming to his marriage bed for the first time. If you think he will be looking at your arms we need to have a quick discussion about men."

"I can't very well wear a gown."

"No. But we have your hair. And we have a bed with plenty of covers." Agnes looked about the room. "And we have far too much kindling for the fire. And too many candles."

The maid scurried about the chamber. She snatched more than half of the tallow candles from the wall and floor sconces and tossed them out the chamber window. The room was doused in little more than faint light. Almost all of the kindling followed. There would be a need for a great many covers this night.

"There. That should help."

She hugged Agnes. "You are a treasure."

Catheryn heard the sound of footsteps approaching.

"Quick, get into bed. Roll over on one side and use your hair for the other arm."

Catheryn did as she was bid. "Oh, Agnes, if this does not work he will kill me."

Agnes smiled. "Oh, lady, do not be afraid. I doubt if he will go that far."

"You don't understand." She'd not told Agnes about her slip of the tongue over de Brye, nor about her fears. She grasped Agnes's hand. "How does a man tell if his wife is a virgin? How does he know if she is pure?"

Agnes's eyes grew round. She leaned closer. "What are you saying, Catheryn? What has happened? What—"

Boisterous sounds of men at the door stopped her questions.

Catheryn bit back a nervous laugh as the priest performed the wasted ritual of blessing the marriage bed. She had little faith that the maid's sly tricks would work. Even if they did not, what would Gerard do if his wife was not innocent? What would she do?

Half carrying and half dragging Gerard into the room, Walter and William stripped the man. Drawing back the covers that shielded her from his gaze, Gerard nodded. "Aye, William, you were right. She is a fine looking woman."

Catheryn longed to yank the covers out of his hand. Fine looking? He sounded like he was appraising a horse or a side of beef.

"Enough, Gerard." William pushed the man into the bed. "Maybe we will see you on the morrow."

Chapter Nine

Gerard watched Agnes and the others leave the chamber. He then turned his gaze to the woman lying at his side. Catheryn—the woman who was now, or soon would be, his wife. *Wife.* The word tripped oddly across his mind.

A thick, uneasy silence had descended at the closing of the door. Now a suffocating stillness filled the room, making it hard to breathe and harder to think.

He'd told her that this would be the night for answers. But it was also a night for promised passion. Which did he want more? Rubbing his throbbing temples, Gerard knew which choice could unfortunately wait.

"Catheryn, it would go easier between us if you would just tell me what frightens you."

She turned her head away. He barely heard her mumbled response. "I cannot."

Why did she have to be so stubborn? So infernally contradictory? How could a woman be so afraid of something he couldn't see, yet stand so strongly against him?

His first impulse was to shake her until her teeth rattled. But he'd learned long ago to ignore impulses. One didn't gain a willing partner by beating them into cooperation.

Gerard leaned over her and ran his finger along her lip. "Does it hurt?"

"A little."

Gently and ever so slowly, he smoothed his tongue over the swelling, and stopped at the rough ridges of a gash. He cupped her cheek and turned her head toward the dim light.

With as little pressure as possible Gerard drew her lip down with his thumb. There were no marks on the inside. She had not run into a wall. He had four gangly sisters who, on occasion, found walls with their faces. And each time they did there was more damage caused by the force of their own teeth cutting into the inside of their lip.

He knew Catheryn had the odd habit of chewing on her own lip when she concentrated, but she would never bite herself that hard. While she might be pig-headed, she wasn't simple. "You did not run into a wall."

The fear glimmering in her eyes was almost more than he could bear. Gerard released her, unable to stop the memories assailing him. Beaten and dying women had that same look in their eyes. And it never failed to turn his blood to ice.

"Who did this?"

She shrank away from him.

"Are you hurt anywhere else?"

In a rush Catheryn shook her head vigorously. "No."

He didn't believe her too-quick denial. Before she could stop him, Gerard tore the sheet from her and tossed it on the floor.

When Catheryn pulled her hair around her like a curtain, he knew she sought more than warmth. She sought to conceal.

It took less than a dozen or so curses for him to charge across the chamber, grab the only branched candlestick in the room and pull it to the side of the bed.

He tore down the bed curtains and threw the heavy fabric to the floor.

With a challenging gaze he dared her to stop him. She gave in with grace. Catheryn closed her eyes, brushed her hair back and let her arms rest at her side.

He sucked in his breath. "It's nothing? A wall?" Gerard ran a finger around the outline of one bruise. "Then tell me, wife, which wall in Brezden has hands?"

"None."

He placed his own hand over the spreading bruise. "These were made by a man."

She nodded.

Gerard straddled her on the bed. He placed one hand on each side of her head. "Look at me."

He waited until she complied. "Who ever was unwise enough to lay his hands on you is a dead man."

Her eyes widened, but she made no comment.

"I will break his neck with my bare hands, Catheryn, and you will watch."

She didn't so much as flinch or bat an eyelash.

"This will not bother you?"

"No."

He'd not been imagining things last night in her chamber. He'd clearly heard her tell someone to go away. Later he'd also heard the click of a door latch. "These marks were not caused by an angry lover, who perhaps became a little too lusty?"

"No, Gerard. No."

It gnawed at him that she had suffered a man's cruel touch. Especially after he had vowed to keep her safe.

"Is the lout within these walls?"

She hesitated and then shook her head. "I do not think so."

"Is it the same man who killed your archer?"

In the bright flickers of light he watched her pale. With great effort she sought to turn away. Her reaction, her silence gave him his answer. It was de Brye. He should feel outraged. Anger should be at the forefront of his emotions.

Instead, he felt drained. Disgusted. Defeated. The ghost of his enemy haunted him even this night.

"A pox on you, Catheryn; how can you protect a man so vile?"

He shoved himself off her and the bed and strode to the fire.

"Because this is nothing. Nothing compared to what he is capable of doing."

Her answer was barely above a whisper. But it felt as if every word had been screamed in his ear. "I know exactly what that blackguard is capable of doing."

He turned around and looked at her. "And with or without your help, I will see to it that no other man or woman suffers his atrocities again."

She sat up. Hugging her arms around herself, she returned his look. "Gerard, I—"

He wanted no more of her half-answers, no more of her meaningless words. "Shut up, Catheryn. If you will not tell me where he is, just keep quiet."

Gerard was surprised. The woman, who thought nothing of calling him a filthy monster more than once, fell silent. He laughed and shook his head.

"You find this amusing, milord?"

"Not at all. Nothing about this day or night has been amusing. But what else am I to do? You refuse to give me the information I seek. And I have not the strength, nor the desire to argue with you. As sorely tempted as I have become lately, I have never beaten a woman in my life and I am not about to start on our marriage night. So what do you suggest?"

"Nothing. Maybe you should just go."

"And provide the entire keep with enough gossip to last a lifetime? You think that would be wise? No, Catheryn, it seems you are stuck with my company this night."

"This night only?"

She sounded far too hopeful. "If you desire, that can be arranged."

"That would suit me fine."

She was infuriating. Maddening. She easily tossed his emotions out on a wind-swept sea without a care. She made him feel as confused and awkward as a boy struggling to become a man.

And she was his wife. Every deceiving, secretive,

beautiful speck of her was his. This was their first night as man and wife. Not exactly how he'd envisioned spending their time together.

While feeding the fire in the stone hearth, he asked over his shoulder, "Do you require anything?"

"No."

"Are you certain you've no other injuries, that you are whole?"

"What are you suggesting?" Her voice sounded strained.

Gerard turned away from the fire and stared at her. Catheryn averted her face, but even in the dim light he could see her jaw tighten and her lips thin tightly. "I'm simply trying to determine if there were any injuries to your person that I could not see." He walked toward the bed. "What are you hiding? What do you not wish me to discover?"

"Nothing."

"Then what do you think I was suggesting?"

The fierce look she directed toward him took him aback. He'd seen her angry, flustered and sad. None of those expressions came close to describing the look on her face now. Creases marred her forehead. Uncontrolled fire flashed in her eyes. Her lips were drawn tightly together.

She raised her head higher, then spread out her arms. "Just let this be over with."

He took one step toward and stopped when she flinched. Was she using this odd, misplaced bravado to hide her nervousness? Gerard frowned. What did she think he was going to do to her? He approached her slowly. In a low tone he asked, "Catheryn? What is this about?"

"Come, Gerard. Let us end this not knowing. Bed me. Take me. Do whatever it is you do and let us discover whether I am a virgin or not."

He paused before her. "Let us discover? I would think you should know."

She shook her head. "Well, I do not know." Catheryn

lowered her arms and wrapped them around her waist. "I do not know."

The fierceness left her expression, but the anger remained. Anger and something he couldn't put his finger on. As her words fully registered in his mind, his own anger flared. He took a step away from her. And tried to step back from the sudden pounding of his own heart.

"How can you not know?"

When she didn't answer, Gerard closed his eyes against the increased throbbing in his head. This day had been too long. Too much wine, too much food, too much everything. Now this. "It is simple, Catheryn. Either you have lain with a man or you have not."

Looking back at her, Gerard was amazed to see confusion cloud her face. Nothing made any sense to him.

"What game are you playing, lady? If you are seeking to have this marriage annulled, be warned—you will lose all, not I."

"It is no game, husband." She made the word *husband* sound like a curse. "You do not trust me any more than I trust you. I thought only to get this question out in the open. Perhaps I spoke too quickly."

"Obviously." Then again, maybe she'd simply had far too much wine herself.

"I could have remained silent."

He couldn't help but laugh at the truth in her statement. "And hoped I couldn't tell?"

Her brows rose in question. "Could you?"

Gerard slapped one hand to his chest, then staggered backward in mock horror. "You wound me. My pride is crushed."

Catheryn had but one wish on her mind—that she *could* wound him. "You make light of this? You make fun of me?"

The smirk faded from his mouth. "No. The knowledge

that my wife may, or may not, have lain with another man is not a joking matter. I find little humor in that."

She swallowed a sigh of disgust when he swaggered back to her as only a man could. "But I promise you, I would know."

Catheryn turned away, unable to continue the conversation she had so rashly started.

And unwilling to do anything to discover the truth of the matter.

Gerard placed his hands on her shoulders. "Catheryn, I know not what fancies flit about inside your head..."

"Fancies?" She ducked out from under his touch and grabbed the cover from the floor. She wrapped it about her shoulders before saying, "I am not given to flights of fancy."

"If I could finish?"

"Oh, please do." She flapped a corner of the blanket at him. Suddenly wishing he would do something to cover himself.

"What makes you think you may have bedded another man?"

Did he realize that when he paced about, the muscles in his legs bunched and relaxed in a most interesting manner? Catheryn dragged her attention back to the matter at hand and asked, "Were you not the one to find me the night you attacked Brezden?"

"Yes."

"Was I not senseless?" She watched as his recollection brought understanding.

"So, you think this attack upon you included rape?"

The urge to run her hands over his chest proved nearly impossible to resist. Catheryn shook her head. *What was wrong with her?* "I have reason to believe that may be so."

"And you believe I would hold that against you?"

"But what will they say in the morning when there is no

blood on the sheets?"

He came nearer. "Blood comes from many places."

"Wouldn't they know?" She was finding it extremely difficult to swallow.

"This marriage was forced upon us. I care little what someone else may think they know."

"But..."

He laid a finger over her lips. "If you were pregnant with another man's child right now and I was to say in the morn that I was well satisfied, no one, not William, the Church, nor the King, would question me."

The warmth from his hand brushing against her mouth and chin did little to help her think. "I am not."

"Not what?"

"Not carrying another man's child." This much she knew for a fact.

He cupped her cheek and turned her face toward his. "That is good." His breath whispered across her lips.

She placed her hands against his chest for balance and leaned closer. "Gerard?"

This time it wasn't his finger that silenced her, it was his kiss. His lips, so warm and gentle against her own, took away her words, her thoughts and her breath.

When he stopped his soft caress, Catheryn rested her forehead against his shoulder. "Who gave you this power over me? Surely I am bewitched. You touch me and I cannot think."

"This is not a night for thinking." He held her in his arms and slowly moved them back toward the bed. "Tomorrow you may think all you like. But tonight, Catheryn, let it rest. Let everything rest."

"Let it rest? The words are easy to say. But I wonder; what will you do if I am not your virgin bride?"

Faster than she could blink, he stripped the cover from her again, backed her onto the bed, and loomed above her.

"Listen to me, for I will say this only once. If in truth you were forced, it does not matter. I will not forsake you. You are mine, Catheryn, and nothing that may have happened before this moment means anything. Do you understand me?"

The strength of his words and the seriousness of his gaze brought tears to her eyes. She stroked his cheek. "You are an odd man, my husband."

Gerard rolled onto his side, bringing her along with him. "Perhaps, but I am all you have been given."

An exaggerated sigh escaped her lips. "Then I suppose I will have to keep you."

She laughed at his low growl and stopped laughing when he brushed his thumb over one breast.

Now he was the one to laugh. "You were saying?"

Catheryn leaned into his touch. "Nothing."

He swept his hand over her belly, across her thigh, behind her knee and back up. She closed her eyes at the warm shivers he created as he repeated the caress.

Were the arrows shooting through her veins tipped with ice or fire? She couldn't be certain. Maybe they were laced with both.

Gerard nipped and kissed the sensitive skin along the side of her neck. His lips kept the flames alive. His hands danced, up to a waiting breast, then down to tangle in soft curls. Catheryn tipped her head back, moaning low, as she offered her neck to his attention.

He pulled her tighter into his embrace. His moan came from deep inside his chest, vibrating against her breasts. He claimed her mouth with his. Passion swept her along. Even though he kept his touch light, his kiss left no room for any other thoughts in her mind.

If she were to die this night, she would never forget the heat of his body next to hers. Never forget the way his hard mouth softened to devour her eager one. Never forget how a dark look could consume her.

She wanted to be enveloped by the essence of him. To breathe in the heady aromas of sandalwood and smoke that surrounded him. To feel his hands stroke fire into her blood. To taste the wine that had flowed over his lips and tongue. She wanted to look upon this beautiful warrior she had married and become lost in his returning gaze.

His hands were everywhere, coaxing a response and igniting fires each place they touched. His kiss demanded complete compliance and she let her whole being melt to his wants.

Lights flicked behind her eyes when a callused palm cupped a breast, lifting it to meet his descending mouth. Her legs parted, as his searching hand found the soft, moist warmth they had sought. While his fingers deftly performed the dance his body would soon take up, she felt like a tiny boat being buffeted by a stormy sea.

Catheryn gripped him to her tightly and marveled at the undulating waves threatening to carry her away.

Through a murky fog Raymond de Brye's evil face loomed before her. His hands clawed at her breasts. She gagged on the smell of his fetid breath.

"You are mine. I will kill you before I will share you with another."

Catheryn froze. The warm, swelling waves crashed against a rocky coast. The fire turned to cold, fear-filled shards of ice.

She fought against de Brye, yelling, "No. Stop. Please, stop." She pushed against his shoulders and cried out with relief when he released her. She tried to escape him.

But he restrained her and grasped her head between his hands. "Catheryn, open your eyes."

Slowly she blinked away the fog, and gasped in horror at what she had done. "Oh, my God. Oh, Gerard, I am sorry."

Catheryn longed to wipe the look of anger and sadness

from his face. She reached up to stroke his cheek. He brushed her hand away and rose from the bed. "Do not."

How could she have been so lost in memories? How could she have let a nightmare intrude? "I am sorry. Forgive me, it will not happen again."

"Stop it." He didn't turn around to look at her. Instead he retrieved his clothes and hastily began to throw them on. "Don't grovel, Catheryn, it doesn't become you." He stepped into his boots. "And don't lie."

"I swear..."

Gerard came back to the bed and leaned over her. "Go to sleep."

She grasped for words to keep him here. "But this is our wedding night."

He sighed as he pulled the covers over her. "Yes, it is. But I'll not share it with a third person."

"I said I was..."

"Sorry? I know. So am I."

She knew that nothing she said would make him return to their bed. What she didn't know was whom she hated more— herself, or de Brye? "Where will you sleep?"

Gerard shrugged. "Not here."

"What will William and the others say?"

"I care not."

"But we haven't, we didn't—"

Gerard finished the statement for her. "We haven't consummated our marriage?"

Catheryn nodded.

His laughter rang bitter in the chill of the chamber. "And we won't." He laid his hand on her cheek and stroked his thumb over her lips. "Not until you crave me and my touch so badly that there is no room for anyone else in your mind, or in your soul."

Chapter Ten

Catheryn snuggled closer to the warmth at her back. She'd spent a long cold and dark night cursing her fate, her life and de Brye. Then she'd cursed her childish belief in dreams.

She'd barely fallen asleep, wrapped in as many covers as she could find, when Gerard crawled into bed with her. She knew him from his scent of sandalwood and spice. From his possessive, yet ever so gentle caress that briefly stroked her hip. No one else could mimic his touch. No other hand would ever feel as welcome to her as his strong, callused one did. No one but Gerard—

Gerard?

Instantly awake, she scooted away from him. "I think you must be lost, milord."

"Keep your voice down." He pulled her back to his chest and wrapped his arm over her waist. "William is on his way to bid us farewell."

"The sun has not yet risen. He cannot wait?" The steady beating of Gerard's heart tapped against her back. His breath brushed warm across her ear. He molded his long legs behind hers, the coarse hairs tickling the back of her thighs.

When she squirmed to escape the mild irritation, she realized they were both undressed. Her next realization chased all thoughts of William and the placement of the sun from her mind.

She held her breath as the warmth nestled against her backside hardened and grew hot. "Oh, my." She quit moving about, the irritation against the back of her thighs forgotten.

Her breath quickened, along with the beating of her

heart. She could hear Gerard's breathing keep pace with her own. And she could feel his heart echo the same rhythm.

He hooked one leg over hers and easily turned her onto her back. Dizzy with anticipation, she closed her eyes. She wanted him to touch her, to stroke her flesh. She longed for the feel of his hands on her skin. The taste of his lips on hers. The fire. The ice. She waited for the thrill of both to rush through her.

But he didn't move. His hand remained motionless on her stomach. He did not kiss her, nor did he move the leg still entwined between hers.

Catheryn opened her eyes in confusion and stared into the burning gaze looking down at her. Anger? Desire? She wasn't certain. "Gerard?"

Slowly lowering his head, he said, "I don't know where you go when your eyes are closed." His kiss was brief. "But I know I'm not there and I like it not."

She stroked his stubble-covered cheek, seeking to assure him that the incident of last night would never be repeated. "Gerard, I—"

The boisterous sound of men approaching the chamber stopped her words.

Gerard threaded his fingers through her hair and whispered, "Now is the time for your lies and half-truths, Catheryn. Show William how well-pleased you are with your marriage."

"Why you—" He stopped her vocal outrage with his lips. She pushed at his shoulders, but could not budge him. His chest shook with laughter at her futile attempts to make him release her.

The moist, insistent caress of his tongue sweeping over her own weakened her desire to fight. He settled his leg more firmly between hers. He pressed the hard length of his thigh against her soft mound and Catheryn found the fire and ice she'd waited for only moments ago.

Now, instead of pushing at his shoulders, she clasped him more tightly to her. The world began to slip away. Her breathing became ragged.

Gerard deepened their kiss, imitating the age-old dance she hoped they would soon repeat with their bodies. He released his hold and stroked the fiery ice into her flesh, into her blood. Wherever his touch fell, she burned for more.

An unknown urgency filled her. She tore away from his kiss and gasped, "Oh, Gerard, please—"

The chamber door banged against the wall, permitting William and four of his men entrance. "See, men. I told you they'd not killed each other."

At that moment Catheryn knew she would gladly murder the earl where he stood.

With a short laugh that sounded oddly unsteady to her ears, Gerard tucked the covers about her and turned toward their unwelcome guests. "Why would you assume that, William?"

After motioning the other men from the room, William ignored Gerard and turned his attention toward Catheryn. "How are you this fine morning, milady?"

She fought to still her jagged breath and racing heart. "Morning?" She glanced briefly to the window opening. "I see no sun yet, Earl William. But I am fine this night."

"Gerard, your wife appears a bit grumpy before the light of day."

Gerard reached under the blankets and grasped her fisted hand. His touch gave her little reassurance; she still retained the urge to commit murder.

He agreed with the earl. "Aye, seems you are right. Perhaps lack of sleep explains the mood."

Catheryn unclenched her teeth. "What can we do for you, milord?"

Only the fractional lift of his eyebrow gave any indication that William took offense at her direct question.

"I came to bid you farewell and to see how married life settled on you, Lady Reveur."

Married life? Why didn't he just come out and ask her how the bedding had gone? She clutched the covers and began to sit up, but Gerard tightened his grasp on her hand. She took that as a silent warning and willed her overwrought temper to settle before replying.

"I find marriage—" She paused, searching for the right word. Gerard pressed his fingers into hers. "Fine. Simply fine, milord."

If William didn't believe her, he said nothing to give his thoughts away. Instead he nodded and turned his attention to Gerard. "I apologize for leaving in such haste. But I've received word from York that requires my immediate attention."

Gerard released her hand and rose from the bed. Pulling on his clothes, he asked, "When will you be ready to travel, William?"

"All is ready now. My departure awaits only my word. By the time the sun rises I hope to be well on my way."

Gerard's slight hesitation caught Catheryn by surprise. She had no idea what bothered him, but she knew something did.

"So, you've been busy all night making plans?"

The look William directed toward her and then to Gerard told more than his words did. "Yes. And I'm not the only one who's been occupied with tasks outside of the normal this past night."

Catheryn felt her heart painfully skip many beats. He knew. Somehow the earl knew that Gerard had not spent the night in his marriage bed.

Gerard did not back down from William's pointed look. Instead, he shrugged. "Things normal to one person may not be considered so by another."

The earl accepted Gerard's non-explanation with a curt

nod. Before quitting the chamber, he said, "I bid you farewell, Lady Catheryn, and I hope to see you again."

"God speed, William."

Gerard returned to the bedside. "Go back to sleep, Catheryn."

Her pulse jumped when he leaned over to place a kiss on her forehead. "Will you come back here after William leaves?"

"No."

Her body cooled as if someone had thrown a bucket of ice-cold water on her. "Why not?"

He stood and looked down at her. "Nothing has changed, Catheryn."

He was wrong. His earlier reaction to her left little doubt in her mind that he desired her, that he wanted her. Then why—an awful thought came to her.

"This was all for William's benefit."

"Partly, yes."

Humiliation, anger, regret all raced to the fore. She couldn't tell which controlled her more. Fighting to master the emotions battling inside, she clutched the covers tightly and sat up. "Why you—you are nothing but a—" Words vile enough to describe what he'd done escaped her.

"I am a what, Catheryn? A man?"

"Is that what you'd call it?" She longed to shove him from the room. To never look at his face again. But to do so she'd have to stand up and release the blanket. She'd be damned before giving him the opportunity to look at, let alone touch, her body again.

"I told you before that I was no one's dream. I am a flesh and blood man, with a man's wants and desires. Something you should realize now instead of later."

He dared to throw her dream sachet in her face? "I don't disagree. You are no answer to any dream."

"Tell me, wife, where was the passion we were to build

this marriage upon? Are your promises always given so lightly?"

If she twisted the covers any tighter between her fingers she would reduce the fabric to threads. "I am not the one who left the chamber last night."

"True. But I brought no one else to our bed."

She gave up trying to remain in control. "I told you it would not happen again!"

"If you wish, I could open the door. Then the entire keep would be certain to hear you."

Vexed beyond rational thought, Catheryn cursed. Not even de Brye at his worst made her as angry as this, this— this *man*. Fulfilling William's request would prove the easiest task she'd ever performed. "Get out, Gerard."

He laughed, but didn't move.

"Blast it all, you toad. Go away and leave me alone."

"I will."

"When? After you've tormented me a little more?" When he did nothing but stand there and look at her, Catheryn sighed with resignation. She realized that arguing with Gerard would prove her death one day. "It was all a waste of your time anyway."

"What was?"

"The show you put on for William. It was a waste. He knows."

Gerard raised an eyebrow in question. "Does he? How? I didn't tell him. You said nothing." He stepped away from the bed. "Your appearance when he entered the chamber told him otherwise."

"My appearance? What has that to do with anything? I am in bed, where any sane person would be at this time of day."

He shook his head. "I find your lack of knowledge interesting, wife."

Catheryn longed to wipe the smug look from his face.

"What are you talking about?"

"I am talking about the look of a woman in the throes of passion." He continued as he headed toward the door. "Lips swollen from kisses. Eyes glazed with longing. Fast and ragged breathing. It was obvious, Catheryn."

Rage-filled blood coursed hotly through her veins. Loud, heavy pounding drummed in her ears. "And I succumbed to your experienced touch so well, did I not?"

"Yes, you did."

"And what about you, Gerard? You felt nothing? Just doing your duty, husband? Covering up our lack of marriage?"

He paused with his hand on the door latch, then he turned back to her. A smile crossed his mouth. She saw the gleam in his eyes and wished she knew what emotion lurked there. Humor? Desire? She decided it didn't matter, for at this moment she hated him.

"You are not that stupid, Catheryn. It is a little hard for me to disguise my desires."

"Then why humiliate me so?"

"I said I only did it partly for William's benefit."

"And the other part?"

The gleam brightened. "When I told you last night that I would not take you until I knew that I alone filled your mind, body and soul, how did you think I was going to know when that moment arrived?"

"I gave it no thought." He was making no sense to her. How would he know? How would he not know? Why did she care?

He opened the door. "And how did you think I had planned to ensconce myself, my kisses and my touch in your mind and soul?"

"Why would you go to so much trouble?"

"Perhaps, Catheryn, you should give both questions some serious consideration."

Speechless, she stared at the empty spot he had just vacated. Falling back down onto the bed she wondered if he planned to torment her until she died.

~*~

And torment her he did. For a week—seven long days—Gerard invaded her thoughts. At night Catheryn lay alone in his bed and remembered the feel of his hands on her body. Her heart pounded with the memory.

It proved impossible to think of anything except his touch. Everything; his lingering scent, the feel of the sheets against her skin, the soft breeze that gently lifted her hair—reminded her of Gerard.

If the nights were unbearable, the days were no better. A flash of his smile quickened her pulse. A brief encounter in a dark alcove brought his lips down to cover hers. At meals his fingers would brush against hers and linger when he handed her a goblet.

He'd warned her. Gerard had told her that he intended to invade her mind and soul. She'd just had little idea how effective his methods would be.

How much longer did he intend to continue this attack on her senses? Catheryn knew that in this instance she was weak—powerless to stop his assault.

She swallowed a bitter laugh. Weak? Powerless? It was more than that. He was like a drug. A potent herb that beckoned her near, only to send her away when she answered the call.

There was no escaping him. She'd toss and turn until the wee hours of the morning, only to fall into a restless sleep filled with dreams of him. She'd awaken in the morning as tired as she'd been the night before.

Yet this morning something was different. The screams of women and the shouts of men tore her from her slumber.

A thick, noxious smoke swirled into the chamber.

Catheryn grabbed her gown from the floor and threw it over her head while she raced to the window. The sight that met her worried gaze caused her knees to go weak and her stomach to roll.

Flames, angry red and orange tongues of fire, engulfed the stable in the outer bailey.

Men, women and children had formed a line and moved buckets of water from the well to the stable.

"Catheryn. Lady Catheryn." Agnes's urgent cry spurred Catheryn into action. She ran past her frantic maid, down the stairs and out of the keep into the bailey.

Hot embers and ashes pelted her. The smoke, thick and cloying choked her, stinging her eyes, nose and throat.

The discomfort of her body was nothing compared to the fear threatening to overwhelm her.

Where was Gerard? She scanned the human water line even though somehow she knew he'd not be amongst those fighting the fire from this distance.

No. He'd be closer to the stable. She fought her way through the mad rush of men leading frightened, rearing horses to safety and darted closer to the fire.

Someone grabbed her arm. "Lady, no. Stay here."

It took a few heartbeats to realize the ash-blackened man holding her was Walter.

Catheryn shook off his grasp and ducked away from Gerard's captain.

Her heart pounded against the inside of her ribcage. She'd cursed her husband's very existence a short while ago. "God, forgive me. I meant him no harm."

Wicked tongues of fire sought freedom from the confines of the stable. They shot through the roof and window openings, reaching toward the sky. And toward nearby buildings. Buildings Gerard and the men had just recently rebuilt after the last fire.

The crash of timbers from inside gave the flames more height, more heat. Catheryn shielded her face and shrank away from the living inferno.

Men ran from the stable, coughing and stumbling blindly. They escaped to the safety of the bailey. One unlucky soul exited to the sound of his own screams as fire ate the clothing and flesh on his back.

His frantic motions fed the flames, giving them free reign to consume him. Catheryn lunged toward him and knocked him to the ground. Buckets of water instantly drenched both of them.

She rose sputtering. But the unrecognizable body lying in the dirt and mud didn't rise. He didn't sputter. And since he no longer screamed with his pain, she knew that at least one man had lost a brave fight this day.

Unable to stand the not knowing any longer, Catheryn screamed over the din of shouting voices. "Gerard!" She snagged the first man she turned to. "Where is he?"

Her worst fears were confirmed when he motioned toward the stable. While the sight and smell of burnt flesh had not revolted her stomach, the mere thought of Gerard being inside the hell on earth that had been her stable brought bile to her throat.

Sweat, more from fear than heat, trickled down her back and stung her eyes. Her heart raced so hard and fast she thought it would burst from the effort.

Her mind shut out all other thoughts but one. Get her brave, but stupid husband out of the stable now. Whatever else was left inside needed no rescuing; it could not be alive.

She stared at the building before her. Even though it was almost entirely engulfed in flames, she knew where the door was. Catheryn took a deep breath before she grasped her gown and held the hem to her face.

"No."

Walter left her no choice this time. He pulled her around

and captured her in a bear hug.

She kicked at him. Twisted in his hold. Pounded her head against his chest. All to no avail.

The tears she'd been holding back since she'd seen the smoke from her chamber burst through her will. "Let me go to him. He needs help."

She thought to beg him, but when she looked up Catheryn swallowed her words. The tears falling from her eyes were mirrored in his.

The world spun around her. A loud, insistent buzz throbbed in her ears. The yells and actions of those still battling the fire disappeared in a haze of pain. Her legs buckled. Had it not been for the strong arms holding her, she'd have fallen to the ground.

"Oh, God. Oh, God, no." She railed against the obvious. Then silently, she begged. "Oh, please. Tell me you did not send me a dream simply so I could watch him die."

A touch, light and filled with promise, wrapped around her heart. The slim thread of hope was all she needed. She caught Walter off guard. Catheryn broke free from his hold and rushed to the side of the stable.

Smoke poured from the doorway. But the fierce flames were still growing, seeking to match the rest of the fire in size and strength.

A huge form, covered in dripping wet horse blankets, stumbled and cursed its way from the building.

She grabbed one corner of the sodden mess, while a shocked Walter tugged on another. The odd shaped form was Gerard and his war-horse.

The destrier's wide eyes rolled with obvious fear. But as long as Gerard kept his hand wrapped in the thick mane, the animal offered no harm.

"Gerard." His name rushed from her lips in a breathless whisper. Her gaze ran the length of him, looking for signs of injury. She shook with relief and offered a prayer of thanks.

Catheryn knew that throwing herself at him would look foolish, but she cared little.

He ran one filthy hand through her hair and clasped her to his chest briefly before pulling her away. "There is no time."

She cringed at the sound of his voice. Hoarse and raspy from the smoke; Catheryn knew it had to pain him to speak.

He turned around, pulled someone from the horse's back and gently handed the nearly lifeless body to Walter.

She'd been so intent on Gerard's safety that she'd paid little attention to anything else. Catheryn gasped when the cover fell away to reveal sparse locks of thin, gray hair.

"Ephram." Horrified, she barely caught the saddlebag he tossed her before it hit the ground.

He waved them away and ordered, "Go."

She tugged at his arm. "Come with us. Let me—"

He pulled his arm away and shook his head. "No. Go."

As much as she wanted to argue with him, she knew that now was not the time. He had little voice left and still had orders to give. And she had a trusted servant to attend to.

Before leaving, Catheryn gave her own orders. "Gerard. Be careful. If you come to harm, I will kill you."

A line of white flashed across his blackened face, but he just pointed toward the already departing Walter.

Catheryn tossed the saddlebag over her shoulder and chased after the man. A mewling whimper escaped the leather.

"What the devil?"

She pulled the bag off her shoulder and opened the flap. A small, dirty, frightened kitten hissed at her from the bottom of the bag.

"Shh, hush, little one."

She closed the flap and shook her head. Who but her husband would think to rescue something as small and useless as a kitten?

After entering the keep, she handed the bag to Agnes. "Clean this up a little, give it something to eat and put it in the lord's chamber."

She held back a laugh when Agnes opened the bag and peered inside. "Gerard rescued it from the stable."

"Milady."

Agnes and the kitten were forgotten at the sound of Walter's voice.

Catheryn approached the hastily made pallet and asked, "How is he?"

Walter cleared his throat and shook his head.

She dropped to her knees. Memories of a strong, capable warrior filled her mind. Old as he was, Ephram was her last connection to her father.

Tears clogged her throat when she brushed some of the soot and ashes from his face. Nothing would lessen the pain twisting in her chest, but she vowed not to let her father's trusted man see the fear on her face.

He turned his head toward her light touch and opened his eyes. "Lady Catheryn."

Her name, spoken in such a hoarse, ragged voice, nearly broke her heart. She forced a smile to her lips and asked, "Is there anything you want? Anything I can get for you?"

He shook his head. That little effort brought spasms of coughing to his slight frame. He wasn't strong enough, or young enough, or healthy enough, to recover from the smoke he'd ingested, or the heat that surely had seared his throat and lungs.

Walter handed her a cup of water and helped her to lift Ephram to a half-sitting position. The man took but a swallow or two before turning away from the remainder.

After they laid him back down and saw to his comfort as best they could, he tried to speak.

"Milady, I saw—" Ephram's throat constricted with his effort. But he closed his eyes tightly and swallowed slowly.

She pushed a lock of hair from his face and sought to bring him some sense of peace. "Hush, Ephram. It matters not what you saw."

He weakly grasped her hand. "I must." The look on his face told her that he knew he was about to die.

She owed him much. This man had no business trying to fight a fire. But when had he ever shirked any task? Never. The least thing she could do was listen to his last few words. She leaned closer to him, lifted his hand to her lips and kissed his crooked, age-bent fingers.

"I am listening." Catheryn despised the waver in her voice, but knew not how to stop it anymore.

"Save Brezden."

Her lips trembled with her smile. "I will."

"I saw him."

"Who? Who did you see, Ephram?"

"The fire."

The old man's eyes widened. She heard the strangled sounds coming from his throat and knew his time was close at hand. Yet, he sought to do his duty as he saw it. "The fire."

He clutched at her hand and closed his eyes. Catheryn felt the tears run down her cheeks. She brushed away the droplets that slipped onto his face.

Ephram's pale eyes met hers. With an effort she knew she'd not possess he finished his accusation.

"De Brye."

His words were barely above a whisper, but she heard them. And they brought a sickening chill to her veins.

"Ephram, that is not possible."

He didn't respond. His grip went slack in her hold. She laid one hand on his chest and leaned over to place her ear against his mouth.

He breathed no longer. Ephram was gone. Catheryn rested her head on his shoulder and let the terrors, fears and pain of this day fall.

How? How could de Brye have started the fire? Why? He was after her, not the innocent people of Brezden.

Guilt piled in on top of all the other sins weighing heavy on her heart and soul. If she'd just done as Pike and de Brye had demanded, none of this would have happened.

Brezden would not have been attacked. Gerard would not have been forced to take a wife he did not want. The stable would not have burned. Ephram would be yet alive.

She had to get away. There had to be a way to escape this assault on her heart and mind. There had to be a way to make everything right again.

She released Ephram's cold hand, stood up and met Gerard's icy stare.

"Gerard, I—"

She ceased speaking the instant his jaw tightened. His tortured gaze matched her own suffering.

Catheryn knew that he'd heard Ephram's final words.

Gerard pointed to one of his men. "You. Take your lady and lock her in a cell. Do not let anyone in, or her out." When the man hesitated, Gerard shouted, "Now!"

Shock nearly swept the floor from beneath her feet. Before the guard could reach her, Catheryn staggered toward Gerard. "Why? Why are you doing this?"

Defeated and humiliated, she beat on his chest. "Damn you, answer me."

Gerard closed his hands over her arms and pulled her to him. As if in a strange, confusing nightmare she felt him pass his lips across her forehead before he handed her to the guard.

"Gerard!"

He closed his eyes for a moment.

Catheryn nearly fainted when he reopened them. Any previous evidence of pain, or remorse had been replaced—by the blankest and coldest look she'd ever seen on any human being.

After motioning for Walter, he turned and left the hall.

Chapter Eleven

Why did doing the right thing, the things that had to be done to protect Brezden and its foolhardy lady, suddenly seem so wrong?

Gerard ignored the guilt twisting in his gut and stared down at Catheryn. For two days he'd avoided her. The shame of it had threatened to eat him alive.

Sunlight poured through the cell's arrow slit, casting a hazy glow about the sleeping woman. She looked like an angel surrounded by a halo of light.

He knew better.

Her tangled, unkempt hair flowed across her pillow and pooled onto the floor. Drawn to the silken waves, he knelt down. He lifted the curtain of hair and moved it back on to the mattress serving as her bed. He permitted his hand to linger, to caress the wild curls that entwined about his wrist and fingers.

Unable to resist the urge to touch more than just her hair, Gerard stroked the back of his hand across her cheek. Relaxed with sleep, the skin was soft, pliant and warm. He brushed the pad of his thumb over her lower lip. The swelling from their wedding day was now gone. The only reminder of de Brye existed in his own mind.

Catheryn opened her eyes. In the fog between sleeping and waking, she smiled at him. A soft, sensual smile that stole his breath away and sent his heart to racing.

He knew the instant the fog cleared. Her smile flattened. Creases marred the smooth skin of her forehead as she frowned at him. She jerked away from his touch and asked, "What do you want?"

Peace. A quiet life. A home. A family. The same things he had always wanted. Things Pike and de Brye had stolen from him.

Instead of voicing his thoughts, Gerard brutally pushed them back into the realm of useless dreams and rose to his feet. "Ephram's burial service is today."

"Will I be permitted to attend?"

"With me, yes."

She sat up and glared at him. So far her wary gaze was the only evidence of her agitation. How long before she unleashed her tongue the way she had the last two nights?

"Should I feel honored?"

"Catheryn, I did not come here to argue with you. Either you attend, or you do not. It is up to you."

"Of course you didn't come to argue. Why bother? Just point a finger and your commands are carried out. No questions asked. No explanations given. Fair, unfair, the reasoning matters little."

Actually, when she held her head at that defiant tilt and her eyes flashed with fire, she was quite charming. This was one reason he enjoyed goading her so. But he gained little enjoyment from their current situation.

"Are you coming, or do I have to drag you?"

She ran a hand over her hair and then held out her arms. "I can't go like this."

"A bath awaits you in our chamber." He reached out his hand to assist her to her feet.

"Our chamber?" She ignored his offer of help. Catheryn stood up and brushed her ruined gown into place. "You mean *your* chamber." She waved toward the mattress. "I believe this is my room."

"Only when necessary."

"What does that mean?"

He'd hoped to avoid this conversation until later in the day, but since it now loomed before them, he answered, "As long as you remain at my side, you can leave this cell."

"At your side?"

"I believe that's what I said."

"Like a trained hawk tethered to your wrist?" When she narrowed her eyes, he knew her temper was close at hand.

"I never said that."

"Then explain it to me."

"It is simple, Catheryn. A good commander keeps the enemy within his sight at all times. If that is not possible, he ascertains their whereabouts and keeps close track of their movements."

She backed up a step, placed a hand on her chest and asked, "I am the enemy?" Then she pointed at him. "And you are the good commander?"

Before he could respond, she waved one hand in the air, closed her eyes for a moment and took a deep breath. "Let me see if I have this correct. I am so dangerous that you see fit to keep me locked up under guard."

"Men have died because of your lack of action."

Her head snap back as if someone had struck her. She looked at him as if he had just sprouted a second head. "You cannot blame me for that fire. I would never bring harm to anyone at Brezden."

"No?" Gerard cleared the distance between them. He was certain she could hear the blood rushing through his veins. "Three men have died because you saw fit to protect a murdering traitor. A man you still seek to protect."

She stared up at him without flinching. "More will die if I talk."

"Then through your association you are also considered a murdering traitor."

Tears welled in her eyes, but they did not fall. "That is not true."

"Is it not? Good. Then it will not bother you to attend the funerals of your victims."

"You bastard."

He laughed at her weak verbal attack. "That is all you

can come up with? For the last two nights I have heard you use curses that I'd never heard even on a field of battle. And now all you can do is defame my mother?"

Her eyes widened with surprise. She backed away from him. "What do you mean you've heard?"

"Who do you think guards your cell at night? Who do you think sits outside this door and listens to your ranting and raving? My men? I would not subject them to that."

"You? You sat out there and never bothered to answer me?" Her voice rose and Gerard knew any further reasoning would be useless.

"Answer your curses? I will not argue with you any more. It serves no purpose."

Now the tears she had been holding in check fell. "Dear God, forgive me; I hate you."

As she turned away, Gerard reached out and grabbed her arm. He pulled her against his chest and whispered, "Good. That just makes everything easier."

He was surprised at how strongly her cries tore at his heart. And at how hard it was not to tell her that he lied. But until he had the information he so desperately needed, she'd not know that he kept her in this cell for her own safety. He could not guard her every moment of the day and a locked cell seemed the only answer.

If de Brye thought little of killing innocent people, Gerard doubted if killing Catheryn would bother the man greatly. From the moment he'd heard Ephram's confession, he had known losing Catheryn would destroy him. Just the thought shook him to his very soul.

"Come. You need to clean up."

She shook her head and tried unsuccessfully to pull away from him. "Leave me alone. I do not want to go."

"You sound like a spoiled child. Have you not yet learned that we don't always get to do what we want?"

"I did not kill Ephram." Her broken words caught on a

sob.

The ragged sound sliced through his will, admonishing him to soothe her fears. Gerard gathered her closer against him, buried his face in her hair and whispered, "I know you did not. Catheryn, can you not understand? If I cannot be at your side, I must be certain you are safe."

After releasing her abruptly, he ignored her questioning glance. Instead, he turned her toward the door. He'd already told her more than he'd intended. "Your bath water is getting cold."

Catheryn stood in the middle of their chamber. His admission of seeking to ensure her safety surprised her. His declaration overwhelmed her anger, pushing the pain and hurt into the shadows. While she was eager to question his motives, she was not willing to tax her emotions any further this moment.

She turned her attention to her bath and gasped softly. When Gerard had said a bath awaited her, she'd expected a simple bath. Not this.

Instead of the small wooden tub she normally used, someone had brought up a very large oval one. What would it feel like to soak comfortably in a hot bath without having her knees drawn up to her chin? Or without having to sit on an uncomfortable stool?

Oversized drying cloths hung by a blazing fire. Even if the water in the bath grew cold, the cloths would be warm.

She had little fear the water would be cold. Steam curled up from the tub, attesting to its warmth. The mist carried a heavenly scent, rich with an unfamiliar spicy and exotic aroma.

Alongside the tub was a table set with an array of combs, a thick bar of soap and a small bejeweled decanter.

Unable to ignore the beckoning warmth and heady scent any longer, she crossed the room and dipped her hand into the water. A sigh escaped before she could swallow the sound.

To cover her display of pleasure, she asked, "From whence did all this come? It is not mine."

No answer met her question. When she turned around to ask again, she stared at Gerard. The deepest shade of red colored his face. *Embarrassed? Gerard?*

He looked everywhere but at her. "It is yours. A cache of supplies arrived from my mother."

"Your mother?" It was hard to imagine her husband with so doting a mother.

"Yes. My mother. The woman you so recently cursed."

Ashamed of herself, she ignored him and ran her fingers over the combs before picking up the decanter. She pried off the cork stopper and lifted the bottle to her nose. This was what scented the water in the tub. "Your mother has wonderful taste."

Afraid she'd drop what had to be expensive perfume, she carefully set the bottle back on the table. "I could understand her sending food, clothing, or household goods. But, Gerard, a tub?"

"'Tis one of the simple pleasures she enjoys."

"How odd." She cast her attention back to him and wondered what he was so embarrassed about. Again, a dull flush had crept up his neck and covered his face.

"Yes, well, she does have odd notions at times." He motioned toward the cooling bath. "They are awaiting our arrival, Catheryn."

She glanced around the room. "Where is Agnes?"

"Your maid has been retired from her duties for a time. I will have to suffice."

"What?" She was not taking a bath with him standing there.

"You heard me. Now get into the tub."

Her heart tripped inside her chest. Her throat constricted, making breathing difficult. "By what right do you dismiss my maid?"

He crossed his arms against his chest. "By right of lordship."

She noticed the bulge in his arms as he flexed his muscles and wondered if she'd lost her ability to reason. Was it wise to argue with someone who could snap you in two? What if William had been wrong in his assumption? What if someday Gerard lost the temper he so rigidly held in check now?

She pulled at her bottom lip with her teeth. While Pike and de Brye had always been cruel, neither man was as large and muscular as her husband was. With little effort, he could—

"Stop it."

She tore her gaze from his chest and arms and warily looked at his frowning countenance.

"Your emotions run plainly across your face." He approached her and deftly untied the laces on her gown before she realized what he was doing. "You have given me more than enough reason to beat you. From the first day I found you in your chamber, I had every right to do with you as I saw fit."

She tried to move away, but he snatched the skirt of her gown, effectively thwarting her escape.

"You are headstrong and possess a tongue that would make an asp kneel with admiration. For all your bravado, you are still smaller and weaker than I."

He lifted one hand before her face and spread his fingers wide. "I could crush you with one grip." He then curled his hand into a fist. "Or kill you with one stroke."

She gasped and leaned her head away. From another man, his words might sound like outrageous bragging. Her blood froze in her veins. This man spoke only the truth.

He uncurled his fingers and cupped her cheek. "Ah, Catheryn, who would torment my days if I was ever so foolish?"

She forced a breath into her air-starved lungs and willed her legs not to fold beneath her.

"You should know by now that I will not raise my hand against you in anger."

The palm resting so warmly against her cheek spoke not of a harsh, cruel man. It was not his hands, nor his fists, that brought her fear. The demon she feared lay deeper than his flesh.

She could grow to love this man she professed to hate.

Once she allowed him into her heart, into her soul, he would not have to employ physical force to bring her harm. It would take no more than a word or an absent-minded gesture to hurt her. Pike and de Brye had taught her that the pain caused by words sometimes caused a wound that would not heal.

"I swear, Catheryn, I will never harm you."

The harm he spoke of was not the pain she feared, yet his oath did mean much. She looked up at him. He appeared so serious, so intent on making her believe his words that she couldn't ignore him. "I know you will not strike me." She rested a hand against his chest. "Gerard, sometimes words have more power than might."

He nodded in agreement. "Then we need to find a place where even words hold no power."

"Where might that be?"

After glancing about the chamber, he asked, "Does this room hold any entrances other than the chamber door?"

"None that I am aware of."

"Then why not declare this a room of truce?"

"Your chamber?"

He rested his forehead against hers. "Our chamber."

"How can words have no power in here?"

"If we do not fight, if we do not argue, if we do not bring spite into this room, then the words we speak in here will not be filled with anger."

As childish as the idea sounded, she had to admit it held interest. "Sometimes it will be hard to leave the ire at the door."

He brushed his lips across hers. "Do you hate me?"

She hesitated a moment, then answered. "Sometimes I think I do."

Gerard slid his fingers through her hair, tilted her head and slanted his lips over hers.

About the time she thought her knees would buckle, he lifted his head. "What about now? Do you hate me now?"

Breathless, she grasped the front of his tunic for support. "Oh, heavens, how do I know? I cannot think."

He swept her into his arms and laughed. "That, my dear wife, is how we will leave the ire at the door."

"Then perhaps I will need to anger you daily."

"I am certain it will not require much effort on your behalf."

This strange, marvelous idea of his might contain a flash of brilliance. Then again, she wondered if it would be wise to agree to something that would, with an absolute certainty, chip away at her resolve not to care too much for him.

"Catheryn?"

Startled out of her reverie, she focused her gaze on him. "Yes?"

He lowered his hand to her gown. "Is this worth saving?"

The gown was torn, stained with soot from the fire and beyond repair. "Not unless you can perform miracles."

A smile lifted his lips. A glow of mischief lit his eyes.

Before she realized what he had suddenly found so amusing, Gerard grasped the hem of her gown and tore the fabric up past her breasts.

She whirled away from him. "What are you doing?"

Hand over hand he took up the slack of the gown, pulling her back to him. "Something I've always longed to do."

Catheryn slapped at his hands. She tried not to laugh at the devilish look on his face. "What might that be?"

"Stripping a gown off a woman's back." He yanked the fabric between his hands and succeeded in tearing through the neckline.

While running a finger around the top edge of her under gown, he looked at her and lifted one eyebrow in silent question.

She cocked her head. "If you destroy it, you will have to replace it."

"I will replace it with two."

Catheryn closed her eyes and tried to ignore the sound of more fabric tearing.

The cool air rushed against her heated flesh, causing her nipples to pucker and a shiver to run the length of her body. He chased away the cold with his hands and body.

Gerard slipped his fingers under the shoulders of her ruined gowns and slid them half way down her arms. His mouth was warm against her neck. Embers of fire trailed along her shoulder and back up to the sensitive flesh below her ear.

"Open your eyes, Catheryn. Know it's me."

Lord, how could she think it was anyone else? She did as he asked. Through eyes glazed with desire, she looked at him.

Here stood the man who'd tormented her day and night. He'd seated himself so firmly in her mind that she could think of no one but him.

Here stood the man she wished she could hate. He wore such an expression of want that at this moment, she'd gladly give him all he desired.

Here stood the man who'd had her locked into a cell

because of de Brye. His touch was so tender, she longed for nothing more than to feel his hands upon her flesh.

Here stood the man who'd attacked her keep. His kisses easily made her forget the destruction he'd wrought.

She'd needed him. She'd called him here and he had answered her call. But he wanted answers to questions that would bring nothing but death to Brezden's men.

She bit her lip to keep from crying. She hated him. She wanted him. She needed his help. She could not help him. If this is what it felt like to go mad, she would rather die.

He brushed the tears from her cheek and drew her face against his chest. "Oh, Catheryn, what am I to do with you?"

Gerard pushed her dress off her arms and tossed it on the floor. "Your body claims that you desire me as much as I do you."

She wrapped her arms around him and held him close. The well-worn cloth of his tunic rested softly against her face.

"Your eyes tell me something different."

No words came to her lips.

"At this moment I would like nothing more than to shake all of your fears and doubts from your mind." He stroked her back before resting his hands on her shoulders. "It would be useless. You would only hold your tongue until I'd shaken all the teeth from your head, and then you'd look silly and I'd not know what to feed you."

He purposely sought to chase away her concerns with foolish words. She tried desperately to hold in the laugh at his welcome attempt. It slid out despite her will. "Gerard, you have lost your mind."

"I know." He brushed his lips over hers. "Since the moment I saw you, I have been a senseless dolt."

Slowly moving away from the circle of her arms, he glanced toward the tub. "I would imagine they are growing anxious for our arrival. I will leave you to your bath."

As much as she longed to sink into the scented water, she did not want this moment to slip away. "Stay."

The flush that had covered his face earlier returned. "You do know why that tub is so big?"

"Because your mother liked to soak her entire body in comfort?"

His hoarse laugh rang loud. "No. She enjoyed sharing it with my father."

Catheryn's breath caught in her throat. The bath did appear big enough to hold two people. The visions springing to her mind caused her own cheeks to heat. Visions that did not appear as distasteful as one might imagine.

She narrowed her eyes and walked backwards toward the tub. "This will fit two people?"

He backed toward the door. "Yes. Easily."

"When was the last time you had a bath?"

Gerard closed the distance between them in a few quick, long strides. He lifted her in his arms and hungrily claimed her lips in a kiss that sent the world spinning away.

She clung to his shoulders, frustrated that his tunic separated her skin from his.

When he moved his lips to her breast, she sank her fingers in his hair, seeking to hold him close.

He slipped one arm beneath her knees and cradled her close for a heartbeat, before lowering her into the bath.

The now lukewarm water served to snap her out of the haze of desire. "Gerard!"

He placed one last, slow kiss on her lips. "We have not the time. However, do not for a moment think I will forget the invitation, Catheryn."

He tossed the soap to her. "I would like nothing better than to wash every speck of your body." Gerard breathed an exaggerated sigh. "In fact, I might enjoy the task more than you."

Just the thought of his soapy hands running over her caused the cool water to be forgotten.

He rose and headed back toward the door. After flashing her a quick smile, he laughed. "Pull your mind away from those thoughts, milady, and finish your bath."

Gerard closed the door to her chamber and stopped. *What had just happened?* He wasn't certain, but he did know that his conversation with Catheryn had not worked out as he'd planned.

He looked back at the chamber door. Had he told her that until de Brye was captured—or killed—she'd have no freedom? He'd only remembered hinting at it.

Now that he thought about it, there were many things he'd not said. He turned back to the door, then paused. The simple thought of her in the bath fired his blood with lust.

No. The things he'd not spoken could wait. At least until he was better able to control his feeble mind.

What happened to him when he was in her presence? Instead of focusing on the safety of Brezden and those who depended on the keep's well-being, he found his attention drifting to her mouth. Or her eyes. Or the way her breasts rose and fell with each breath.

He was supposed to be angry with her. He had been—for about a dozen heartbeats. He was supposed to have laid down the law—his law. Her tears had reduced that intention to rubble.

If he wasn't more careful, if he didn't maintain a tighter grip on his wandering thoughts, he would lose this keep. If he could not find his usual sense of control, it would be an easy thing for de Brye to destroy all—including him and the woman who was driving him mad.

Gerard motioned to the guards waiting further down the corridor. "If anyone tries to enter this chamber I expect your shouts to be heard in the bailey. No one enters or leaves without me at their side. Understood? No one."

Chapter Twelve

Catheryn looked down at her father's grave. Would she ever be able to visit this site without experiencing the twist of heartache?

Five days ago, at Ephram's burial service, the swelling of her heart had surprised her. Emotions—grief, loneliness, anger over her parents' deaths—had rushed to the fore with all the intensity of a raging river.

She'd wanted to visit her mother and father's graves that day, but Gerard had insisted they wait. Ephram's daughter had invited those from the village to join her at the cottage she had shared with her father. Gerard wished to be among those making a final farewell to Ephram.

At first, the mourners had been shocked by the appearance of the lord and lady of Brezden, but Gerard's easy way with the men vanquished the edginess from the crowd.

She'd been glad they'd attended. Catheryn hadn't had much contact with many of those outside the keep for years and was grateful for the chance to renew old acquaintances.

But did it have to take another five days before he had the chance to bring her back to the grave sites? True, he'd been busy rebuilding the stables, but she could have come alone.

She swallowed a laugh. Alone? She'd not been alone in five days now. If she wasn't at Gerard's side, she had Walter as a shadow. But having either man watch her was better than sitting in a cell.

Today she'd had to shame her husband into bringing her to the cemetery. His dark looks made it clear that he'd not liked her high-handed actions one bit. Would she ever understand Gerard's moods? Maybe in a dozen life times.

A beam of sunlight danced off the etched metal adorning the cross marking her father's burial site. Dead vines and weeds from the last two years' growth twined about the cross and covered the grave. She'd not been permitted to care for this small, sacred plot of ground.

Pike had forbidden it. The small, jagged scar on her arm burned with the memory. Any who saw the ill-healed wound would assume it'd been obtained from a childhood accident. They would not think the bite of a lash had caused the disfigurement. She'd only sought to protect her mother, who in turn had been seeking to protect her headstrong daughter. Neither had come away from the incident unscathed.

Her gaze wandered to another cross just outside the wooden fence protecting the consecrated graves from rooting animals. "Oh, mother, what am I to do?"

No answer was forthcoming. None had been expected.

"Do about what, Catheryn?"

She gave him only a cursory glance, before centering her attention on the mountaintops far beyond Brezden. "Nothing, milord."

How she longed to be a bird. A falcon with the ability to spread her wings and soar into the clouds hanging low over the mountain peaks. The freedom to come and go at will. The power and the right to live her life without constraints. She tried to shake off the strange, unusual longings coursing through her, but they only grew stronger.

The responsibilities and limitations of her life descended like a thick, heavy mantle about her shoulders. She was a woman. When had she ever been free? Had the decisions to come and go, to stay or leave, to even eat or to sleep, ever been hers to make? She would never be permitted such freedoms.

Gerard stepped into her line of vision. No. Never. And suddenly the coming days stretched out long before her.

Each day would blend into the next and before she knew it, she would be lying in the cold dirt. She would die never having known freedom. Never having tasted love. They would cover her with the earth before she had a chance to touch her simplest dream.

Her breath caught in her chest. What could she do?

Nothing.

Catheryn closed her eyes against the useless moisture building behind her eyelids. She fought to swallow beyond the pain thickening in her throat.

Gerard gripped her shoulders. "Catheryn."

Unshed tears blurred her vision and cast a misty glow around him.

"Talk to me." He gestured toward the graves and tilted his head. "Tell me of your parents. Talk to me."

Confusion swirled about her mind. "I thought you were angry with me."

"I am." He shrugged. "I am asking you to do nothing more than to tell me of yourself."

"There is not a great deal to tell." This was not important to him, so why did he insist upon knowing?

"Were your parents kind to you?"

"Yes."

"You had no brothers or sisters?"

"No."

"You learned to read and write?"

"Yes."

"Mathematics? Religion?"

"Yes."

After making himself comfortable on the grass, he pulled her down beside him. "A one word answer is not talking."

To quell her sudden nervousness, she pulled out some of the weeds covering her father's grave. "I find it odd that now you wish to talk about meaningless things."

"You are my wife. Is it not natural for me to be curious?"

"I would not know, milord."

"Gerard."

She looked at him blankly.

"My name is Gerard."

"Oh." What was this man seeking? He appeared serious. No trace of amusement, not even a smile, crossed his face. "I would not know what is or is not natural for a husband or wife, Gerard."

He plucked a weed from her hair. "What was it like growing up at Brezden?"

"The same as it was anywhere." Her childhood seemed so far away. It was hard to remember, harder still to find words. She pulled another vine from the ground and tossed it aside. "People here used to laugh. Even after a hard day of work, there were things to talk and smile about."

Gerard glanced toward the keep. "And some day they will again."

"I find that hard to imagine." She shook her head. "No. The laughter and the love were beaten out of Brezden a long time ago. It would take a miracle to bring them back."

"Not so much as a miracle, Catheryn. Trust would bring life back to these people."

For a reason she could not name, his assumption grated on her. Jealousy? Possessiveness? "You presume much for a new lord."

He chewed on a blade of grass for a few moments before answering. His eyes seemed to flicker with some kind of life and she swore she could see the thoughts running around his mind.

Finally, he said, "I think you are wrong."

"What do you mean?"

He ignored her question and posed one of his own. "Who beat the life from Brezden?"

The hairs on the back of her neck rose. Catheryn now saw the dangerous ground he was headed toward and liked it not. "I'm certain you know the answer to that."

"Humor me."

"Baron Pike."

"And what of de Brye?"

"Not until later."

Gerard moved to the other side of her father's grave and began to yank at the weeds too. The look he shot her was not one of patience. "Do not force me to drag every sentence, every word from you."

She fought to keep the anger from her voice. "Why do you want to know this?"

"Brezden is my home, too."

"And you want the people to like you."

His laugh caught her off guard. "Like me? What has liking to do with anything?"

"Would it not make things easier?"

"How long ago did your father die?"

"Almost five years ago. Why?"

"So you were a child of what? Thirteen? Fourteen?"

"Fourteen." Catheryn tossed her hair over her shoulder. "And I was not a child."

Gerard rolled his gaze briefly to the sky. "Your actions and experience make you an adult, not your age. I would wager at fourteen you were closer to a child than a woman."

Briefly comparing what she knew about life now and what she'd known then, she conceded him this one. "Go on."

"And you probably believed everyone liked your father."

"They did." She could think of only a few who disliked him.

"Why do you think that?"

"Everyone laughed and joked with my father."

Gerard lifted his eyebrows in obvious disbelief. "Everyone?"

"Almost everyone."

He shrugged. "Then your father was probably a weak, ineffective leader."

She was tempted to throw the clump of weeds and dirt she held in her hand at his head. "My father was a strong leader of men. No one ever thought to naysay his orders. Never do I remember an argument about any decision he made."

"The freemen who followed his orders, do you think they enjoyed having someone tell them what to do? Do you think they did not chafe under orders?"

"Whether they chafed or not, they did as they were told."

"Because they liked your sire? Because he could tell a good joke? Because he knew how to laugh?"

"No. They did it because he was their lord and they—" She glared at him and cursed silently. In the future she'd have to be more careful. "You made your point well, milord. They trusted him."

Instead of gloating over his victory, Gerard merely nodded. "And I need them to trust me. Do you understand that? I care not if they like me."

"Yes. I understand."

"Do you also understand that I need them to follow my orders without question, without hesitation? Mostly I need them to not be concerned about what you might think or do about those orders."

"These are my people."

"That may be true. However, I am responsible for their safety now. Not you."

Regardless of the sun warming the day, Catheryn grew cold. "What are you saying, milord? Do you wish to take all away from me? All responsibility, all decisions are to be yours? Are you seeking to cut me off from my own people? Will you succeed in finishing what Pike started? Do you think I will stand by idly while another lord treads on Brezden?"

A clump of dirt landed in her lap. "Give over, Catheryn. Had I sought to tread on Brezden, the deed would have been accomplished by now."

Exasperation tinged his words. She searched his face for signs of anger, but found only a tired countenance looking steadily back at her. Still, she needed to understand what Gerard was after. "Am I not your wife? Is not Brezden as much my responsibility as it is yours?"

"Yes, in most instances it is, but you are not going to lead any men into battle. You are not going to meet de Brye on the field. You are not going to take up arms at the gates."

"Will you not be leading your own men into any battle that may arise?"

"How many men do you think came with me on this mission? You have seen them in the hall and the bailey. Surely you realize there are not enough to keep Brezden safe from any and all attacks."

"Where will you get more men? Mine are—" She stopped. What could she tell him?

"Yours are mysteriously absent from the keep. And seemingly nowhere to be found."

Catheryn averted her face. "You've looked?"

"Of course."

"And you found no one?"

"Not a soul."

Her heart fell. Even though de Brye had told her that the men were held under his guard, she'd hoped that a few had somehow escaped. That hope died with Gerard's declaration.

He reached across the grave and with the crook of his thumb turned her chin so she again faced him. "You expected me to find them?"

"No. I had only hoped."

"Do you know where they are?"

Unable to meet his searching look, she jerked her chin

away from his touch.

"Catheryn, did you send them away?"

"Yes." She studied the vine twined around the cross.

"Did they make it to safety?"

Her throat burned. Her heart ached with the knowledge of what she had done. She took a deep breath, hoping to steady her voice. "No. They did not."

She expected him to rail at her, but his silence piqued her curiosity. Warily she glanced at him. The frown on his face made her wish she'd not looked.

After a few more silent moments, he sighed and shook his head. "Tell me of yourself, of your childhood."

"Do you wish to know of Brezden, or of me?"

A half smile lifted one corner of his mouth. "Both, if you please."

Not seeing any harm in his request, she told him of her lessons, of learning to ride a horse, and the horrendous chore of learning to sew. He was easy to talk to, because oddly enough he appeared to listen.

He laughed when she recounted tales about learning to fight with the stable boys and again when she confided in him about the squire who'd tried to teach her how to kiss.

She explained what she could about the changes her father had made at Brezden upon his return from the last crusade. How he had declared the upper chambers were better suited for his family as they afforded a small measure of privacy. He'd even returned with enough household furnishings to turn their dwelling into a small but comfortable keep.

Catheryn shivered with revulsion when she told Gerard about Baron Pike's introduction to Brezden.

The baron had come seeking refuge with his long-lost cousin by marriage. At least that's what the man had called her father. The Lord of Brezden had no reason to doubt Pike's claims and had welcomed him with open arms.

Within a short time Pike started carrying on about holding a tourney at Brezden. Soon, everyone was looking forward to the event and her father had little choice but to bow to the fervent pleas of the men.

When she fell silent, Gerard prompted, "This is where your father was killed?"

"Yes. Somehow a sharpened knife had replaced the blunted one in Pike's belt. Before all in attendance, the baron delivered an instantly fatal blow to my father."

A look of confusion fell upon Gerard's face. "No one questioned the man?"

"Only the squire responsible for the baron's weapons. The boy was slain immediately after being branded a murdering knave by Pike."

"How did the baron come to remain at Brezden?"

Catheryn's laugh tasted bitter as it rolled off her tongue. "He petitioned King Stephen. Since the King could not be bothered to come to so small a keep as Brezden to investigate the mishap for himself, he simply granted Pike's petition."

"Your mother did not issue a plea to King Stephen?"

"Yes, of course she did. The King had been convinced that she was too distraught to know what she was talking about."

He shook his head. "I cannot fathom Stephen blindly accepting Pike's words."

"Do you doubt that it happened? Was Pike not here when you attacked Brezden?"

"Yes, he was, but it still does not explain how the petition was granted so easily. Nor can I understand why your father's death was not questioned more closely."

"You did not know Pike. He was clever. He played upon your emotions so effectively that you were not certain what you thought, or what you felt. In that very moment of uncertainty, he always found a way to drive his will over your own."

"And de Brye?"

"He arrived much later. It soon became obvious that if Pike was clever, he had learned it from his master—Raymond de Brye."

"If your lady mother knew from the beginning how dangerous de Brye was to Brezden, why did she not send her plea to Earl William?"

"By the time she had proof that de Brye's outward acts of kindness were naught but a ploy, it was too late."

"Too late? How?"

Catheryn attacked the vines twined about the cross. She wished that de Brye's face was beneath her clawing fingers.

"He was kind, even pleasant to us at first. Whenever Pike would fly into a rage, de Brye would soothe the baron and protect us from harm."

"Your mother appreciated his efforts?"

She broke a nail and winced. "No. From the first day my mother said he was too nice, too kind. She trusted him not, but went along with his act, always waiting for his darker side to come forth."

Gerard stayed her now bleeding fingers with his hand. "What about you? What did you think?"

Guilt, humiliation and anger fed the force of her admission. "I thought he was sent from God."

"Catheryn, you were too young to know any better." He released her hands and moved to sit behind her. "The man who'd always protected you was gone. The new lord knew not the meaning of kindness. Who could fault you for thinking de Brye a welcome reprieve?"

She stiffened when his arms came around her, but she didn't pull away. "My father had been gone nearly two years. I was not too young. I was old enough to have been married and have had children running about my own keep. Instead of listening to my mother, I made our lives a hell on earth."

"How so?" His question fell softly on the nape of her neck. She longed to lean back against the broad chest behind her, but the lingering wariness teasing at the back of her mind kept her upright.

"He treated me like a favored child, when I wished to be seen as a woman. His warm glances, honeyed words and lingering touches were reserved for a woman who had little use for any of his attention."

"Your mother."

She couldn't bring herself to say the words. Yet that did not stop them from ripping her heart to shreds. *Yes, her own mother—the woman who had given her life, who had seen to her care and happiness. The woman who had protected and comforted her...had become her enemy.* To this day Catheryn did not understand her own actions back then. Did not understand them; nor could she forgive her actions, or herself.

The strong arms around her tightened. Gerard pulled her against his chest.

His heart tapped a steady beat against her back. His fingers were warm against her skin as he stroked her cheek and gently coaxed her to relax against him.

Temporarily safe in his protective embrace, she drew in a shaky breath. The scent of sweet woodruff filled her senses with a modicum of peace.

A breeze ruffled her hair and Gerard smoothed the windswept tresses back into place. "How did he react to your mother's rejection?"

"No more." She struggled to twist free from his hold. "Please, Gerard, let me go. Ask me no more."

His hold fell away. Before she realized what he was doing, she found herself seated across his lap. Before she could protest, he covered her lips with his own.

Catheryn wanted to scream with outrage. She wanted to

melt against him. She wanted his kisses to stop—tomorrow.

She knew that he would not cease his renewed assault, nor this calculated seduction, until he'd learned all. The knowledge made her want to sob. Aware that her will could no longer stand a chance against his, she surrendered with a silent cry.

He gently pulled her tightly against his chest. Engulfed by his sweet, warm caress, she clung to the safety he offered. Safe. Protected. Things she'd never thought to feel again.

Too soon Gerard broke their kiss. The cold, sharp pang of abandonment swept over her. The warmth of his touch against her cheek banished the chill.

"Catheryn, my shoulders are large and well able to bear any weight you see fit to place upon them. I am your husband and as long as I walk this earth there is no burden you need carry alone."

The tears she had wanted to shed earlier slipped past her closed eyes and down her cheek. Oh, how she longed to believe him. To know she was not alone. To have someone she could trust without doubt would be a dream realized. But she had been told that dreams were for children and never came true.

Never.

An oft-repeated verse rang in her ears. *Thou pretty herb of Venus's tree, thy true name is yarrow.* The image of a dark knight thundering toward her raced through her mind.

A tear cascaded over Gerard's fingers. He leaned toward her and kissed it from his hand, then from her lashes.

He rested his forehead against hers and whispered, "Ah, Catheryn, you will rip the heart from my body with these tears of yours."

Trust. It was naught but a small word. Yet, so much rested on so few letters.

She opened her eyes and looked into the shimmering

dark ones so close to hers. His gaze was steady. No anger, no mocking glance, no look of disgust met her perusal.

She brushed her fingertips across his cheek before threading them through his hair. *Oh, dream knight of mine, fate may yet prove you wrong.* She may take the first step toward trusting him, but Catheryn doubted if he'd ever come to trust in her dreams.

Not wanting to watch his expression change when she told him of her mother's death, she lowered her head and rested the side of her face against his shoulder.

"When my mother rejected de Brye, he turned mean. Crueler than Pike had ever been."

Gerard tilted his head and rested his cheek against the top of her head. He ran his hand over her hair, letting it come to rest for a moment at the nape of her neck. The heat of his body radiated through his tunic, warming her. The steady drumming of his heart calmed her racing pulse.

She burrowed into his embrace, seeking solace from the memories chasing her.

"It was then that I realized my mother had been correct. Raymond de Brye was lower than vermin. By then it was too late. He had already seen my childish jealousy and sought to use that against us."

She paused, searching for words to describe those last few days with her mother. How could she explain the guilt she bore or the terror she felt? How could he understand?

"Catheryn." His deep voice broke into her thoughts. "Do not think about what to say. Just say the words as they come."

"I had—I was—" She took a slow deep breath, fighting to gain a measure of control. "I had nearly hated my mother and she had acted only out of love and concern for me. She had sought to protect me. I was unworthy of her love."

"That is nonsense. You will never convince me that your mother ever, for one heartbeat, thought you unworthy of her love."

She couldn't stop the harsh laugh from escaping her lips. "She said as much herself."

"You did not listen?"

"I was too busy sobbing onto her lap to listen to her words."

His chest shook. She didn't need to look to know he was chuckling. "You find that humorous?"

"No, Catheryn, not at all. Somehow I find the picture of you sobbing on her lap very easy to imagine."

She ignored him and continued, "She made me vow not to leave my chamber that night. She also made me promise to always look after Brezden. The keep was my responsibility and so were those who'd spent their lives making Brezden all that it was."

"We will, Catheryn. I promise you, we will always look after Brezden."

"No. Don't you see? She made *me* swear. Me. Gerard, just me. I have failed her, and Brezden and its people."

"You failed no one."

Unable to bear his comforting words, she pulled away from him and stood. Catheryn looked at her mother's grave and then back to him. "You do not know just how badly I did fail."

"Then tell me." Gerard leaned back on his elbows and looked up at her. "Convince me that your miserable, childish sins were failures."

"She died that night." She wrapped her arms about herself and tightly gripped her waist. "I hid in my chamber while she screamed." Bile rose to her throat, nearly choking back her words. "While de Brye shouted and raged, I cowered in a corner with a cover pulled over me."

"Catheryn." Gerard rose. When he sought to touch her, she moved beyond his reach.

"Their fight moved from her chamber to the hallway

outside my door. I could hear his slaps through the door as they landed on her. Every word they shouted at each other reached me with ease."

She shook with the memory of that night. Even though she'd not seen the horror with her own eyes, her mind readily supplied the vision.

"When de Brye said he'd take me as his wife instead of her, my mother told him it would be only over her dead body. He responded by telling her that did not pose too great a difficulty. Then next thing I heard was her screams as she tumbled down the stairs." She covered her mouth to hold back the sobs. "Then there was silence. Nothing but deathly silence."

Gerard reached out for her. Catheryn backed away, not seeing him. Fog swept across her vision. Suddenly de Brye stood before her. The blood dripping from his hands belonged to her mother. "No! Stay away."

Before she could evade the demon coming toward her, he grabbed her arms and pulled her against him. She struggled against his hold of iron. When kicking and twisting did not gain her freedom, she pummeled his sides and back with her fists.

"Catheryn, I am sorry. Forgive me."

She paused at his words. Forgive him? Why would de Brye ask for forgiveness? The arms around her were not de Brye's. The stench of stale wine or ale did not assault her nostrils. When she looked up at the man holding her, the mist that had temporarily clouded time cleared from her vision.

What had she done?

Drained of emotion, and of the strength to stand, she sagged against him. "Gerard, I am sorry."

"You have no reason to be sorry."

"But—"

He cut off her words with a brief kiss. "Now hush." He

lifted her in his arms, walked over to a tree and sat down against it.

After settling her on his lap, he rested the back of his head against the tree and closed his eyes. Catheryn nestled into the cocoon made by his chest and arms.

The steady rise and fall of his chest and the warmth of his embrace lulled her into an easy peace that bordered on slumber.

She would have been content to stay like this forever. Never having to worry about another thing. Far too soon the clamor of horses approaching Brezden cruelly drew her from her wishful thoughts.

Gerard sighed wearily and opened his eyes. "What now?" He glanced toward the road and cursed at the armed party filing in through their gates.

Catheryn felt his heart leap and asked, "Who is it?"

"Earl William."

Chapter Thirteen

Each step Catheryn took closer to Brezden filled her heart with dread. The urge to turn around and run nearly overwhelmed her. It wasn't the twenty or so strange men milling about the bailey that threatened her composure. It was their manner of dress.

The battle armor and weapons did not foretell a social call.

She swallowed hard, hoping to quell her trepidation. Countless questions formed in her mind. Questions that made her lose concentration on the uneven ground beneath her feet.

She stumbled. Gerard turned around at her soft curse.

"Lady Catheryn." Her attention flew from the men in her bailey to his face. He clasped her hand and shook his head slightly. "Think on anything else, but pay them no heed."

Her gaze traveled from him, to William's men and back. "But—"

Gerard draped an arm across her shoulders, pulling her to his side. "You don't wish them to think we've any cause for worry." He smiled and nodded at the earl's men before resuming their approach to the keep.

While what he said made sense, it did little to ease her fears. Catheryn fought to paste a haphazard smile on her face, before whispering, "We don't have cause for any worry." At least none that she could think of.

"I know that." He drew his thumb along the side of her neck.

Her cheeks warmed. Her pulse quickened. Would she ever grow accustomed to his touch? Somehow she doubted it. Before she forgot the matter at hand, she asked, "Why do you suppose the earl is here?"

"I've not the slightest idea. Perhaps he missed our company."

Catheryn shot him a look of irritation before trying to move away. He simply tightened his hold to keep her by his side.

Before walking into the great hall Gerard ducked into an alcove, pulling her along. She wrapped her arms around him and rested her cheek against his chest. She was more than willing, at this moment, to take whatever strength he could offer.

He placed a kiss on the top of her head and brushed his cheek across her hair. "Catheryn, there is no need for fear. All will be well."

"I am not afraid."

His chest shook with subdued laughter. "No?"

She shook her head. The gesture was useless, that much she knew. He was well aware of her fear, but telling the lie fed her a measure of bravery.

"Good." He placed his hands on her shoulders as if to move her away. "Then maybe we should join William in the hall."

She tightened her clasp about his waist. "No. Not yet."

"Count Reveur!" William's yell shook the keep and took away the option of waiting any longer.

She frowned. Something was not right. On his last visit William had never used Gerard's title.

Catheryn stiffened against her husband for a moment before releasing her hold. She audibly drew in a breath before squaring her shoulders. Pointedly staring at him, she said, "It does not sound as if all is well, Gerard."

He nodded in agreement, before offering his arm to lead her into the hall. "Shall we?"

The hand she placed upon his forearm shook slightly. Reaching across his body, he covered her hand with his and squeezed it gently. "We are not feeding lions, Catheryn."

She shrugged. "I wouldn't be so certain of that."

Walter approached from the doorway. "Milord, should I summon the guard?"

Gerard shook his head. "No. If William meant harm to Brezden he'd have announced his intention outside the walls. We'll wait and see what he is about."

She was thankful that Walter stayed close at hand. It had already become obvious to her that it would require a small army to remove Gerard's captain from his side when danger threatened.

When they stepped into the hall the look William turned on them would have stopped another man in his tracks. But her husband was not another man. His steps did not falter.

One glance at the Earl of York's expression told Catheryn more than she wished to know. She'd been correct; the angry visage on the man across the hall did not foretell of a social call.

Before she or Gerard could issue a greeting to the earl, William pointed at her, nodded toward his men and ordered, "Seize her."

Her breathing ceased for one or two painful heartbeats. She'd done nothing to be taken prisoner. It was if time came to a standstill. A curse froze on her lips.

Not on her husband's. His oath echoed in the hall. All in the same movement, Gerard grabbed the sword hanging at Walter's side, yanked her behind his back and brandished the weapon before him.

William's men stopped their advance.

"What is the meaning of this, William?"

She wanted to do nothing more than to hide her face in the fabric covering Gerard's back. The need to stand up for herself forced the thoughts aside.

Catheryn stepped away from his protection, only to find her wrist caught in a near bone-crushing grip. The gentle, caring man of earlier was gone. She required only one glimpse at Gerard's face to realize the warring knight had returned.

The earl pushed his own men aside as he crossed the hall. The anger that had been evident a moment ago grew to rage. He didn't stop his approach until the point of Gerard's sword rested against his chest. "You would protect a traitor to your king?"

Catheryn gasped and stepped back behind her husband. Gerard lowered his weapon. "Of whom do you speak?"

William's already red face darkened even more. He raised his arm and pointed a meaty finger at Gerard's shoulder. "That murderous bitch cowering behind you."

Catheryn flinched against Gerard's back. She sunk her fingers into his tunic and grasped the fabric with a hold that could tear the linen to shreds.

Traitor? Murderous? She closed her eyes. Surely, the world had gone mad. There was no other explanation for the earl's accusations.

Gerard's muscles tensed beneath her touch. She opened her eyes and watched in horror as he leveled his sword and twisted the tip against William's chest.

Friends or not, the moment he'd married her, Gerard had fallen under William's lordship. Had he suddenly lost his mind? His action would put not only himself but all in danger. William of Aumale had a tendency to be cruel to those who incurred his wrath.

Everyone present gasped at Gerard's audacity. The sound echoed in the otherwise silent hall. The earl's men took a step closer. Walter motioned to Gerard's men standing behind him. Instantly obeying their captain, the men advanced. One handed Walter a weapon.

"Milord," Gerard paused. His hesitation told her that he was carefully choosing his words. "Surely someone has told you a falsehood. My *wife* has not been out of my sight since our marriage."

It was almost the truth. While she'd not exactly been in his sight every moment, Catheryn knew she'd not visited the privies without his knowledge.

William flung the sword tip away from his chest. "That lie is almost laughable coming from a man who spent his wedding night in the stables, Count Reveur."

True or not, the earl's statement banished the worst of her fear. Where her husband did, or did not, spend their wedding night was none of William's business. For him to announce such a thing in a crowded hall was more than tasteless.

Catheryn stepped out from behind Gerard, ignoring his tightening hold. She glared at William. "How dare you presume to know what took place that night? You know nothing."

If the earl's cold stare had been harsh before, it grew more fearsome now. His eyes widened and then narrowed to mere slits. A tick, strong and steady, pulsed rapidly in his tightly clenched cheek. He tightened the grasp on his sword hilt.

It was all she could do not to take back her words and retreat to safety. But where did safety lie? Behind her husband? At what cost? His life? Their lives?

No. She stiffened her spine. She'd see this sham through to the end—regardless of what it cost her.

After beating back her fear, she stepped forward. Gerard released his hold on her wrist and stood beside her. Walter took up the position on her other side. Both men used their swords to shield her from William and his men.

Catheryn blinked at the sight of two menacing weapons crossed before her, then raised her eyes to the earl. "I may be guilty of many things, milord, but treason is not among them."

"You think not?" William looked from one sword point to the other. "I am an envoy of King Stephen." He nodded toward the weapons. "This is not an act of treason committed for your benefit?"

His voice was smooth. Smooth and supple as a length of perfect silk. The hairs on the back of her neck rose.

"They seek only to protect me."

"Protect you?" His features moved into a mask of disbelief. "If you are innocent, as you claim, why would you require any protection?"

Gerard spoke up before she could answer. "When I was coerced into this marriage, did I not swear an oath to protect her from any threat? Including you, William."

"You also swore an oath to give service to me." A wicked smile crossed the earl's face before he added, "And to your king."

"I have always served my king faithfully."

"Until now. It seems to me that not only have you forgotten your sworn duty, but you have forgotten how to follow orders."

Catheryn felt the exasperation she heard in Gerard's ragged sigh. "What proof do you offer for your accusations?"

The earl motioned to a band of men standing at the back of the hall. With no further prompting, the men carried a bundle forward and dropped it at the earl's feet.

It was obvious the wrappings of the bundle concealed a body. Whose? Part of her wished to know the identity of the dead man and part of her dreaded the knowing.

William pointed at her. "Lady Catheryn, the honors are yours."

She glanced at Gerard. He lowered the tip of his sword as if to flip the covers back. The earl kicked away the blade. "Nay. I want her to see what she has wrought. Then I want her to offer proof of her denial."

Slowly kneeling, Catheryn held her breath and pulled the coarse covering away from the man's face.

"All the way, Lady Catheryn."

She gagged as the stench of rotting flesh seared her nostrils.

Gerard nudged her with his knee. "Breathe. The smell will lessen with each breath."

Bile rose to her throat. His words seemed ludicrous. Unable to bear the smell any longer, she pulled the covers free and stood.

Catheryn turned her face away from the body that would surely be her death.

"*Mon Dieu*, those are Brezden's colors."

William laughed at Gerard's shocked statement before demanding, "Explain this, Lady Catheryn."

She passed her gaze over the green and gold tunic claiming the man to be from Brezden, before letting it fall on Gerard. "I cannot explain." She placed a hand on her husband's chest. "I did not kill him."

"Maybe not by your own hand." The earl held out a missive to Gerard. "This might interest you."

"Where did you obtain this?" Gerard asked as he unrolled the parchment.

"My men found it on the barge they captured."

"The contents are so important that you gathered this evidence and rode directly back to Brezden?"

"You mock me, Count Reveur? You think to question me? I returned directly to Brezden seeking to right the wrong I did by giving you this…this woman as wife."

Gerard narrowed his eyes for a moment before dropping his attention back to the missive he held.

Catheryn leaned toward him. "What does it say?"

The expression on his face as he read frightened her. Like a serpent uncoiling in her belly, the fear grew. Cold and strong it seeped into her veins, chilling her to the bone.

She bent to retrieve the document as it fell from Gerard's suddenly lax fingers. He pinned the note to the floor with his sword.

"Damn you, Catheryn."

His voice was hoarse and hard. His hold on her arms as he grasped her and dragged her upright was brutal.

She sought to pull away, but he jerked her back to him. "Gerard, please, you are hurting me."

"Shut up. At least you are alive."

William added, "For now."

The floor beneath her tilted. The penalty for treason was death by hanging. She clutched at Gerard's tunic. "I did nothing. I swear to you. Nothing."

His pained look tore at her heart. He closed his eyes, as if the pain were too much to bear. Catheryn knew in that instant she'd do anything to take away the hurt. Anything.

The knowledge surprised her. She'd not realized the depth of her feelings for this man she'd married. When had she grown to care? How had he slipped unseen into her heart?

Less than a week ago she'd said she hated him. What she felt now was no where close to hate. No amount of hate caused this wrenching in her chest.

When he opened his eyes, he presented her with an ice-filled stare. She'd expected it and was not surprised. Boldly holding his stare, she asked, "Gerard, what did it say?"

William answered. "Let me fill in the blanks in your memory. It was a list of supplies to be delivered to the Empress. Along with a short missive about the gold and men you would be sending her soon."

Not breaking her gaze from Gerard's, she shook her head. "I did not write that, milord."

The earl's laughter held no trace of amusement. "Are you going to tell me that Brezden Keep is filled with people who can write? Please, Lady Catheryn, do not think me dimwitted."

"I did not write that, milord."

William stepped next to them. "Then who did?"

Gerard searched her face. She remained still and prayed he would find the truth he sought.

His hold lessened. He answered William's question. "Raymond de Brye."

Catheryn nearly fainted with relief. Yet she knew there would be more questions. Questions that this time she'd have little chance but to answer. Answers that would only ensure her men's death.

"Who is Raymond de Brye?"

She turned her head and stared at the earl. "Milord?" Was this some type of jest at her expense?

"This Raymond de Brye; why have I not heard his name before this moment?" William directed his question to Gerard.

"You have. Many times." Before her husband could respond, or stop her, Catheryn pulled out of his hold. "My mother wrote to you of de Brye. She begged you to intercede on our behalf."

William shrugged. "I received no missive from your mother. No plea ever reached my hands. What are you seeking to do, Lady Catheryn? Is it so easy for you to concoct tales to cover your traitorous deeds?"

He dismissed her with a shake of his head, then he turned his attention back to Gerard. "Has she bewitched you? Have you become so besotted by a lovely face that you have lost all ability to reason? There is no Raymond de Brye. He is naught but a cover for her duplicity."

When Gerard did nothing but look at her, Catheryn gasped and backed away from him. "You think me capable of that much deceit?" The pain throbbing in her temples was nothing compared to the ache in her chest.

His gaze moved briefly to the ceiling, before coming back to rest on her. She paused. He was up to something. Her life was in peril and he was plotting? What? At this moment everything rested in his hands.

He could remain silent and send her to certain death.

Or he could defend her.

She wanted to scream, to rage at him. By the smug expression on his face, he knew it. He raised one eyebrow and cocked his head as if daring her to attempt anything so foolish.

Catheryn bit her lower lip. If nothing else, the action would keep her from accepting his obvious dare. He flashed her a look that she could not decipher before he turned to William.

"You are mistaken, my liege." Gerard handed the sword back to Walter and waved the man away. "There is a Raymond de Brye."

Two of the earl's men grabbed Catheryn's arms. Held securely between them, she could not break free.

William raised his hand. "Wait. I want to hear this." The men relaxed their hold, but did not release her.

"So, tell me, Gerard, who is this de Brye?"

Without waiting for an answer William strode toward the table and sat down. Gerard followed him. So did she. But not of her own volition. Her jailers marched her to stand alongside the table.

The earl offered Gerard a goblet of wine and prompted, "Well?"

After waving away the drink, Gerard answered, "De Brye has been a pox on Brezden for years. I have yet to capture the murdering knave."

"Who is this villain? From whence does he come?"

"No one seems to know from where he came. He just appeared a while after the old baron died."

William motioned toward Catheryn with his goblet. "This is true?"

"Yes, milord. We tried to—"

He cut her off with a wave. "Cease. Other than yes or no,

your comments are unwanted."

"But I only—"

This time Gerard stopped her. Without taking his attention from the earl he reached up and placed two fingers over her lips. "Do not."

Under any other circumstance she'd verbally lash out at his high-handed action. But common sense rushed to the fore.

This was not any other circumstance.

Catheryn swallowed her outrage, but couldn't stop the imp who coaxed her to kiss the fingers covering her lips.

His eyes widened.

It wasn't until the men still holding her snickered that Gerard removed his fingers.

William leaned across the table. "Are you two finished?"

The heat on her cheeks flamed hot. What had she been thinking? Obviously, she wasn't. This was neither the time, nor the place to suddenly act the brazen whore.

Gerard shook his head and swallowed his own thoughts before returning to the topic at hand. "I believe Raymond de Brye was with Pike when they attacked Reveur Keep."

"Which one killed your wife and son?"

Catheryn choked on a hushed gasp at the earl's question.

"From Edyth's description I would say de Brye did the act, while Pike may have issued the orders, or was little more than a pawn."

His cold, unemotional tone sent a shiver down her spine. From the snippets of the men's conversation the last time William had ventured to Brezden, she'd gathered that Gerard's wife had meant a great deal to him.

Was his pain still so great that he felt the need to cover it with the appearance of indifference?

William frowned. "Then why is he not dead? How did you not kill him when you attacked this keep?"

Catheryn wished a spell existed that could make her

disappear. She had no urge to be present when Gerard told William of Brezden's secret tunnels. The tunnels she still had not shown to the new lord—her husband.

"Either he was not here, or he escaped before we arrived."

This time she did not think to choke back her gasp. It escaped before she could catch the sound.

William looked from her to Gerard. "I do not believe either one of you." He pulled out a dagger and admired the shining blade. "Count Reveur, you have until I count ten to tell me what is taking place here or…" He grasped the front of Catheryn's gown, pulled her down and held the blade to her neck. "One."

Gerard paled, but did not attempt to stay William's hand. Catheryn gripped the edge of the table for support. She would need it when he learned her secret.

"Two."

"He was here when I attacked Brezden." Gerard pounded the oak table with his fist. "Instead of facing his attackers, he chose to beat and rape another woman."

William lifted a brow. Catheryn managed a slight nod in agreement.

"Three."

"He escaped. I do not know how, William." He ran a hand down his face. "Brezden's guards had long ago been replaced with those loyal to Pike. They could very well have assisted de Brye."

"Ah, but he has been back, has he not?"

Both she and Gerard looked at the earl in surprise.

William shook his head. "Please, do not think for a heart beat that I possess loose wits. You never left my side during your marriage feast, Gerard. Yet your wife, somehow, gained a broken lip."

She was glad she'd held on to the table. Otherwise she'd have fallen forward on the knife. She'd always thought her husband was too perceptive. Now she knew why. He'd probably learned it from William.

"Four."

Stunned back into speech, Gerard admitted, "Yes, he has been back. The day of the battle he beheaded an archer and recently returned to start a fire in the stables."

"Then he must have help from inside." William pulled Catheryn closer. "Are you certain it is not your wife?"

Gerard leaned across the table and laid a hand on top of the earl's. She wasn't certain if she wanted to laugh or cry at the vision of two men holding a knife to her throat.

"Five." The earl's voice belied his anger at Gerard's action.

"I am positive my wife is not assisting de Brye—of her own accord."

"What does that mean?"

"I think he has threatened her, or her people. I think she seeks to protect those dear to her and has unwittingly played into his hands. She will not confide in me, so I am not certain."

She closed her eyes briefly. Perceptive was not quite the right word. It was not strong enough to define how well her husband seemed to know her thoughts, her secrets.

"You are unable to get this woman to tell you what she does without your permission? Do you require help in locating your backbone, Gerard?"

"My backbone is located where it belongs, milord."

To her amazement, William laughed. To her gratitude, he sheathed the dagger. The rush of her relief weakened her knees. Had the two guards not reclaimed their hold on her arms, she'd have fallen across the table.

"Then what we seem to have here is a hindrance which blocks you from accomplishing your mission." William rose. "A hindrance that is easily removed."

Her relief fled. Nausea twisted her stomach.

Gerard stood with such haste that he toppled the bench to the floor. "She is not a traitor."

"I am not certain I believe that. There is a way to prove it true or false."

She wasn't sure she wanted to hear his explanation. Gerard urged him to elaborate.

"'Tis simple. I will hold Lady Catheryn hostage at Scarborough—as a surety that you will find and dispatch the traitor."

"Scarborough?"

"Aye. You heard me correctly. The Earl of Richmond will be in attendance for a tourney, so there will be plenty of people to keep a watchful eye on your lady."

Gerard's expression grew hard. His eyes blazed with anger. "There is no need for that."

The earl disagreed. "I say there is. Would you care to fight me on this, Count Reveur?"

All breathing ceased. Not a sound rippled through the hall. Catheryn watched in dismay as her husband's hand wavered over his dagger. Unwilling to witness what could become a frightening tableau, she whispered, "I will go."

When neither man appeared to hear her, she raised her voice, "Gerard, I will go."

He turned his head toward her. "It is not your decision to make." The sharp edge in his voice told her she'd gone too far.

This time William's laugh was not one of amusement. It sounded like more of a growl than a laugh. "The only decision to be made is whether she hangs here and now, or comes as hostage with me."

Gerard's shoulders fell in a slump. Catheryn released the breath she'd been holding. He was not happy with the outcome, but what did he think he could do against the Earl of York?

Gerard cupped her chin, lifting her head so their gazes

met. Her heart ceased beating. What emotion lurked behind his eyes? Worry? Fear? She wasn't certain, but it frightened her.

He stroked his thumb over the lips he'd tried to silence earlier. "When do you leave?"

"How touching." William mocked Gerard's display. "We leave with first light. Do not think you have this night to devise any plans between you."

Gerard lowered his arm and turned back to the earl. "What does that mean?"

"You may have full run of your keep, Gerard. But she will be under constant guard in her old chamber."

Both she and Gerard shouted, "No."

The earl slammed his fist on the table. The cracking of wood echoed through the hall. "No? You tell me *no*? I am your overlord and you will do as I say."

Catheryn's blood ran cold. Who would kill her first? Earl William or Raymond de Brye? Would she live long enough to make the journey to York, or would she meet her fate this very night?

William motioned to his men. Without hesitation, they tightened their grasp and led her to the stairs.

She watched as Walter gathered Gerard's men into a group and led them from the hall. He was most likely doing the wisest thing. By getting the men out of the keep before they too were placed under guard they would be freer to protect their lord. She hoped Walter could prevent his master from doing anything rash.

Any attempt to rescue her from her own fate would be useless. Either way her life was in immediate danger. Had she confided in Gerard as Agnes had urged, she'd not be in this position. And she did not wish for Gerard to suffer for her own foolishness.

She heard Gerard's already angry voice rise. "You are insane, William."

But it was the earl's outraged response that made her want to weep.

"And you, Count Reveur, have reached the very end of my patience."

Chapter Fourteen

Gerard walked around the two bound and gagged men in his chamber. "What do you think, Walter? Do they not look like a fine pair of trussed hogs?"

"Oh, aye, milord, that they do."

Gerard peeled back one man's eyelid. "Mistress Margaret said they would be dead to the world for the entire night. I just hope her brew doesn't leave them dead to the world forever."

Walter's eyes grew round. "Don't say that, not even in jest."

While heading toward the window opening, Gerard laughed at his man's fears. "It will be fine." He grabbed the rope he'd used to gain entrance to his chamber and tossed one end back out the window.

"Milord? Would it not be easier to just use the door?"

Gerard paused with one leg hanging out the tight opening. He flashed Walter a grin. "Ah, but nowhere near as fun. 'Tis but a short drop to the ground. And since our men still guard the walls, they will look the other way."

While Walter still didn't seem pleased with this entire scheme, he offered no argument. "Just be careful. I would hate to have to kill Earl William because of a senseless prank."

"'Tis not a prank to thwart that man and it is far from senseless. Just see to your duties. As long as everyone follows orders, all will be more than well." Gerard sent his man a quick salute and hauled himself over the edge of the window and out into the dark night.

He'd been right; it was just a short drop to the ground. However, it'd been ages since he'd climbed a rope. At least the descent was easier than the climb up had been.

After Walter pulled the rope into the chamber, Gerard scanned the bailey. Not many wandered about. He crossed the bailey and entered the kitchen.

The cook barely noted his presence with more than a quick nod, before turning away and mumbling something nonsensical about a busy night.

Gerard grabbed a lit torch and slipped through the door that led down to the storage rooms. Two of his men already waited there, but they were not alone.

"Agnes?" What was Catheryn's maid doing here?

Before he could ask, the flustered woman answered. "I only wanted to see Lady Catheryn, milord. I meant no harm."

He waved away her worry. "You know about this tunnel?"

"Yes. I see you do, too."

Gerard frowned. "Maybe I have been seeking answers from the wrong person. Does everyone know about Brezden's tunnels?"

"No, milord. I know only of this one. I used it to reach the kitchens when my charge was but a babe."

He nodded. "That makes sense. You will not be using it this night."

She opened and closed her mouth. "But I—" Wringing her hands in obvious agitation, Agnes tried again, "But, milord, I must—"

Gently, he grasped her hands in his. "I promise you that you will see Catheryn before she leaves in the morning. You have my word."

Her sigh of relief was audible. "Thank you, Lord Gerard."

"Now, go. Seek your bed and sleep well."

After the maid left, Gerard turned to his men. "Ready?" At their nod, he led the way. "Then let the night begin."

~*~

Catheryn lay across her bed, staring out the window while absently stroking the purring kitten at her side.

Jewel, as she'd named the kitten because of its bright emerald eyes, had proven to be a good companion in her hours of solitude. Especially now, when the sun had set and the darkness came, ending an already terrible day with even more gloom.

Turmoil raged wildly within her. It was not strong to be so afraid. There was no honor, no bravery in fear. Yet, she could not assuage the abject fear running rampant in her heart and soul.

After William's men had escorted her to her chamber, she'd tried to be brave. She'd even gone so far as to open the door. Her moment of bravery had been cut short when the guards forcefully pushed her back into the room and threatened to guard her from inside the chamber if she so much as poked her nose out the doorway again.

Their demeanor was not of the sort she'd welcome as company in her room. The possibility existed that they could prove as brutal as de Brye.

She turned to look at the door. If they would have left the locking bar, she'd drop it across to protect herself from the danger lurking outside. Her focus drifted to the alcove. How would she fend off the danger lurking just beyond her chamber wall?

This could not go on forever. This fear of de Brye and what he would or would not do had to end. Why had she not confided in Gerard when she'd had the chance? Surely he would be able to protect her men from de Brye.

Jewel sprang to her feet. Until now the fluffy ball of reddish-blonde fur had been content to lie still at her side on the bed. Suddenly its fur stood on end and the normally gentle animal hissed and jumped from the bed.

A low growl rumbled from Jewel's throat as she entered the alcove. Catheryn's heart froze in her throat. What had the animal heard?

Frantically searching for a weapon, she cursed softly. The chamber had been stripped of any item she could have put to use in her defense.

Should she summon the earl's men for help? Before she could decide, Jewel pawed at the hidden door. Her fur smoothed out and the hissing ceased.

In the short time she'd had the animal, Catheryn had learned one thing—Jewel did not take kindly to strangers. So, whoever was behind the panel was someone the kitten knew.

The pounding of her heart slowed to normal. It could only be Agnes. Her maid was the only person, beside de Brye, who knew how to get from the storage room below the kitchens to this chamber.

Happiness filled her. It would be good to see, to touch a friendly face.

The panel slowly slid back. The well-oiled door made no sound in the quiet room. Candlelight danced off the tip of a sword as it preceded its holder through the doorway.

Catheryn gasped and swung away from the door. Before she could call out for William's men, a hand covered her mouth.

Sweet Mary, she'd expected de Brye to come this night. How had she let down her guard so swiftly? She closed her eyes and prayed for a swift, painless end. *Dear Lord, forgive me, but I am truly a coward.*

The hand over her mouth did not tighten in a cruel or threatening manner. Instead, another hand fell on her shoulder and spun her around. At the same time she heard the panel slide back into place.

A familiar, welcome scent drifted beneath her nose. She opened her eyes just in time to see Gerard bend his head to hers. He gently coaxed a kiss from her lips.

Anger from the fright he'd caused her prompted her to kick him.

He instantly released her. "That is a fine welcome, wife."

She ignored his sarcasm. "How long have you known about the tunnel?"

Gerard's heart-stopping smile spread across his face. "Ephram told me when we were in the stable."

Catheryn glanced toward the chamber door. "We are not alone. William's men guard the door."

"Do they?"

His easy smile sent shivers to her toes. "Yes. If you don't stop smirking at me, I'll kick you again."

He tugged her toward the chamber door. With the hilt of his sword he tapped twice on the heavy wood and then stood back.

Walter opened the door and tipped his head. "All is well here, milord. Are the others in place?"

Gerard responded, "Aye, they are."

Had they lost their minds? "What are you two doing?" She peered both ways down the corridor. William's men were nowhere in sight. "Are you trying to get us killed?"

Gerard pulled her inside and closed the door. "No. I am seeking a night with my wife."

The look on his face said as much, if not more, than his words had. A thrill of anticipation rushed through her. Worry and logic pushed the thrill aside. "Where are William's men?"

He stroked her cheek with the back of his hand. "In my chamber. They are bound and gagged, but unharmed. Your Mistress Margaret has more concoctions at hand than an apothecary."

She leaned into his touch. "What will they think when they awake?"

He cupped her chin and stroked her lower lip with the

pad of his thumb. "They sleep well and will know for a certainty that they were fools."

Catheryn parted her lips; with her teeth and tongue she teased his thumb. "How will they explain?"

He dropped his sword, and pulled her into his embrace. "They will not admit their stupidity to William."

The floor swayed beneath her. She held on to Gerard's shoulders for support. "Why are you here?"

"To banish ghosts." He threaded his fingers through her hair. "To fulfill a promise." He lowered his lips to hers and finished on a whisper, "and to claim my wife as my own."

His statements sent her world spinning. The muscles that normally held her upright folded. His kiss left her breathless.

She longed to make this moment last an eternity...because when the morning came she might never see or touch him again. A strangled sob tore at her throat.

He broke his kiss and held her head steady so he could stare into her gaze. The candlelight glittered like a multitude of stars in his eyes.

A frown marred the smoothness of his forehead. He lifted her in his arms and crossed the room. Gerard settled into the chair placed before the window opening and held her on his lap.

Moonbeams poured in through the uncovered window. It spread a soft, gentle light across them.

She rested her cheek against his shoulder, content to be held in his arms. Jewel landed in her lap for moment before sniffing the two of them and heading off to the comfort of a makeshift bed in the corner of the room.

"Are you going to cry?"

His question startled her. She swallowed back the tears that had threatened and shook her head.

"If you are, do so now."

The invitation was hard to resist, but she succeeded. "No.

I am fine."

"Good. I'd not have you shed tears for something that will never occur."

She looked up at him. "William will not take me in the morning?"

"Of course he will. You know that."

Catheryn lowered her gaze to her lap. She bit her trembling lip. "Oh."

"Look at me."

She did and was amazed to discover that the moisture in her eyes blurred his features. "Catheryn, I know you are afraid. I swear to you, William will not harm you. This is naught but a well-devised ploy to gain my cooperation."

"What if you fail?" Her voice shook.

"He will rage. He will shout. He will swear to strike you dead, but he will not. Trust me on this, he will not harm you." He brushed the hair from her face. "I will not fail."

"It could take years to find de Brye."

He nodded in agreement. "Then we need to make enough memories this night to last that long."

The thought of being away from Brezden, away from her people, away from Gerard for any length of time made her ill. "Oh, God, I cannot bear the thought."

His arms tightened around her. "You will bear what you must."

That was not the answer she wanted to hear. Catheryn turned her head away. "You are cruel."

"I am honest."

"I am frightened, yet you tell me I might not return home for years?"

"You think so little of me?"

She swung her head back to face him. "Think so little of you?"

"I am hunting but one man."

"He is not a man. He is Satan."

Gerard's features hardened, but his voice remained steady. "So I have been told."

"Who? Who besides me could tell you about the evil lurking in de Brye?"

"My wife. Right before she died in my arms." The steadiness of his voice grew as cold and hard as his expression.

"I am sorry."

"Why? Did you give the orders to destroy Reveur?"

Catheryn shrank from the bitterness in his tone. "No."

"Did you beat Edyth to an unrecognizable pulp before raping her and then killing her newborn son?"

"No." The bitter taste in her throat choked her. "I am sorry because I have done nothing to help you find the man who took so much from you."

"You can change that, Catheryn."

"How can I tell you what you need to know without the loss of more lives?"

His deep sigh filled the room. "Do you not think your men are willing to give their lives for yours? Have you so little faith in their loyalty?"

"No. I cannot permit them to die for me." The thought appalled her. Her stomach churned at the idea.

"You cannot permit it? Who gave you the power of life and death?"

"They are Brezden's men. They are my men."

"No. They are not *your* men. Brezden is not yours."

When she moved to stand up, Gerard wrapped his arms tightly around her. "You are going nowhere, Lady Reveur."

Him calling her Lady Reveur shocked her enough to keep her from fighting.

He grasped her face between his palms, forcing her to look at him. "What will it take to make you realize that you are not alone? Catheryn, you are not capable of rescuing our men from de Brye. I am."

She pushed at his chest and cried, "He will kill them."

A mask of anger dropped over his face. He tightened his hold and pulled her closer. "My God, woman. Do you think this man will hold to his promise simply because you do not speak? He will kill them in the end anyway."

His words stopped her heart. "No. He said—"

"Cease. Do not be a fool. Listen to me. He will kill them."

She couldn't break his hold. They were nose to nose. He held her so close that she could feel the heat of his breath. "No. No, he wouldn't…" She stopped mid-sentence.

Yes, he would. Raymond de Brye wouldn't hesitate to ensure no one lived to give evidence against him.

What had she done? Was it too late? One man was injured. Another lay dead in her hall. Both had suffered the cruel hand of de Brye. Her mind whirled. What could she do? How could she stop him?

She stared at the face so close to hers. "Our men?"

Gerard nodded.

"You are willing to help me?"

The hands still holding her face shook. She saw the barely perceptible tick in his cheek jump to life. The silence in the room became nearly unbearable. Finally, through gritted teeth he answered, "I came to Brezden for Pike's and de Brye's blood. That has never changed."

For some unexplainable reason, her heart fell. She lowered her gaze. "Brezden owes you that much for what was done to your family."

His hands slid from her cheeks to the back of her head. Gerard covered her lips with his own. After a brief, albeit all consuming kiss, he rested his lips close to her ear. "You are my family, Catheryn, my future. I will do anything to protect you, but I need your help."

A thrill rippled through her. She was his future? His words flowed warm through her veins. Promptly, before she lost her nerve and the fear of de Brye settled back in place, Catheryn gave him the information he sought. "The entrance to the rest of the tunnels is behind the one in my alcove."

He leaned back and shook his head. "Clever. A secret door behind a hidden panel."

She shrugged. "Yes, well, my father thought it safer to conceal the true entrance to the tunnels."

"So the one behind this chamber..."

She finished his sentence. "Is actually just a quick exit to the kitchens."

"And the other?"

"Others. There is more than one. The tunnel to the left will take you below Brezden, under the postern gate and out to the river."

"To the right?"

She shuddered. "To the stables."

"That's how he started the fire." It wasn't posed as a question, so Catheryn remained silent. "Are there any more?"

"If there are I am not aware of them."

He raised one eyebrow.

Catheryn lifted her right hand. "Upon my honor. I know of no other tunnels."

"Why is the entrance in your chamber?"

"It was easier for Agnes to come and go when I was a babe. My parents took your chamber as their own."

"And Pike left you here because it was easier for others to have access to you."

"I suppose. This had always been my chamber. I never questioned him."

He held her close for a moment. "I am surprised they did not kill you long ago. They could have done anything they wished to you, Catheryn. You could easily have suffered a fate as gruesome as Edyth's."

His look, when it came to rest on her, was not filled with

the anger and sadness evident in his words. Catheryn marveled at the warmth his expression conveyed. She stroked his cheek. "I am truly sorry for your loss, Gerard."

He kissed her fingers as she ran them across his lips. "Why? What reason have you to be sorry?"

His questions made little sense. "She was your wife. Did you not love her? Do you not miss her? Was that not your whole reason for attacking Brezden?"

"Love?" He frowned before shaking his head. "I know nothing of love."

That admission settled heavy on her heart. The heaviness confused her. Should she not be happy that he'd not loved his first wife? Wouldn't that leave room for her to teach him of love?

Now it was her turn to shake her head. What did she know of love? She directed her thoughts back to him. "Do you not miss her?"

"I used to. She filled my mind night and day." A grin worthy of the devil himself crossed his face. "Lately I find myself occupied with thoughts of another."

A flush heated her face. She paused with her fingers resting on his lips. Uncertain how to reply, she said nothing.

Her confusion mounted when he grasped one of her fingertips with his teeth. She gasped as he slid his lips down to cover her finger. The moist, silken warmth of his tongue swirling about her flesh sent flame-tipped arrows to start a fire between her legs.

Catheryn's heart slammed against the inside of her chest. After catching her breath, she asked, "What are you doing?"

He released her finger and moved his lips to her neck. "Banishing ghosts. Fulfilling promises."

The feel of his lips, the heat of his breath caused the fires to spread. She arched her neck beneath his touch. "I don't understand."

"Who asked you to understand?"

As much as she enjoyed his attention, it made no sense to her. She forced the words from her mouth. "How can you talk of Edyth in one breath and seduce me with the next?"

He deftly untied the laces at the back of her gown. "I can do nothing about things that happened before this moment."

The cool night air rushed against her exposed shoulder. "I can do nothing about things that might happen after this moment."

He grazed the tender flesh between her neck and shoulder with his teeth. "I can only act upon what is happening right now."

Her breath came fast and hard. It became an effort to talk, even harder to think. "Gerard, I do not think this is—"

Her words died in her throat as he brushed his thumb across her breast. "Save all your thoughts for tomorrow, Catheryn." He smiled down at her. "Right now all I care about is what you feel."

She sighed. "I feel as if I've died and gone to heaven."

His laugh was soft. "Not yet you haven't." His touch was like fire. "But you will."

The promise of more to come curled her toes. Eager to feel more, to be closer, she pressed her body against him. Soon, even that closeness was not enough to satisfy the longing that pulsed in her veins. "I don't know what to do."

With her in his arms he stood and lowered her to her feet. "Just trust me, Catheryn. Do not be afraid. I will not harm you."

He lifted her chin with the crook of his finger and thumb. "Open your eyes."

"No one else invades my thoughts." She looked up at him.

"Good. Then maybe the ghosts are banished."

What he'd promised for tonight suddenly made sense to her. His words about banishing ghosts and fulfilling promises became clear. The ghost, or ghosts rather, were de

Brye and Edyth. If that were true, then the promise was the one he'd made on their wedding night. The same one he'd so diligently pursued of late.

Embarrassment drew the flames to her face. He smiled. "I see you now remember."

Catheryn tried to turn her face away, but he brought his hand to her chin and held her in place. He repeated his words. "I will not take you. I will not make you my wife until you crave me, and my touch, so badly that there is no room for anyone else in your mind, or in your soul."

Uncertain of exactly what that meant, but knowing he would soon show her, she groaned.

"Are you afraid?"

"No." Fear had nothing to do with the emotions sweeping through her.

"Do you trust me?"

"Yes." The breathlessness of her own voice caught her off guard.

He released her chin and stepped away. "Then turn around."

She turned. Catheryn trembled when he finished untying the laces of her gown. Every place his fingers brushed against her back tingled.

A shiver mixed with pleasure and anticipation rippled down her spine when he slid the gown slowly down her body. The shiver grew to a tremor when her thin under gown followed.

He found the soft spot on her neck with his lips. She tipped her head, permitting him free reign and gave herself up to the indescribable sensations running the length of her.

She leaned back against his chest for support. He trailed his hands along her belly, up her rib cage and cupped her breasts.

Hot and cold. Fire and ice. All collided at her core. She pressed her thighs together to ease the drumming.

Gerard shifted behind her, then he slid his leg between hers. He teased and tormented her with his hands and mouth. Easily, he coaxed a response wherever he touched; from the tips of her breasts to the now insistent throbbing between her thighs.

The heady scent of him invaded her being. It screamed his name in her mind. Even without seeing him, she had no doubt who drove her wild.

His touch alternated between teasing and demanding. From light to hard. From fast to slow. The combination fanned the fires to an inferno.

His warm breath, as ragged as her own, rang loud in her ears. It echoed in her mind, through her body. The pounding of his heart against her back tapped a strong, steady rhythm into her soul.

Time froze. No moment other than this one mattered. There was no yesterday, no tomorrow. No other people, but the two of them, existed.

He nudged her legs apart with his own. She readily complied. Catheryn closed her eyes against the sudden spinning of the room, she gasped when he slid a finger along the warm, wet cleft leading to her core. For one brief heartbeat, he paused just beyond the entrance.

"You are a fool, Catheryn."

The words whispered into her ear held no meaning. She was caught in the haze of need, of desire, and cared little about words.

She turned her head toward the sound and caught his lips with her own. Slowly, he turned her in his arms.

She dug her fingers into the offending tunic covering his body. The throbbing intensified. Her heart pounded. She groaned with need, desire, longing—for what?

He broke their kiss.

She rested her forehead against his chest. "Gerard, please."

"Please what?" His tone, hoarse and ragged, demanded an answer.

She leaned into him. He wanted her to ask for release. Desperate need wiped out any thought of pride. "Take me. End this torture."

Before the pulsing or the longing could lessen, he stripped off his clothes and laid her on the bed. But he avoided the arms she held out to him.

Instead, he slid his body down the length of hers. His breath was warm as it brushed over her breasts and stomach. Yet he trailed his lips and tongue lower.

The inferno raged out of control when he graced her with a too intimate kiss.

Catheryn stiffened. When she tried to rise, he captured her with his hands, one on a breast, the other rested flat over her stomach.

Gerard caught her gaze. "Trust me."

Shock left her speechless. What was he—?

The next touch of his mouth drove all coherent thought from her mind. His lips, tongue and hands were every where.

He touched her in ways that stole her breath away. And when the need to surge against a calling she did not understand overtook her, he steadied her with one strong hand. And answered her need with the other.

The bed beneath her fell away. She dropped into a whirlpool spinning round and round. Her heart raced. Her flesh quivered.

She buried her hands in his hair and called out his name as she burst around the madness stroking her, coaxing her to heaven.

After floating slowly back to her chamber, Catheryn opened her eyes, to find Gerard looming above her. His smile, so tender, brought tears to her eyes.

Tears he kissed away.

She rested the palm of her hand against his cheek, and whispered, "I didn't know."

He laughed softly. "You still don't."

The unsteadiness of his words reached through the haze. Her question died on her lips as her vision cleared enough for her to focus on his features.

Perspiration beaded on his forehead. A bright sheen glittered in his eyes. His chiseled jaw tensed with what appeared, to her, as pain.

She placed her hand against his chest and felt the hard, erratic pounding of his heart. The beat matched the heaviness of his breath.

Catheryn shifted her gaze back to his face, while sliding her hand along the hard planes of his stomach. His eyelids fluttered closed. The smooth flesh beneath her touch quivered.

She stopped. "Gerard? Is something wrong?"

He ignored her question and moved to settle his erection against the still beating entrance to her womb. He rested his lips against her ear. "Catheryn, you were not raped."

He pressed into her warmth. Her body recoiled from the tightness of its own accord. Something was not quite as she'd expected. She braced her hands against his shoulders.

"Ah, love, your body is more than ready for me. Are you?" His ragged breath burned hot against her ear.

She forced her trembling limbs to still.

"Catheryn, help me. Open for me. Do not make me do this alone."

He'd taken her to the heavens and back. At this moment there was nothing she wouldn't do for him. She slipped her arms about his neck. "Kiss me."

He'd already fulfilled two of his promises for this night; he'd banished ghosts, and he'd easily coaxed her into wanting him with every fiber of her being. It was time for the fulfillment of his last promise.

She wrapped her legs around his thighs and whispered against his lips, "Claim your wife as your own."

He came to a stop the instant he filled her.

Catheryn froze for an uneven heartbeat, before the greedy desire beat off the short-lived flash of pain. She dug her fingernails into his shoulders, seeking to lose herself in his kiss.

His muscles shook as he slowly, gently slid out and back in.

There was no more pain. Only a deep yearning for him to repeat the motion. She shivered with the thought of what pleasure that action could bring. After threading her fingers back through his hair, she broke their kiss.

"If this night is all we are to share, then love me, Gerard."

He gripped her face between his hands. "You are wrong. This is not our only night. It is our first." He moved against her, bringing a sigh of pure delight to her lips.

His eyes glistened with the promise of all their tomorrows. His touch gave her the promise of memories that would last a lifetime.

She promised him her body, her heart and her very soul, sealing the promise.

Chapter Fifteen

Propped up on one elbow, Gerard gazed down at the woman dozing next to him.

His wife, in more than name. He cursed the time they'd wasted. They could have had many nights of such ecstasy had he not permitted his pride and temper to get in the way.

He cursed his own failings. He could have had the information about de Brye weeks ago. Had he thought to use a measure of kindness instead of anger? His father's voice ran through his mind. How many countless times had his sire encouraged him to utilize patience and logic when dealing with his headstrong sisters?

It had been many years since he'd had contact with a stubborn female. His father's lessons had fallen to the wayside. Edyth had been the perfect wife. Meek and mild, the thought to raise her voice against him never entered her mind. She had been perfect for a man whose first loyalty was to his king. Somehow, he doubted if this wife would be content if ignored for long periods of time. Ignored? Gerard shook his head. How could you ignore someone who invaded your thoughts night and day?

The candlelight played across her hair, shimmering off the fine threads of gold woven among the others. A frown creased her forehead. Her hand sought him.

The frown vanished when she rested her fingers against his stomach. Her lips turned up in a brief, but satisfied smile.

The sight of her lips and the memories of the night fanned the heat of his desire. He groaned with the need to bury himself in her. To feel her hot, wet flesh tighten around him.

Thought overruled his baser needs. She had a two-day

ride ahead of her. He did not want the agony of that journey to overshadow their night of passion.

Because of that wish, they'd joined their bodies but once during the night. The rest of the night had been spent learning other ways to find satisfaction. Desire could be flamed with nothing but a look, or a touch. Fulfillment could be found—many ways.

Even he had learned something. As erotic and as thrilling as her lips and hands on his body felt, he would rather bury himself in her. And feel her hot, wet flesh tighten around him.

Gerard laughed at his determined mind. So much for controlling his thoughts.

The night grew short. As much as he'd like to stay here and watch her sleep, little time was left.

There were things he wished to tell her. Things about William and the earl's wife Cecily that she needed to know. He stroked her cheek. The skin reminded him of velvet, soft and pliant.

Catheryn's eyes fluttered open. A gentle smile curved her lips. "Good morning." She moved next to him and placed a hand against his chest.

"Not yet, but we must talk."

"We will have many days to talk. Can you think of nothing else to fill the remainder of the night?"

"You are leaving when the sun rises. That has not changed."

"No. I told you what you need to know. There is no reason for me to leave Brezden."

"Until de Brye is dealt with I want you gone from here."

"But—"

"Cease, Catheryn." He took a deep breath, forcing his impatience aside. "Do not argue with me. I cannot devote all my attention to capturing de Brye if I must worry about your safety at the same time."

"So, even though I gave you what you wanted, I am still to be William's prisoner?"

"Yes." He answered her slowly. Something was wrong. He could hear it in her tight voice.

"Will you always use gentle touches and soft words to gain what you want?"

A fist to his gut would not have caught him as off guard as her question did. "Is that what you think?" When she tried to roll away from him, Gerard grasped her arm. "Answer me. Is that what you think last night was about?"

"I don't know." Her words were clipped.

If she was seeking to goad him into a fight, she was close to succeeding. He released her arm and moved to leave the bed.

"I have never been away from Brezden."

The slight tremor in her softly spoken admission stopped him. Shame filled him. Catheryn wasn't seeking a fight with him. She was afraid. He turned and looked at her.

Gerard hated the terror that had fallen across her face. If there was a way he could wipe that expression from her forever, he would. He could think of nothing that would convince her the fear was unnecessary. He could, however, help her to live with it for the time they'd be apart.

He pulled her into his arms, lay back down and cradled her on top of his chest. "Catheryn, all will be well."

She shook her head. "Not until I am back here in your bed."

"That will happen soon."

"Not soon enough, Gerard. I can hardly bear the thought."

Neither could he, but what choice had they? "Then don't. Do not think about it."

She crossed her hands on his chest and propped her chin on top of them. "How do you propose I do that?"

He thought for a minute. Maybe she could use the same

trick he'd learned. "What things bring you pleasure?"

Amazed, he watched a blush color her cheeks before she answered, "You."

"Things you can think about in public, Catheryn."

"Oh." Her brows furrowed in concentration. She shrugged. "A walk in the sunshine. To breathe the spring air. A warm blazing fire in winter. The scent of baking bread. A quiet room. A day with no shouting. A night sky filled with stars."

Jewel landed on the covers next to them with a small squeak. Gerard scratched the kitten's head and was rewarded with a throaty purr.

Catheryn continued, "This ball of fur." She scooted forward and placed her lips on his. "And you."

"That is all?"

"It is enough."

She'd added none of the things his sisters would have listed. No gems, no rich fabrics or furs, no chests of gold, not even a simple piece of jewelry.

Of all the things she did mention, there was not one he could give her to keep as a reminder of Brezden and him.

Gerard glanced out the window, searching for another tack. The fading stars still twinkled in the semi-dark sky.

He drew his attention back to her. "Close your eyes."

When she did his bidding he slowly, gently circled her back and shoulders with his hands. "Picture the night sky filled with stars."

He kneaded her shoulders. "Can you see them?"

"Yes." Her answer came in a hushed, steady whisper.

"Every time you are afraid, whenever you feel alone, close your eyes. Think of this moment."

She opened her eyes. He purposely ignored the sheen of gathering tears and set her aside. He rose from the comfort of the bed, pulling her from the rumpled nest and led her to the window.

"Look at the stars, Catheryn." He stood behind her, with his arms wrapped about her waist. Gerard rested his chin on the top of her head and pulled her close against him. "Every night before you seek your bed, find the stars, search for the moon."

"And you?"

"I will do the same and I will remember this night."

"How long will a memory be enough?"

"What are you asking?"

"In the days since we have been married, we have shared a bed only one of those nights."

Gerard knew where her thoughts were headed, but he wanted them voiced. Here and now. "And?"

She inhaled loudly, before asking in a rush, "How many of those nights have you sought your bed alone?"

If he laughed, she would never forgive him. If he raged, she would think him guilty regardless of his words. What she thought, or what she would do, should not matter to him.

Oddly enough it did. Even though he'd known her less than a month, her thoughts did matter to him. A great deal.

He turned her around in his arms, grasped her wrist and placed her hand against his chest. "As long as my heart beats I will be true to you. I swore a vow that I have not broken and will not break as long as I live."

He held her startled gaze and lifted her palm to his lips for a kiss. "The vow is sealed." He closed her fingers over her palm. "Hold this sealed vow in your hand for as long as your heart desires. Always remember, that no matter what your eyes may show you, or what your ears may hear, that what I have told you and shown you in this chamber tonight is the truth."

"I will hold it longer than forever. I will not forget. Every night I am not at your side I will find the stars and I will search for the moon."

He didn't want to mention the possibility, but he knew William. More than that, he knew Cecily. "What if you are in a room with no windows?"

She gasped, but her voice did not falter. "I will close my eyes and seek them in my mind."

Gerard folded her into his embrace. He held her close. "Catheryn, do nothing to anger William's wife."

She stiffened in his arms. "She is cruel?"

"No, not intentionally cruel." Would it be better to lie to her? No. Neither did he want to give her reason for disliking Cecily before she met the woman and could decide for herself. "She will be jealous of your youth, of your looks and she will not hesitate to be mean-spirited."

"She is married to the most powerful man in this part of England. She lives in a castle fit for royalty. She has no reason for jealousy."

Gerard laughed. "She is married to a man who knows not how to honor their bed." His laughter died. "If William should seek you out—"

Catheryn pushed against his chest, breaking their embrace. Her eyes blazed. "I will run a knife through his black heart."

"Fair enough. Just promise me that you will bite your tongue and do as Cecily asks." He knew it was a mean thing to ask. In the end, it would serve Catheryn better to swallow her pride and let the spoiled Cecily have her way.

"I promise." She turned her head and glanced out the window at the waning night. "The day is arriving."

He brushed a curl from her cheek. "Aye, far too quickly."

Catheryn grasped his hand, tugged him toward the bed and pushed him down on the mattress. He didn't resist. He too wished to steal another kiss, another touch.

Soon another kiss, another touch led to soaring desire. With a ragged curse, he rolled away.

She swept her fingertips down the length of his arm.

"Gerard?" Her voice sounded as raspy as his breathing.

Unable to form complete thoughts, he ground out, "No, Catheryn. The ride... You will not—"

She lifted his hand to her lips and kissed his palm. "For every pain I feel on the coming journey, I want a memory of how it occurred."

Gerard closed his eyes and groaned. He tried to think of anything but the warm, soft woman beside him.

She would not be dismissed so lightly. She gently grazed his chest with her fingernails. He could not stop the shooting desire her motions caused.

"Gerard, I have waited for you a life time. My dreams foretold of your coming. Love me, forget all but this moment and love me."

His will to argue dissolved. He gave himself up to the moment, carrying her with him.

~*~

Catheryn stood alone in the hall and fought her urge to rail against the unfairness of life. She had already bid farewell to Agnes. The leave taking had not been easy, but then she'd not expected it to be.

Since the day she was born she had counted on Agnes's presence. Her nursemaid, her friend, her confidant had always been readily available.

Never had Catheryn been further than the demesne lands surrounding Brezden. She'd always dreaded the thought of marrying someone who would take her away from Brezden.

Regardless of her fears, she was leaving now. Her chests had been packed and loaded onto a cart that was already headed toward Yorkshire.

She turned as William and Gerard entered the hall. The earl looked angry. Her husband looked smug. Was it possible he had somehow changed the earl's mind?

William answered her unspoken question. "Lady Catheryn, your husband and I have discussed the details of your stay at Scarborough."

"Stay? Milord, you make it sound as if I am visiting."

The earl glared at Gerard. "Yes, well, you may be going as a hostage, but your treatment will be one of a visitor."

Gerard added, "A cherished visitor."

She graced her husband with a soft smile of gratitude. He nodded in acceptance.

William looked from her to Gerard and then rested his stare back on her. His attentive gaze drifted from her head to her toes. Red suffused his face. He clenched his hands into fists and swung around to Gerard. "It is not possible."

Surprise crossed Gerard's face for an instant before he dropped a bland look of question over his features. "What isn't?"

"There were guards posted outside her chamber door and at the foot of the stairs."

"Yes. What matter is that?"

"You were not to be permitted into her chamber."

Gerard took a step toward her. "Why is that, William?"

"You have—"

Her husband spoke over William's sputtered answer. "What? Sullied your prize? Destroyed your plans?" He pulled her to his side. "You thought I would be foolish enough to hand my virgin wife over to your care?"

William grasped the hilt of his sword. "You were supposed to rid Brezden of traitors."

Gerard grasped his own sword. "So, now we finally come to the meat of this matter."

"You disobeyed orders."

"I did not. I captured Brezden and dispatched Pike to his maker."

"You permitted the other traitor to escape."

"You think to punish me by taking my wife hostage?

What do you have planned for her?"

William had the nerve to look affronted, but he said nothing.

"Do you have another betrothal already arranged? Has the church issued their consent for the annulment of her existing marriage?"

The earl shook his head. "No. Neither."

Gerard released his sword. "Then what were you going to do with her? Kill her?"

William glanced at Catheryn with a look that chilled her blood. "By all accounts she is a traitor." He directed his stare toward Gerard. "And you are a lovesick fool."

The smug laughter that sprang from Gerard's lips froze the blood in her veins. "Lovesick? Because I make certain that you cannot hand my wife over to another as an unsullied virgin?"

Catheryn's heart ceased to beat. Had she been wrong? Instead of using her for a means to discover the whereabouts of de Brye, had he used her instead to thwart Earl William? Had Gerard only used her for his own ends? She swallowed against the pain ripping through her heart and her chest.

"Maybe if you are not panting after her like a rutting stag, you will be able to find de Brye."

"Maybe I won't. What then?"

"King Stephen will come in with an army and tear this keep down to the ground."

His bald statement, spoken with utter certainty, should have angered or frightened her, but her feelings were numb. Her emotions nonexistent. Catheryn didn't care what they did with Brezden, or with her. She just wanted to leave this place. Now. Before her wounded heart fell from the open gouge in her chest.

"You have informed the king of your discovery?"

"No. I wanted to give you the chance to prove Brezden's loyalty to the crown."

"It gives you the perfect opportunity to prove who is in charge."

William nodded. "Yes. We are not in Normandy. Nor on our lands in France. This is England and we are not on equal standing here. This is my region, under my control. From this moment forward, Gerard, when it comes to Brezden, you will take your orders from me."

"Until I return to my own lands, I will follow your orders concerning Brezden only. You will issue no orders regarding my wife."

"Your wife *is* Brezden. She *will* remain in my hands until this matter is over."

"You harm one hair on her head and I will make all the days of your life miserable. Your sheep will die. Your vineyards will burn. Your dikes and canals will fall into disrepair."

William's eyes widened. "'Tis a little much for a woman you profess not to love."

"I will protect and defend this wife with a vengeance lacking in my first marriage."

The earl remained silent for the space of a few heartbeats, before finally saying, "Defend your wife all you wish. Regardless of what you do, Gerard, someday the woman will still die."

Gerard agreed with William and added, "Not at your hands. Not before her time."

Catheryn gasped softly and wished the day was now.

William looked at Catheryn. "Bid your husband adieu and let us be on our way."

As if in a dream, a nightmare with no end, she turned toward Gerard. William strode toward the door, giving them time for a brief farewell.

Gerard pulled her into his embrace and held her close. She kept her arms at her side.

"What is this, Catheryn?" He spoke softly, so only she

could hear.

It took a few deep breaths to gather her courage and to get past the hurt constricting her throat. Before she left, she had to know. From his lips to her ears, she wanted to hear his words. "Do you care for me at all? Was last night nothing more than a game to thwart the earl?"

He stepped back. She caught a brief, fleeting glimpse of confusion cross his face before he dropped his mask in place. "Already you have forgotten."

It was not a question. He did not wait for an answer.

"Think what you will then. I care not."

The words he'd spoken in front of the window earlier this morning floated into her memory. Before she could stop him, he turned and walked away.

"Gerard!" Her call did not make him cease his hasty exit. He walked by William without pause and disappeared out the door of the keep.

"Lady Catheryn." William called to her.

With the burden of guilt and shame resting heavily on her shoulders, she slowly joined him at the door.

The look he gave her was full of pity. She hoped he would let this incident pass without words. He shook his head and said, "That was not the way to encourage him to be quick about finding de Brye."

She bit sharply on her bottom lip to keep her thoughts from escaping. What difference did it make? Even if he found and killed de Brye this very day, he'd not want her back. Not today. Maybe never.

William lifted her chin with the side of his hand. "Lady Catheryn, do you not wish to return home, to Brezden?"

Home? She gazed about the hall. This had not truly been home since her father's death. It had been a prison—little more than a large, over-crowded cell.

Until Gerard's first brutal coming. Even with the attack, he'd brought a measure of life back to Brezden. And she'd just tossed his offering to the dogs.

"No, milord. It might be better if I never returned."

He dropped his hand. "A day from now you will regret having spoken those words." Then he led her out into the bailey.

Men, women and children lined the path leading to her saddled and waiting horse. She looked beyond them, searching for the one person she desperately wanted to find.

Gerard was absent from the bailey. He did not stand in the crowd. She could not locate him along the path, nor by her horse.

She slowed her steps, unwilling to leave until she could set things right. Or at least gaze upon the chiseled face that had become so dear to her.

William nudged her shoulder, interrupting her thoughts and her search. Irritated, she frowned before transferring her attention to him.

He pointed through the crowd, toward the gates.

She shifted her gaze in that direction and found Walter standing along the wall. Gerard's captain met her look and pointed up.

There, leaning over the wall stood Gerard. His back was to her, but he was there and that mattered greatly.

Her heart fluttered with hope that he might yet bid her farewell.

As she mounted her horse and followed the earl and his men out of the bailey, her hope died. Its death brought only more pain, and more guilt.

Clear of the gatehouse she turned in her saddle and craned her neck, still seeking her husband. Tears blurred her vision, but she easily picked him out of the men lining the wall. He was the one who stoically met her frantic search.

After lifting her arm to wave farewell, she paused and then held her hand high in the air and curled her fingers into a fist. She would hold his sealed vow tightly until the day she died. One question burned furiously in her heart. Had he used her last night, or had he loved her?

It took only a breathless moment for Gerard to return her gesture and douse the flames threatening to sear her heart.

Chapter Sixteen

Scarborough Castle, Yorkshire, England

For the second day since her arrival, Catheryn watched the hordes of people pour into William's castle. When he'd said there was to be a tournament held, she'd thought that meant fifty or so men.

More than that had already set up tents. As far as her vision could travel there were tents of every size, shape and color. Still more people entered Scarborough's gates.

While she desperately missed Brezden, Agnes and Gerard, at least she could fill her time with watching the participants for the tourney. Men practiced everywhere. The inner and outer yards, in the grass outside the castle's walls, even in the barren fields.

No amount of entertainment could dilute the fact that William's lady detested her. From the moment Catheryn had entered the castle, Cecily had seen fit to mock and degrade her at every turn. Even though her door was guarded, it became a welcome respite to seek the solitude of the tiny chamber she'd been given.

Here, away from the noise and bustle of the crowd, she felt a semblance of peace. The room itself beckoned feelings of ease. From the soft, over-stuffed mattress on the bed, to the flowers and herbs painted on the walls, the chamber had the ability to soothe and to quiet a worried heart.

"Lady Catheryn?"

She jumped away from the window at William's question. She'd not heard the door open. "Milord?"

"Is there anything you require? Anything you want?"

Taken aback by his sudden concern, she frowned. "No, not that I can think of. May I ask why?"

William fidgeted. He looked around the room. He put his hands behind his back only to fold them before him again. He gave the appearance of a child who'd been caught in the act of mischief. She shook her head to clear the mistaken picture from her mind.

"Earl William? Is something wrong?"

"No. Lady Catheryn, we seem to have a bit of difficulty."

Her heart skipped a beat. What had happened? Did Gerard fail? He'd only had four days, not nearly enough time to locate, capture and kill de Brye.

William took one look at her face and closed the distance between them. "Oh, no. No, milady, it has nothing to do with you." He grasped one of her trembling hands. "I am sorry. 'Tis King Stephen. He and his queen are due to arrive at any moment."

Catheryn's heart, which had resumed beating, skipped again. This time, not with fear. Excitement caused her heart to trill. The chance to be presented to the king and queen did not happen to everyone. "Queen Maud and King Stephen are here?" She was awed to be in the presence of such nobility.

"Aye. Don't you see, there lies the problem?"

Problem? Why was he telling her about any problem at Scarborough? Unless—she hung her head, mortified at her earlier thoughts of meeting the king and queen.

"I understand, milord, it would not be seemly for you to have one as lowly as I in your hall."

"My God, woman, do not seek to put words in my mouth. You don't understand at all." He lifted her chin with the side of his thumb. "Lady Catheryn, you are far from lowly. Was your sire not a baron? Did he not fight at the king's side? I cannot find words to tell you how sorry I am about not coming to yours and your mother's aid when you so desperately needed me."

She was shocked. The man truly seemed remorseful. "It

was not your fault, milord. You did not receive the missives."

"Regardless, I should have come to see for myself how the baron's family fared." He laughed softly. "Now I hold his daughter hostage. Don't you see? That's where the problem lies."

"Because I am a hostage?" It still made little sense to her.

"Because I never wished for Stephen to discover that fact. I wanted, I expected no crisis to arise from this situation."

Now the problem became clear. Somewhat. "No crisis? To whom? 'Tis a crisis to me. Release me and all will be forgotten. Your problem would then be solved."

He dropped his hand. "If only it were that simple. Your husband must understand who rules. Here, in York, I give the orders, not Gerard. I cannot have my men running about doing as they please, when they please."

"I am the tool you will use to teach him?"

The look he shot her spoke volumes. "Aye."

"So, what do you propose?" She guessed at what he was going to say, but she wanted to hear it.

"This chamber is far from where the king and queen will reside for the few days they are here. I cannot, I will not, allow you to leave this room."

Catheryn breathed a sigh of relief. "Gladly will I remain within these walls." When he looked at her like she'd gone mad, she explained, "I thought you were going to lock me in a cell."

"Do not speak too soon, Catheryn. This will be a cell of sorts. I cannot leave the men posted outside the door. It would draw attention."

She stepped back. "A woman alone in a bedchamber will not prove to be an open invitation to those—"

William cut her off, "No. Gerard would kill me. *I* would kill me." He pulled a large ring of keys from his belt. "I will have to lock you inside. The others will be told this room is useless, in terrible disrepair."

"How long will the king and queen be here?"

"A few days at the most. It will not be long."

She watched in confusion as he opened the door of the chamber and permitted a man carrying lumber, hammer and nails to enter.

"What are you doing?"

"A woman leaning out this window will give the lie away." He then waved the man to his task.

It took little time before thick boards choked off most of the breeze and the light that entered the chamber. Only a small slit between the boards remained.

William dismissed the man and peered out the narrow opening. "You can still catch a glimpse of the comings and goings from time to time if you so desire."

Not knowing what else to say to the man who'd just cut off her link to the outside, she muttered, "Thank you." Catheryn then tried to think of anything she might require in the next few days. "What about food, drink and," she felt her face flush, "the necessities of life?"

He scratched his head and furrowed his brow. "It looks as if the Earl of York will be your personal maid for a time."

She wanted to laugh at the look on his face, but he'd brought this on himself. "As long as you don't forget, milord. I get angry when not fed."

He laughed at her reply and headed for the door. "I promise, I won't forget."

She watched the door close behind him and listened to him turn the key in the lock. Her heart lurched. She was, in essence, a prisoner.

Catheryn forced her breathing to remain even. It was only for a few days. Anyway, what would she have to say to the lords and ladies present? What could she discuss with them? She doubted if they'd relish hearing about Pike or de

Brye. For a certainty they would laugh at her mooning about a husband she'd known for less than a month.

It was better this way. Truly it was.

Her justification fell aside. She failed miserably at convincing herself in the logic of this decision. Silently, she raged. This wasn't fair. When else would she get a chance to meet the King and Queen? Because William wanted to hide his actions from King Stephen, she had to pay with imprisonment?

The blast of a horn called her to the window. She leaned her forehead against the wood and peered through the narrow opening between the slats. The view was not sufficient enough to gain a broad panorama.

She scanned the instant formation of men in the bailey. Her gaze swept over the perfect lines of men standing at attention, she glanced at the procession riding past the men.

There was no doubt that royalty had entered Scarborough. From the many pennants fluttering in the breeze to the men guarding the procession, it was a show that screamed "The King has arrived!"

This far up in the corner tower, she was unable to discern individual faces. Only the many bright colors of clothing, horse trappings and standards.

Her gaze drifted from those now entering the yard to the groups still outside the far walls. Her heart tripped over itself. Green and gold. Surely she was mistaken. She squinted to better see the men, then she gasped.

Green and gold standards fluttered in the breeze. Silken tabards, that she herself had once helped to sew, covered the chests and shoulders of the men in a small party toward the rear of the line.

She tore her gaze from the approaching men and raced to the door.

"Damn!" She beat on the locked door with the palm of her hand. "Rot in hell, William!"

He'd tricked her. Gerard was here. It would have been easy to hide what the two men did from the King. They would simply say nothing. There was no need to lock her inside this chamber. The next time she saw William, she'd burn his ears with curses.

She rushed back to the window and tried to scream through the slats. The wood must have effectively swallowed her voice, because not one head, not one set of eyes so much as glanced up at the tower.

She tugged uselessly at the boards. The long, thick nails held them securely over the window. The only damage she'd caused was to her own fingers. She'd torn her nails into jagged, broken ends.

Catheryn fought the urge to throw herself on the bed and scream in rage. It would gain her nothing. She rested her head against the barrier once more and consoled herself by watching her husband approach.

Gerard closely watched the people lining the road that led into Scarborough. Hundreds of faces, and not one of them his wife, waved and cheered the procession entering the castle yard.

He sought one other face as he rode through the gates. That one he found easily. Gerard dismounted, handed the reins of his horse to his squire, then he approached William.

The earl seemed shocked to find him here. Gerard knew better. King Stephen had sent messengers to all of the barons requesting, nay demanding, their presence at Scarborough.

Clasping William's shoulder in greeting, Gerard leaned in close. "Where is she?"

"Safe from you."

He smiled and nodded at those passing by. "In a cell?"

"Not exactly."

"Shall I ask Stephen for assistance?"

Now the earl smiled. "If you do, I'll hand over the

evidence branding her a traitor. 'Tis a fine day for a hanging, don't you agree?"

Angry, Gerard squeezed the earl's shoulder a little harder than necessary. "I will find her."

"Fine. If she comes up missing I'll send an army to take her back."

"You do that, William."

He bowed. More to mock the man who used to be called friend than anything else. Then he entered the castle. He'd find Catheryn if it took all night. Even if he had to dismantle the entire building.

He'd had recent experience at dismantling things—especially walls. There probably wasn't one wall left in Brezden untouched. It had taken no more than a few hours after Catheryn left to discover that there were more tunnels than the three she knew about. One way or another he'd find every one. Or he'd die trying.

Now, where would that blackguard William keep his wife? If not in a cell, then where? He glanced up the spiral staircase. Before he could make his escape, King Stephen called for an immediate gathering.

Hours later Gerard knew three things.

One—William would not be holding his tourney. Too many men could be injured and the king needed all the men whole and preferably in one piece.

Two—they would all be leaving for Northampton in the morning. It was time to gather everyone together and attack Empress Matilda.

Three—he had but a few hours to find Catheryn.

He left the hall, seeking air. A fresh breeze might stir some thought in his mind. Walking about the bailey, Gerard looked up at the castle. At first he paid no attention, but something drew his gaze back to the tall, stone building.

Almost every window opening on this side of the castle glittered with candlelight. All but one or two.

He stared harder at those two windows. A larger figure, a man perhaps, stood in one. The other appeared empty. No. A tiny slit of light peeped through. The opening was covered. Gerard frowned. On a night like this, with the mild breeze, one would think the occupant of that room would want to take advantage of the warming spring air.

Unless whatever covered the window could not be removed.

If that was where Catheryn was held, he'd never be able to scale the wall. There had to be a way to find out who was in that room.

He sought Walter in the stables. "Where is Catheryn's gift? Find me something to pick a lock with."

The captain handed him a medium sized wooden box. "Here. She's getting riled at her confinement."

Gerard lifted the hole-filled lid and caught the reddish-blonde bundle as it tried to jump out of the box. "Come, Jewel. I have a job for you." After putting the crying cat back into the box, he closed the lid.

After Walter handed him a length of long thin metal, Gerard told his captain, "If anything untoward should happen and I am not in attendance in the morning, gather the men and head for Reveur."

"But, milord—"

Gerard waved off Walter's words. "I have no time for questions and answers. Just do as I say."

He left the speechless man standing there and headed back to the castle. It was easy to slip in past the crowded great hall. He was nothing more than another figure walking about. No one took any notice of him.

He took the steps of the spiral staircase two at a time up to the third floor. He was amazed that William had no guards posted. The man was mighty sure of himself, to think no one would snoop about these chambers.

As soon as the thought left his mind a heavy set of

footsteps approached. He ducked into a shadowed doorway and held his breath, praying that Jewel would make no sound.

How often did the guard make his rounds? Would he have enough time to locate the door and trick the lock into opening?

He waited. As still as death, he stayed in the doorway and counted. The man didn't round the corner again until Gerard reached one hundred. It was little time, but it would have to be enough.

As soon as the guard turned the corner, Gerard pulled the cat from the box and walked to the door he was certain was Catheryn's. He placed the cat on the floor and waited.

And counted.

At first Jewel walked away. When a noise drifted through the door, the cat turned back and sniffed. It took but a moment before the animal started pawing at the wooden door.

He grabbed the cat and held his fingers around its mouth to stop the sudden cries. Gerard raced back to his hiding spot and waited again until the guard passed and out of sight.

He pulled the slim tool from his belt, then stuck it in the keyhole and tried to turn the lock. For a moment he panicked, certain he'd reach one hundred before tripping the lock and opening the door.

At the count of ninety his heart slowed as he finally unlocked the door. He bolted inside, then handed Catheryn the box before softly closing the door and lifting a finger to his lips.

He added another fifty to his count of one hundred before using the tool to lock the door from the inside.

"You do enjoy teasing death, don't you, milord?"

Her words lacked the sarcasm he knew she meant. He could hear the tears before he saw them.

Gerard turned to face her and opened his arms. "You left before I could bid you farewell properly."

She was in his embrace before he could even smile. He carried her to the narrow bed. "Your keep is in ruins."

Catheryn touched his face. She kissed his chin, then his lips. "I care not."

After laying her down on the soft mattress, he covered her with the length of his body. She felt so good. So soft. So inviting. It was hard to believe that in four days time, he could miss anyone this much. His heart ached with an unfamiliar longing. "I will fix Brezden before you return."

"I am certain you will." She ran her tongue down his neck. "It matters not."

"We have been searching for de Brye without end." He tasted her eyelids, her cheek, before seeking to meet her lips.

He was lost. Lost in a kiss that promised him all. The promise took his breath away. Her kiss, her touch called to his heart in a way that was frightening.

What if she truly was in league with the devil?

He pushed the thought away. Surely he could guard his heart long enough to discover the truth.

Jewel jumped up on the bed. Her purr, loud and insistent, roared in his ears. The kitten had not seen her mistress in days and it was obvious she was not going to give up.

With a groan, Gerard broke away. He traced a finger down Catheryn's heated face and whispered, "If there were time I would make love to you all night."

The animal squeaked when Catheryn hugged it close to her chest. "I would be happy with but a few moments."

"We cannot chance being caught this time. We are not at Brezden."

She held the kitten with one hand, sat up and ran her other hand down his chest. "Who would know? What could they do? We are husband and wife."

He grabbed her hand and placed a kiss on her palm. "You are a hostage. William vowed to give King Stephen the evidence if I so much as seek you out."

She slipped her robe off her shoulders.

He pulled it back into place—slowly and with great regret. "How have you been treated?"

She ran her cheek across Jewel's back, before shrugging. "I am not harmed. Cecily is unkind. I survive by staying in this room."

"Damn him! That was not our agreement." His blood boiled with anger. No one could treat his wife in this manner and not pay for it.

Catheryn rested a hand on his arm. "It is my choice, Gerard."

He looked about the chamber. "It is your choice to stay in a locked room with one small candle for light?" His rage grew with every word he spoke. "No window for air? If this was your choice, what was the other option?"

"No. You misunderstand. I have free run in the keep. When there are no royal guests. I choose to stay up here, because I am then away from Cecily's sharp tongue."

He knew William's wife could be temperamental. He also knew that Cecily carried a grudge against him and would not hesitate to take it out on Catheryn. "I am truly sorry for all of this."

"It isn't your fault. It is mine for not telling you what you needed to know immediately."

Gerard never expected to hear that admission from her. "No, Catheryn. I think we must both shoulder the blame for this."

"How so?"

He pulled her onto his lap and scratched Jewel's head before threading his fingers through Catheryn's hair. "That first night, when I attacked Brezden, I should have forced you to speak the truth."

Her laugh was small, but it sounded like music to his ears. "You think you could have?"

He used his forehead to tip her head back. Then he lowered his lips to her neck and nipped the tender flesh. "I know I could have."

"Prove it, milord."

She squirmed in his lap and he doubted if the movement was an accident. Even if it was, the effect would have been the same. His blood surged to his groin and he knew she could feel his erection. Her low throaty moan gave away her intentions.

"Behave, Catheryn."

"I will not—"

He swallowed her words with his lips. Despite all his will, all his promises to himself to not spend too much time in this chamber, he found himself and her naked within a few breathless heartbeats.

As his heart swelled with emotion, he heard his own hoarse voice as if through a fog, "God, I have missed you."

~*~

Catheryn jerked awake when the door to her chamber opened. William, Cecily and the carpenter entered.

Had last night been a dream? No. She knew by her tired, sluggish body that Gerard had definitely been there.

She hid her smile and bid good morning to the trio. "What brings you here this morn, my lord?"

While the carpenter removed the boards from the window, William answered her query. "We are setting off to join King Stephen."

"The king has already left?"

"Aye. With the first morning light. Your confinement is at an end, Lady Catheryn. There is none here who can do anything to help your cause."

Her heart lurched, but there was truly little else Gerard could do. He'd brought her Jewel for a visit. He'd made sweet desperate love to her. He'd bid her farewell, properly this time.

"You will be leaving, too?"

"Yes. Cecily will see to your welfare."

She wanted to laugh out loud. If Cecily didn't have her strung up from the closest tree by nightfall, things would be well.

As if reading her thoughts, William added, "You will come to no harm." He looked at his wife while continuing. "Upon my word as the Earl of York, you will come to no harm."

Catheryn wasn't too certain that would help matters much, but it was better than nothing. "Thank you, milord. Have a safe journey and wish my husband well."

"Oh, speaking of your husband," William ducked back out into the hall for a moment and returned with a wooden box. "He left this for you."

She had to choke back tears as she opened Jewel's cage and pulled the kitten to her chest.

"That animal will not reside within these walls!" Cecily's screech surely resounded over all of England.

William sighed. "Please, Cecily, let the lady and her cat be. I will vouch safety for both of them."

His wife turned away in a huff that did not bode well for Catheryn.

Earl William took his leave, then he left the two women alone. As she wrapped her robe about her, Catheryn walked to the window. Cecily stood next to her and they stared out at the assembly below. The men were mounted and waited only for William's orders to leave.

Catheryn watched silently as the earl joined the group. The procession then headed out the gates. All but one lone rider.

She smiled, leaned on the window ledge and thrust her arm out the window. While holding it high, she closed her hand into a fist.

The rider still motionless in the yard mimicked her odd wave before joining those now leaving Scarborough.

"Who do you shake your fist at, Catheryn?"

She buried her face in Jewel's fur, hid her smile and answered, "No one."

CHAPTER SEVENTEEN

"I want that cat out of here." Cecily sneezed, again.

Catheryn looked about to make sure the kitten was not round. "Cecily, Jewel is in my chamber."

"Did you not hear me? I want that cat out of my keep. If you refuse to do it yourself, I'll have it taken away."

She stared at William's wife before turning to go back up to her chamber. She'd listened to this woman's ravings for little over two months now and she was sick to death of it.

How much longer before the men returned and Gerard could set about finding de Brye? How much longer would she be held hostage by a man with a shrew for a wife?

She'd be happy to give up her freedom for the relative quiet of a cell.

"Where do you think you are going?"

Catheryn paused. "To my chamber."

"No. First of all, it is not your chamber. And we have some arrangements to discuss."

She closed her eyes, counted to ten before returning to sit back down and ask, "What arrangements are those, milady?"

Cecily titled her head in a way that said she was so much better than any other living person. She looked down her nose at Catheryn. "I am having a party at the hunting lodge in three days and you will attend."

"A party? Your husband is gone and you hold a party?" She rose from her seat on the low stool beside William's wife. "I hope your gathering is a success, milady. But I will not be attending."

She made it as far as the stairs this time before Cecily's snide tone of voice stopped her. "Either you will attend or I will inform William of your husband's visit the night before they all left."

Catheryn caught her breath, hoping to calm her racing heart. "I know not of what you speak."

"And I have already questioned a stable boy who heard your husband and his captain talking."

"He must have been mistaken. It wasn't my husband he overheard." Wishing she had the stable boy's neck between her fingers, Catheryn resumed her climb toward her chamber.

"I am quite certain that William promised to turn you over to King Stephen as a traitor if Gerard so much as looked for you."

When that didn't stop Catheryn's escape, Cecily walked to the bottom of the steps. "How do you think you'll look in a noose?"

That was not something she wished to discover. Catheryn turned and came back down the steps. "I still say the boy was mistaken."

"Say what you will. I believe the lad and so will William."

Catheryn accepted defeat. "What am I required to do?"

An evil smile, one that reminded her of an old crone, crossed Cecily's face. "Serve."

She swallowed. "Serve?"

"Yes. You think yourself too high and mighty to serve food and drink at a party given by an earl's wife?"

"Well, not exactly. But serve?"

Cecily leaned closer, so they were nose to nose. "'Tis that or hang."

Catheryn knew when to give up. She took her pick. "Fine, milady, I will serve at this party of yours."

A commotion in the bailey drew both women outside. William and his men rode through the gates. Heart racing, Catheryn searched the returning party—Gerard was not among them.

Cecily rushed to the earl's side and threw herself into his arms with apparent glee. "Oh, you are home at long last."

Catheryn wanted to vomit. Cecily had not mentioned her husband in a kind, or wifely, sort of way since the moment the men had left.

But William gazed down at his wife with the look of a man obsessed. "Yes, I am." He glanced up and saw Catheryn. "And how have the two of you been fairing?"

Catheryn remained silent.

Cecily, however, did not. She waved at Catheryn as if she were dismissing a servant. "Oh, you can go now."

Lifting her eyebrows in question and amazement at the woman's gall, Catheryn remained where she stood.

"I said, you can go now. Get you gone from my sight."

Catheryn shook her head. "No. If you wish me to leave, you will have to do more than issue churlish commands."

"Why you—"

William tore himself from his wife's embrace. "Enough!" He ushered both women back inside the keep.

The moment they entered the hall, he turned toward Catheryn and pointed a meaty finger at her. "You will give my wife the respect due her."

Then he loomed over his much smaller mate. "If this has been happening during my absence it will stop now. You will cease treating Lady Catheryn like a common serf."

"Then, dear husband, lock her up like the prisoner she is supposed to be."

"Hostage, Cecily. She is a hostage, not a prisoner."

A familiar argument. When she'd first arrived at Scarborough, William and Cecily had discussed it more than once. And oddly enough it was an argument that William never won.

In an aggravating sort of way, it amused her. Catheryn found it hard to believe that the man who'd accused Gerard of being a love sick fool was wrapped around his own wife's calculating, conniving, finger.

This man was the terror of York? This man had been instrumental in defeating the Scots at the battle of Standard? As far as Catheryn could tell this man gained more from his over-large build than from any claim to bravery or strength.

She rolled her eyes as Cecily batted her lashes and gazed adoringly up at her husband. "Yes, William, a hostage. I do forget." The woman fluttered her hands as if seeking words from the air. "It is so hard to remember when she is so, so..." Cecily peered around William to glance at Catheryn. "When she is such a common and plain sort of wench."

"This common and plain woman you speak of is Count Reveur's wife. Forget that not, Cecily."

"Ah, yes. Whatever possessed a healthy, strong, enticing man like Gerard to take on a wife like her?"

"I did." William's words sounded forced. As if they'd been issued from between clenched teeth.

"Oh, silly me, that is right." Cecily stroked his arm. "Tell me, beloved, why could you not find someone like Edyth? At least she knew how to enjoy life."

Without asking leave, Catheryn fled the hall. She knew that if she didn't get away from Cecily, she'd be sorely tempted to strangle the woman.

She escaped to the only secluded spot she'd found other than her chamber. The tower facing the water gave her a wide vista on which to gaze.

Catheryn stared down at the waves crashing against the castle's walls. Huge, white crested mountains of water roared toward the walls and upon contact with the immovable stone shattered into countless, broken droplets.

A servant. A personal maid to the Lady of York. That's all she would be if she attended Cecily's party. But in truth, she had little choice. The thought galled her.

It wasn't that she minded the work. It was not as if fetching and carrying could be considered work. When allowed, she'd performed more physical labor at Brezden.

But then Catheryn didn't have as many people to order about as Cecily did. That was where her rebellion lay. The Lady of York had many servants that could easily be ordered to work at this coming party. Why her?

She leaned against the wet stone wall. Catheryn's gaze roamed the ocean waves. How long before she could return home?

"What is taking him so long?" she murmured aloud.

"If you will remember, he has been with the king."

She almost fell over the tower wall into water far below at this unexpected answer to her almost unspoken question. After catching her breath, she turned and stared—at William. "I know that. But you are here now, so where is Gerard?"

"He has been at Brezden for over four weeks now."

"And?"

William extracted a missive from the inside of his fur-lined cloak. "And, he has located de Brye's base of operations. It seems, milady, Brezden is a paradise for smugglers and traitors."

Her already low spirits sank even further into the deep, cold well of despair. Smugglers? At Brezden? If Gerard did not find de Brye, she would surely hang.

He waved the message in front of her face before putting it back into the safety of his cloak. "And, before you ask, I'll tell you. No, he has not found de Brye." He turned to leave, adding over his shoulder, "He did mention something about your men though."

Catheryn watched his retreating back for a moment before his words sunk in. Spurred into action, she ran to catch up with him. "William. My lord, please."

She grabbed the tail of his cloak before the door of the tower closed. Without turning he asked, "Is there something you want? Something I can do for you?"

"What else did Gerard say? About my men. What about my men?"

When he did turn around the look on his face made her wish he hadn't. It was obvious from his furrowed brow, reddened face and the tick in his cheek that he was in a fine rage.

She needed to remember who this man was. Regardless of what she thought of him, or what she thought of the way he handled his wife, he was the Earl of York. And her life rested solely in his good graces.

"Tell me, Lady Catheryn, why were your men not in Brezden the night Gerard attacked?"

A lie would serve no one. "Because I sent them to safety."

"How?"

The truth would serve few. "There is a tunnel which leads out of Brezden." It wasn't a complete lie. She just didn't mention that there were numerous tunnels leading out of the keep itself.

"And how did you know they needed to seek this safety?"

"Because I dreamed of Gerard's coming."

William's eyes widened before he snorted and turned back around to leave.

"No, wait. 'Tis the truth, milord. I had the village midwife sell me a magical sachet so I could dream of my true love." She paused. Somehow the words sounded ludicrous to even her ears. "Have not you seen children make such charms?"

"Children, yes. Grown women, no."

"It was all I had left." She tried unsuccessfully to keep the despair from echoing in her voice.

William faced her. "All you had left? What does that mean?"

"Pike and de Brye made my life a living hell. Fanciful

dreams were all I had left. But instead of dreams, I had nightmares of the destruction to come."

"And you believed these night terrors to be true?"

"Weren't they?"

He nodded. "In this case, yes. But do you react to all your dreams as if they are real?"

"No. There was a difference with this one. It came every night and would not leave me alone."

William pulled the missive from his cloak. "What will you give me for this?"

"I have no gold."

"You possess more than simple gold, milady."

She gasped in shock and placed both of her hands over her heart. "You promised Gerard you would not harm me."

"We are not speaking of harm."

It took all the strength she possessed to back away from him and the page he held in his hand. "I will not lay with you."

His intent perusal slowly drifted from her head to her feet. "I admit the thought has crossed my mind. It has been an entertaining notion, to be sure." He laughed at her outraged hiss. "But I was not asking for a share of Gerard's leavings."

If he was trying to goad her to anger, it was working. Her blood pounded hot in her veins. "Then what do you want, milord?"

"Me? Nothing." He teased her with Gerard's note by holding it out, only to snatch it from her reach. "However, Cecily requires your presence at her next gathering."

"Cecily has already spoken to me of this." Catheryn shuddered to think of what that woman had already told William. "I have agreed to attend. But I still don't understand what is so special about this party."

William smiled and she knew the answer would not be to her liking. "She is holding an intimate party at the main hunting lodge."

How appropriate. "And what will she be hunting?"

"Knowing my wife," he shrugged. "Anything she can catch."

The earl and Cecily's idea of marriage sickened her. "And you, William, what will you hunt?"

At that question he laughed. "I? Nothing. I do not attend Cecily's private parties and she does not inquire as to how I amuse myself those nights."

"How quaint. Do neither of you fear the fires of hell?"

He stepped so close to her that Catheryn had to tip her head back to meet his irate glare. "What about you? Does the thought of hanging or burning at the stake bring you any fear?"

"I fear many things." She backed up. "But your threats are not among them."

"You can be quite bold at times, Lady Catheryn. Do you have enough bravado to attend one of Cecily's gatherings?"

He kept saying *attend*, not *serve*. So, the Lady of York kept her own secrets from her husband. "I will not be intimate with any of her guests. I would rather be confined to one of your dark cells."

"No one will force you." Her pulse quickened nervously at his grin. "But, if you should find one or two guests to your liking, no one will stop you from enjoying their attentions."

The nervousness his grin had caused dissipated with the return of her ire. "I would never dishonor my husband so."

"He would never know."

"It matters not. I would know."

William waved the missive under her nose. "Will you attend Cecily's party?"

Even though she didn't understand why her presence at this event was so important, she needed to know the fate of her men. She longed to touch something that had been in

Gerard's hands. She wanted to see the words he had written.

After closing her eyes, she nodded. "Yes. I will."

William placed the letter in her hand. "The gathering is in three days."

She did not open her eyes until she heard the door close.

She held Gerard's note close to her heart and looked up at the darkening sky.

As she had done every night, without fail since leaving Brezden, Catheryn sought the moon and found the twinkling stars.

~*~

She stood in the dark. Lost and alone, Catheryn sought escape from the terror hunting her.

The pounding of her heart echoed into the murky blackness and returned, louder and stronger than before. Her fear was a living, breathing monster. It sucked at her strength and at her very will to live.

Shouts and the wild crashing of men coming closer and closer drowned out the sound of her throbbing heart. They laughed, jeered wickedly and reached out for her. One grasped her arms and dragged her to the ground.

Her cries of fear ceased. It fell to a hushed whisper of a prayer. A useless prayer for mercy, for a quick end to the horror, floated from her lips to the darkened sky.

Men, their faces covered with bawdy masks, stripped off their clothes. Drunk with thoughts of lust and blood, they fell on her.

Her scream split the night. One word tore from her lips.

"Gerard!"

"Catheryn!" His answering shout ripped him from the clutches of the nightmare.

Sweat drenched his body. His heart drummed loud in his ears. Gerard drew in great breaths of air, willing his heart to slow, his blood to cool, his fear to abate.

He released the crumbled sheets entwined in his hands. A small, square bundle of cloth fell from his fingers.

He retrieved it from the bed, then he turned it over in his hands. Where had he seen this before? One edge was scorched, as if it had been tossed into a fire and rescued from certain destruction.

"You had no choice but to answer the yarrow's call."

Her words, the night he'd attacked Brezden, floated into his memory. It was her dream charm. The sachet had been beneath the pillows on her bed. The very same bed he had slept in every night since he'd returned to Brezden.

Were the legends true? Could one dream of his true love by simply sleeping with this sachet?

Gerard laughed weakly at his sudden fancy. It was nothing more than lack of sleep and the long hours spent searching for de Brye that set him on edge.

He swung his legs over the side of the bed. Then he rose and walked to the window. The night air was cool on his naked flesh.

He beat his fist on the wall. He missed her. They'd been apart for several weeks and already it felt like a lifetime.

Stephen's march to capture Empress Matilda had come to an abrupt halt in Northampton, where the King had fallen ill. Relieved of duty, Gerard rode straight back to Brezden to resume his search for de Brye.

While he had located de Brye's hiding place and a few of his men, the villain himself had been absent. If Raymond de Brye was in league with the empress, it was likely he was at her side. He'd return; and when he did, Gerard would be waiting.

In the meantime Gerard searched the other tunnels and caves, looking for Brezden's men. His efforts turned up not the men, but enough evidence to hang his wife.

There was no doubt in his mind that de Brye had planted

Brezden's jewels, maps of tunnels, gold, weapons and forged missives to the empress. Had anyone else found these items, Gerard knew they'd have come to one conclusion—that Catheryn was a traitor.

The chance existed that King Stephen and Earl William would not listen to reason. He couldn't take that chance. He wouldn't take that chance with her life. The only solution was to capture de Brye and to do it before any more incriminating evidence surfaced.

Gerard turned away from the window and donned the clothing he had earlier draped over the bench. He tucked the discarded sachet into his belt. After leaving the chamber, he climbed the steps that led to Brezden's tower.

A chilled wind buffeted him. The cold air helped to dispel the lingering remains of his nightmare.

"Milord."

He did not need to turn around to recognize Walter's voice. Had he known he'd not be alone, with only his thoughts for company, Gerard would have looked for solitude elsewhere.

"Walter."

"The men have stowed the jewelry in your chamber."

"Good. An inventory was taken?"

"Yes, the clerk will have the list for you in the morning."

Gerard leaned on the ledge of the wall. How many times had de Brye entered the keep without anyone knowing it? Any one of them could have been killed. Murdered while the lord of the keep was busy searching in all the wrong places. Raymond de Brye had been within reach all this time and Catheryn had kept that knowledge to herself.

He had permitted this woman to get too far under his skin. She had slipped into his blood, into his heart too easily.

Danger lay in caring too much. If she would keep secrets that could cost them their lives, what else would she do?

The thought twisted at his innards. He needed to force Catheryn far enough away from his heart to give his mind distance to work. How?

He had to find a way. Because once this mission was complete, once de Brye was dead and she returned to Brezden, things would be different.

No more would he plead with her. No more would he permit her tears to weaken his will. No more would he seek to allay her fears when so much rested on information she withheld.

No. When she returned she would find a husband she could not deceive. A man she could not bend. She would become the obedient wife she always should have been.

It all sounded right to his mind. His heart snickered at the thoughts.

His gaze drifted to the night sky.

"Gerard!"

The hair on the back of his neck stood on end. He searched the wall, but could see no one except Walter. He shook the strangeness from him and leaned back on the ledge.

"Gerard!"

His blood raced ice-cold through his veins. He touched the dream charm. The bag pulsed with life. Heat suffused his fingertips. Fog misted his vision.

She stood in the dark. Lost and alone, Catheryn sought escape from the terror hunting her.

His heart swelled, then stopped with unexplained fear.

Shouts and the wild crashing of men coming closer and closer drowned out the sound of her throbbing heart. They laughed, jeered wickedly and reached out for her. One grasped her arms and dragged her to the ground.

Now his heart crashed against the inside of his chest in a wild, frantic pace.

Her scream split the night. One word tore from her lips.

"Gerard!"

He closed his eyes, but he could still see her. The scent of her terror seared his nostrils. The fear evident on her face pierced his soul.

He pounded the wall before ordering, "Walter, gather the men. Arm them well."

"Milord?"

He turned to face his confused captain and forced himself to keep his voice steady. "We ride to bring the Lady of Brezden home. Tonight."

Walter blinked once before answering, "It is about time, milord."

"There is never a time for committing treason."

"We could ride for France. The men would not begrudge a return home."

"A coward's escape? Walter, I never thought to hear you offer the easy way out."

"Not cowardly, milord; expedient."

Gerard choked on his laughter. "Expedient? Or safer for your neck?"

His captain had the grace to look confused. "Milord?"

"My lady mother would hang you if anything happened to her son." He pinned Walter with a knowing stare. "Surely you did not think I was that ignorant?"

Walter said nothing, but his gaze darted everywhere except to him.

"Since my father's death you may have been my captain, but you have ever served my mother. Tell me she issued no orders in reference to my welfare."

"You are her only son." The man's reply was mumbled, but Gerard had long dealt with Walter's muffled answers and was well able to discern the words.

"Yes, but her son has outlived the need for a nursemaid."

Walter's complexion darkened. "Has it been that obvious?"

"Obvious? Lord, man, you have walked in my shadow since Edyth's death. If danger came from anywhere, it came from breaking my neck as I tripped over you."

"But—"

Gerard raised his hand, effectively cutting off the other's words. "I am not chastising you. I am trying to tell you that I am whole. The crazed grief is gone, Walter. You need not watch my every move."

His captain nodded, but said nothing.

Gerard clasped the man's shoulder. "I would have no other guarding my back."

Walter's smile eased Gerard's guilt for making the man uncomfortable. "Thank you, milord. I will be certain to inform Lady Reveur of your well-being."

"Good." Gerard turned to look back out over Brezden's lands. The darkened forest caught and held his attention.

"Walter, be certain to tell the men what we go to do. Give them the choice to come or remain at Brezden. I will not force them to take up arms against the earl."

"Think you it might be wise to prepare them for a swift ride out of England?"

Gerard stiffened his shoulders against the weight of the crime he was about to commit. Then he nodded. "Yes."

The door to the stairway opened. Instead of leaving, Walter added softly, "Do not lie to yourself, milord. You are not yet whole. A piece of you resides at Scarborough."

Wearily, he sighed at the truth in his captain's words. "I know that."

Once his captain left, Gerard gazed up at the dark sky.

As he had done every night, without fail since Catheryn left Brezden, he sought the moon and found the twinkling stars

Chapter Eighteen

"William."

The earl did not lift his head up from the accounts on the table before him.

Gerard took another step into the lord's private solar. "Milord Earl."

Still not looking at him, William asked, "What do you want, Gerard? Why are you here?"

"I am taking my wife home."

After slamming the ledger closed, William stood. "By whose orders?"

"My own."

"And de Brye?"

"He is not presently at Brezden. His men are watched."

"They are not yet captured?"

A detail that nagged at Gerard. "No. I want de Brye."

"You are dressed for battle. I can assume your men await your return?"

"How astute, William. Yes, they do."

The earl's jaw clenched and unclenched. "Do all from Brezden possess unruly tongues?"

"Ah, my wife has unleashed hers a time or two?"

"I am amazed Pike or de Brye did not kill her for it."

"They tried."

"And you. Why do you permit her to continue?"

Gerard could not mask his impatience any longer. "Because I find it a refreshing change from the bland females at court. Where is my wife?"

"You think it that simple? You walk in here dressed in mail, helm, and spurs, draw your sword and demand her release?"

"No. I don't think it simple." He hesitated. How much

could he tell William without seeming insane? "My wife is in danger and I intend to remove her from harm's way."

"Danger?" William's expression revealed his surprise. "She is in no danger here."

"William, I can not explain other than to say that I know, with all my fighting senses, that danger stalks her even here."

The earl frowned. "I have never found cause to fault your judgment in battle, but this is no battle, Gerard. Perhaps lust for this woman has set your normally keen senses askew."

"Lust has nothing to do with it." Desire maybe, but not lust. "Where is my wife?"

"Again, I ask you, did you think to walk in here, demand her return and then simply walk out?"

Gerard shook his head. "No. I had planned on attacking your castle. I'd resigned myself and my men to committing treason to take back my wife." He paused to gather his thoughts a moment before admitting, "As I rode up to your walls I remembered that once we had been friends."

He sheathed his sword and continued, "I recalled that our lands border each other in Aumale. I thought about all the times we shared the work of harvesting. I remembered that once your mother and mine were close companions."

The earl ran a hand down his face. "I knew giving you Brezden would never suit. How am I to keep my reputation intact with you around?"

Before the smile reached his lips, Gerard bit it off. "I could leave. I could return to Reveur."

"Stephen would have both of our heads. This rebellion with the Empress requires all the men and gold he can lay his hands on."

"King Stephen already knows my plans."

"And?"

"The missive was only just sent two days past. There has been no time for a reply."

William sat on the edge of the table and toyed with the writing quill. "What did you tell him, Gerard?"

"Never fear. I told him nothing that will bring his wrath down on your head."

Both men shook their heads at that statement. Not knowing when to employ any measure of wrath was one of Stephen's biggest downfalls.

"So, he knows nothing of holding Lady Catheryn hostage? Nothing of your quest in attacking Brezden? Nothing of de Brye's escape and subsequent smuggling?"

"No. He knows only that I wish to remove my wife from England and that after doing so and seeing to her safety, I will return."

"You think he will agree to your absence for such a flimsy reason?"

Gerard smiled. "I sent the missive to Maud."

"To the queen?" The shock in William's voice was evident.

"Of course. Why not? It is worded as a matter of love and Queen Maud will bend over backwards to see that Stephen permits my humble request."

"How you gained that woman's good graces, when I could not, is baffling."

"'Tis simple, William. Maud enjoys the role of mother. So, instead of treating her like a woman unworthy of my attention, I set about finding things only a mother can take care of and present them to her."

William's face registered disbelief. "I never treated Maud as unworthy."

"No, you give her all the respect due a queen and none due a woman."

"You have listened to far too many troubadours."

"Have I? Tell me, William, who has the queen's ear and who does not? Who do the other men trust around their wives and daughters and who do they not?" Gerard rested his palms on the table and leaned across the expanse of oak. "Where is my wife?"

Lost in apparent thought, William answered, "At one of Cecily's parties."

Gerard bolted upright from what felt like a physical blow to his stomach. "What?"

"She is at a gathering."

"Catheryn, my wife, is at one of Cecily's gatherings?"

William stood up and stared down the length of his nose at Gerard. "You heard me correctly. She is attending a party. She had been given the choice and freely accepted."

Gerard stepped back, then slapped his gloves on the table. "I want answers. Now." He'd known William too long to believe any claptrap about choices. He could imagine what her choices had been.

"It is useless to argue. She is there."

Blood rushed to his head, causing his temples to throb and his vision to blur. He blinked to clear the red haze. "How long has this…party…been going on?"

"A while." William's tone matched the vagueness of his answer.

"All day?"

"No. Actually, it should just be starting about now. Are you worried, Gerard?"

"About my wife's fidelity? No. About her level of shock? Yes."

"You are now referring to *my* wife."

"William, we are speaking of a woman who lives to love. Do not play innocent with me. We both know who taught her those ways. That is the only reason you do not run a sword through her."

"You go too far, Count Reveur."

"Are you going to tell me that my wife and yours have become such good companions that they enjoy spending time together?" Gerard couldn't wait to hear the lie that would leave William's lips.

"Well, they do get along"

"Get along? Like fire and oil?"

"I give up." William threw up his hands in mock surrender. "My wife hates yours. However, she recently admitted that she found Edyth charming."

At that Gerard laughed. "Please. Edyth was horrified by Cecily's actions at our wedding. It isn't every day a guest tries to seduce the groom."

"She meant nothing by it." William's red, tightly held face belied his calm voice.

"Where is this party being held?"

The earl scanned the room as if looking for a place to hide. Gerard's heart thumped in his chest. "William, is it here, within the castle?"

"Not precisely."

It was obvious that William was not going to volunteer any information on the topic. "Where?"

"In Yorkshire."

An urge to fling himself across the narrow space between them and beat the earl to a mewling mass nearly overwhelmed him. Instead, Gerard grasped the hilt of his sword. "Play no more games with me."

William backed off and sat on a bench by the fire. "Gerard, you worry greatly for naught. She is doing nothing wrong, simply attending one of Cecily's gatherings."

Dread rushed in where anger still boiled. "Where?"

"The main hunting lodge."

"A bathing party?"

William nodded.

Memories of the first party he had attended at the lodge assaulted him, nearly knocking him from his feet. While the party was—educational—he certainly didn't want his wife there.

He retrieved his gloves, turned on his heel and headed

toward the door, stopping only when the earl called out his name.

"Gerard!"

Without turning, he answered, "I must go. Whatever you have to say will wait until I return to England."

"You need not leave the country. I will not come for your wife, but you must find a way to capture de Brye before Brezden's name is besmirched with rumors of treason."

"You tell me nothing I do not already know."

~*~

Catheryn stared at the sight before her. No amount of blinking cleared away what her eyes told her existed. No amount of wishing made what her ears heard disappear.

How had she let Cecily coerce her into doing this? Easily. Earl William had ordered her to attend this disgusting party with his wife. They insisted that it was an honor to be chosen to act as a servant at one of Cecily's gatherings.

Catheryn stared at the revolting tableau before her and wondered where the honor lay? Surely not here. She'd had little choice though; it was this or take up residence in a cell.

She'd seen Scarborough's cells. Catheryn knew she'd not last a day enclosed in one of the dark, tiny rooms tucked so far beneath the keep. If the dark didn't drive her mad, the rats scurrying across the dirt floors would have.

Now she wondered if she'd made the right choice.

From the many kettles of water kept warm on fires outside to the numerous, huge tubs filling every room of the lodge, there was an over-abundance of everything—laughter, food, drink, baths.

And far too much exposed flesh.

The sight of such wantonness repulsed her. She did not find the crude display exciting. Not only did it embarrass her; she found that any respect she might have had for those in attendance died a quick and easy death.

They displayed themselves as if walking about naked were an everyday occurrence. Had they no shame? No pride? Simple decency would demand they cover themselves.

The only thing covered on the bodies inside the lodge was their faces. Every guest wore some type of mask or hood. Some were adorned with feathers and some were nothing more than scraps of decorated fabric tied around the wearer's head.

Their secrecy bothered her more than their nakedness. Other than being well able to determine male or female, she knew not whom she served.

A wide slat of wood balanced across the middle of each double-sized tub. It was there she was to place the food and drink. Her hands shook while she carried trays of wine goblets. She twisted and turned to avoid grasping hands as she walked between the tubs. Her wits nearly left her when it became obvious that not all of the seeking hands belonged to men.

They were drunk. Or they were under the spell of some herb. Incense burned in every corner of the lodge. Fear that the sweet, strong smell was to blame for their behavior kept her well away from the thin columns of smoke.

There had been one other serving girl helping inside with the food and drink, but she'd easily been coaxed to join the bawdy fray.

Catheryn's face burned. She tried to avert her gaze, but everywhere she looked couples were seeking their pleasure in a variety of ways. In the tubs and on the pallets Cecily so thoughtfully provided.

Catheryn stood by a window and breathed in the cool night air. She leaned against the wall and stared up at the dark sky. Wisps of clouds partially covered the moon, but she could see the twinkling stars against the inky blackness of the night.

As she had done every night since she'd been away from her husband, she whispered, "Oh, Gerard, hurry."

She closed her eyes for a moment and decided she'd had enough of this senseless entertainment. Just as she went to tell Cecily she was done serving, someone shouted at her.

"Wench, more wine."

Catheryn swallowed a deep breath of air. Maybe, maybe if she kept her thoughts on just the serving and pretended this was all nothing but a bad dream, she could still avoid a cell.

"Wench!"

After first grabbing a pitcher of wine, she approached the shouting guest.

She backed away from his wayward hand and then backed into another seeking palm. When she slapped at that man's hand, she found her wrist captured in a hard grasp that she couldn't break.

The first man snaked his hand up inside the hem of her gown. Fear, shock, and disbelief held her momentarily still. He stroked and caressed her ankle, calf, and moved up toward her thigh.

She jerked her leg from his touch. "Earl William said I did not have to entertain. Get your hands off of me."

The second man, the one holding her wrist, laughed. "William is not here, is he?"

Cecily waved from the next tub. "Oh, Catheryn, relax. Enjoy yourself." The woman's eyes were glassy and red-rimmed.

Catheryn fought to keep her wits intact. "Milady, your husband said—"

"Nothing. He said nothing." Cecily's brittle laugh boded nothing but ill will. There'd be no help coming from her.

The first man continued to paw at her leg. At the same

time, the second man cupped her bottom and squeezed.

Catheryn brought the wine jug down on the first man's head. She then held the broken jug toward the second man. Just as she was about to thrash him with the jagged pottery someone else grabbed her arm.

Her gaze raked the new intruder. This man towered at least a head over her. An elaborate hood adorned with black feathers and jewels worthy of a king's ransom concealed his face.

His gaze burned through her. Something felt familiar about his eyes. They seemed to pierce her. Catheryn's heart raced. Her breathing quickened with fear.

He reached out and slapped away the other man's hold and pulled her away. He kept his hand firmly around the back of her neck while he escorted her toward the stairs leading to the upper floor of the lodge.

Her breathing ceased. "Release me. Now."

She struggled against him, but was no match for the hold he had on her.

When they reached the steps leading up to the private chambers, she stiffened her legs. She'd not willingly mount those stairs. She'd not willingly commit adultery. She'd rather die.

The disguised man bent to lift her in his arms. She swung around and slipped from his hold. Catheryn ran to the door of the lodge and sighed a breath of relief when her hand fell on the latch.

Her relief had come too soon.

He grabbed her from behind, opened the door and pushed her out into the night.

His laugh froze her blood.

She recognized the tone and the laugh. Her stomach churned. The scream building in her throat could not fight its way past the bile choking her.

"Ah, sweeting, I have waited far too long for this night.

You will not escape me now—or ever again."

~*~

Gerard led his men swiftly across William's land, through the town, past the fields and into the secretive, dark forest. His heart drummed in unison with the horses' hooves. Steady and strong, the pounding rhythm echoed a common goal into his mind and soul.

Find Catheryn.

And find her they would. Before the terrors of his nightmare became a reality.

He'd not needed to ask directions to the lodge. He'd attended one of Cecily's gatherings there and remembered the way.

It was impossible to believe that Catheryn had willingly gone to this party. What trick did the earl and his lady use as coercion? Catheryn would be like a fish tossed up upon the shore—out of her element and helpless.

She was nearly an innocent in the ways of lovemaking. Their few nights of shared passion could not have prepared her for what she would witness at the lodge. He himself had been shaken to the bone the first time. And he'd not been a green boy in the arts of seduction.

The sight of unending flesh entwined with flesh had left him speechless. From one partner to another the guests would find their pleasure. The gatherings here rivaled a roman orgy. He'd found it embarrassing to witness at first.

But, with the help of two lusty bawds, his youthful embarrassment had swiftly dissolved. And his education had been broadened.

But he did not want his wife exposed to such acts. Not without him. And not outside the privacy of their own chamber.

Her presence at this party had no purpose other than to

humiliate her and anger him. It was a shameful and a dishonorable way to ensure his outrage.

Amazed at the strength of his conviction, Gerard shook his head. Surely he was getting old. When had the wicked, randy follies of youth become something shameful?

Immediately, he found the answer—since he'd left youth behind and become a man. Since he'd married and discovered someone who depended on his honor and needed his protection.

His protection. Now, there was an odd, misplaced thought. How well had he protected Edyth and his son? Not at all.

Regardless of his will to avoid the thought of that event, the memories swept over him. He steeled himself against the scenes forming in his mind as he rode, but that did not stop them from coming.

The wound opened anew. It throbbed with the intensity of a fresh gash. As if it had happened only just now.

He'd been so full of himself. So sure of his duty to his king above all else. Duty had been more important than the birth of his first child. More important than Edyth's well being.

Or, what he'd thought was duty.

A missive had arrived at Reveur. A command from King Stephen ordering Gerard to join him at court—a three-day ride away.

He had to go. Duty called him. Honor and loyalty to his king compelled him to answer the missive. So he'd left his laboring wife in the hands of a midwife, gathered his men and departed.

Barely a day out, a wounded squire from Reveur found him and reported the terrible news. Reveur had been attacked. The babe murdered. Edyth lay dying. She waited only for her husband to return.

And return he did. He and Walter had ridden like

demons. They covered the distance back to Reveur in less than half the time.

The keep had to have been attacked almost the moment he'd ridden out of sight. With few men left to defend the gates, the intruders had gained quick and easy access.

Everywhere he'd looked he could see their mark. From the burned stables, ruined baileys, and dead bodies, the scene screamed of destruction.

But that scene was nothing compared to what had awaited him inside the keep. All of the servants, the midwife and the friar lay dead in the great hall. Their bodies had been mutilated; some were unrecognizable. He'd prayed that they had found death before the unspeakable acts had been committed upon their persons.

In a private alcove at the rear of the hall, Edyth lay close to death. She'd sworn to await his arrival and somehow, with a strength he'd not known she possessed, she had managed to keep breathing—barely.

"No."

Gerard spurred his horse faster through the forest. Low-hanging tree limbs buffeted him. But the branches did not distress him as much as the memories battering at his mind and soul.

He'd not relive that day again. Not in his mind. Not in his heart.

It was enough to remember that his wife died in his arms. That she'd never once pointed a finger of blame at him. She'd not needed too. When he later discovered the missive had not come from King Stephen, that it'd been forged, he'd pointed the finger of blame at himself.

And he'd lived with the guilt every day since.

He'd not be guilty of another wife's death. His heart constricted with the thought. And a new guilt gave birth and tore at him.

Was the missive that now branded Catheryn a traitor also

forged? Had the same hand composed both the message last year and the one recently found at Brezden? Catheryn could die because of his lack of trust. He could lose her because of his own stupidity.

As much as Edyth's death had grieved him, just the thought of Catheryn facing the same terror threatened to rip his pulsing heart from his body.

He'd known Edyth all her life, nearly all of his own. They'd been betrothed at her birth, when he was but three. She'd learned the art of housekeeping at his mother's knee for years before they'd wed.

Edyth was almost as much of a sister as his blood sisters were. He had teased and goaded her, the same as he had them.

He'd known Catheryn but a few months. He'd attacked her keep. He'd deserted her bed on their marriage night. He'd locked her in a cell.

Yet, of the two, Catheryn was the one he would die for now. It was the Lady of Brezden who held his heart in her hand. How would he protect her?

The fires burning outside the lodge drew his attention to the problem at hand—getting Catheryn away from Cecily, away from William and back safely to Brezden. He could worry about the rest later. After she was safe and back in his arms they could sort out the truth from the lies. Together they could dispatch their common enemy to the devil he served.

They thundered into the clearing, drawing their swords as they came. Frightened servants scurried out of the way as the destriers' hooves knocked caldrons of water from the fires.

Guests, copulating under the stars, paused in their acts to stare blankly at Gerard and his men. Their unfocused gazes confirmed his worst fears. Reddened and glazed, their eyes spoke of Cecily's incense of lust. When lit, the opium-laced herbs emitted a sickly sweet aroma that beckoned one into a world of uninhibited passion.

If his wife had been exposed to the drugged herb, she'd not be responsible for her actions. But, still, he'd kill any man who'd touched her, and deal with her later.

Gerard ignored the masked guests who were too lost to be of any harm and entered the lodge. After kicking the door open, he guided his great destrier inside.

The horse shied away from the smoke permeating the air. Gerard shouted, "Catheryn!"

Chuckles rumbled from those guests who bothered to pay attention.

Walter slid in the door, squeezing past the destrier with care. "My lord, I do not think—"

Gerard glared down at him. "Good. Then don't. Find my lady and let us be gone from here."

His staid captain, after displaying a brief expression of horror, warily ventured further into the lodge and headed toward the stairs. Gerard guided his horse around unconscious bodies, not caring if they were passed out from an over-abundance of wine, or dead from the cloying smoke.

If he could not locate Catheryn, maybe he could find Cecily.

What had Catheryn thought when she'd witnessed this vile orgy? Had she been shocked? Had she been angry? Or had it captured her interest? No. That thought was unfair. While another woman might find the sights and notions here intriguing, Catheryn would not.

He steeled himself against the knowledge that he might very well find her entwined in another man's arms against her will. It would take all the will he had not to kill the foolish miscreant.

No. He drove those thoughts away too. She would not be in another man's arms. He would not find her entwined with anyone else.

"Gerard!" Her voice screamed in his mind. He started backing the horse out of the lodge. She would not be here. He would find her somewhere dark and dank. Somewhere private, secluded, not in this overcrowded lodge. A curse built in his chest and raged from his lips.

He shouted for his captain. "Walter!"

His man appeared almost instantly, dragging a naked, angry Lady Cecily with him.

"What is the meaning of this, Gerard?"

The sound of his name coming from her mouth nauseated him. Gerard stared down at her. "Whore, let my name not cross your lips again. Where is my wife?"

"Whore?" She screeched at him like a fishwife. "Who are you to call me whore?" She waved her hand about. "Is my mind suddenly ailing? Do I not remember you, Count Reveur, enjoying the pleasures of this lodge?"

He ignored her baiting and repeated his question, "Where is my wife?"

When she refused to answer, Walter shook her.

"She left. With a man, Count Reveur. A big, strong, capable man. One who will not look down his oh, so holy nose at her."

His hand convulsed over the pommel of his sword. William would be angry if he found the Lady of York dead. Even though he'd soon replace her with another.

Before he did something he'd regret later, Gerard ground out another oath, wheeled his horse around, knocking one staggering man to the floor, and left the lodge.

The forest was vast. There were many places she could have been taken. Where would he find her? Would he get to her in time? Or would fate repeat itself?

While circling the clearing, he fought to control his raging emotions. Fear was something he'd not often felt and it clouded his thoughts.

Never in or before any battle had he felt this weakness, this horrible pounding of his heart or the cold sweat that now coursed down his neck. Never before had he been unable to form coherent thoughts. Nor had he ever been unable to devise a plan that would bring victory to him and his men.

He stopped his mount and took a deep breath. Gerard then gazed up at the sky, seeking the moon and finding the stars. He closed his eyes.

Where are you, Catheryn? Where are you?

Chapter Nineteen

Catheryn opened her eyes to stare into nothing but complete blackness. No light broke the cold darkness surrounding her, enveloping her in a thick cloak of dread.

Her back rested against icy, damp stone. Stiff from being in this slumped position for God knew how long, she groaned with the effort to move.

A chain rattled across the hard floor as she tried to cross her legs before her. She reached out and felt the metal links firmly circling one ankle. She was chained in the dark like an animal.

Her heart raced. Sweat covered her body. An emotion stronger than fear shot through her limbs. Terror. Horror. Unable to breathe, she gasped, forcing her lungs to fill with air.

Disoriented, she could discern nothing. She wondered if de Brye was sitting somewhere within reach.

Panic overwhelmed her. She would die. Without ever seeing Gerard's face. Without ever touching him, or kissing his lips again, she would die.

And he would never know how much she loved him.

It was irrational to love a man she'd only known a few months. Insane to love a man who'd attacked her keep and locked her in a cell. Unreasonable to love a man she'd only spent a few nights with.

Irrational, insane, unreasonable...but true.

But there was no one else she'd rather be with, or share her life with. No one but Gerard could make her knees go weak with a smile. Or set her pulse racing with a look. Or send her blood soaring with a kiss.

No one else but Gerard would listen to ramblings about her parents, her childhood. No one else had ever bothered to ask. No one else had claimed to care.

And who but Gerard would tell her to find the stars and seek the moon and know all was well?

Aye, he'd attacked Brezden, but he'd rebuilt the damage. True, he'd locked her in a cell, but he'd guarded that cell each night himself and had seen to her well-being. And yes, he'd left her on their wedding night. But he'd more than made up for it, her last night at Brezden.

And when all was said and done, she'd called him here and he had come.

Catheryn buried her face in her hands, willing herself not to cry. If her tears fell now, they'd never stop.

The pain from clenching her teeth was almost her undoing. Agony shot through her jaw like an arrow. He'd hit her. Outside the hunting lodge de Brye had hit her and she remembered little else.

Vaguely she recalled being slung over the back of a horse like a sack. The bitter taste in her mouth brought a blurred memory of someone forcing a vile liquid down her throat. But that was all she could force from her groggy mind.

When she moved her jaw back and forth, her stomach rebelled at the pain, but she was relieved to find the bones were not broken. She was only bruised. And sore.

She feared he would kill her; but that was the least of her worries. The idea that he would torture her before he killed her frightened her beyond words, beyond rational thought.

Catheryn swallowed down a sob. *I will not cry. I will not show that vile slime my fear.* To do so would only inflame his desire to see just how far he could build upon her terror.

Catheryn ran her hands down her body—poking and prodding. For right now she was whole. She could detect no damage, no pain except for that in her jaw.

Whatever de Brye planned, he was saving it until she had awakened. She slumped back against the wall, hoping he would think that she was still lost in forced slumber. Maybe she could gain enough time to gather her strength and her courage. Both would be needed, along with her wits.

"It will not work."

Catheryn froze. He was here and probably had been the entire time. She remained silent, unwilling to make it easy for him to find her in the dark.

She nearly fainted when a hand grazed her shoulder. His approach had been silent. She hadn't heard his footfalls over the sound of her harsh breathing or the roar of blood in her ears.

De Brye drew one finger up the side of her neck, across her cheek and down her chin before closing his fingers around her throat.

She gagged at the smell of his rancid breath and fought the urge to scream.

"You will die, sweeting." His hand tightened, cutting off her air. She refused to struggle and simply closed her eyes against what she already could not see. But her mind supplied the vision.

And it terrified her.

In the semi-dark chambers of her mind, she saw his evil grin. And she saw the mad light shoot from his eyes.

His grip relaxed, slightly. "But not before you beg me to end your life."

She flinched when his other hand closed around her thigh. His fingers dug into the tender flesh; gritting her teeth did little to fight off the pain.

De Brye caught her chin between his teeth and bit hard enough to draw a gasp from her. He released her chin, then moved his lips closer to her ear and whispered, "Fear not, my love, you will scream for me. I have longed to hear the sweet melody tear from your lips."

He moved his hand up higher on her leg.

If she fought him would he kill her outright? Or would he

only beat her until she could no longer move? Until she could no longer fight? Until she no longer cared?

When his hand came to rest between her thighs, she lost control of her will and could not remain still beneath his squeezing fingers. Surging wildly against his touch, she threw him off balance.

An oath echoed in the darkness.

"You will pay for that, sweeting."

Catheryn twisted around and came up on her hands and knees. She could only hope that if she kept moving, he would not be able to find her.

She'd not taken the chain into consideration.

Instead of seeking her in the dark, de Brye found the length of chain. Slowly, steadily, he dragged her back to him.

She clawed at the wet, smooth floor, praying her fingers would find something, anything, to latch on to. But nothing marred the flat surface beneath her.

Fire burned at her fingertips as they dug at the rock floor, breaking nails and gouging her flesh. The stone scraped her knees as he pulled her across its hardness.

She screamed and kicked when de Brye latched a hand onto her ankle and finished pulling her to him. She'd not give up. Not without a fight.

He grabbed a handful of her hair with one hand. "'Tis truly too bad that I have no time for this now." His voice held a tone of true regret. "I would so enjoy giving you a small taste of what is to come."

"You will burn in hell." Her words barely left her mouth before his hand cracked against the side of her face, sending her forcefully back down to the floor.

Her head bounced against the hard stone. Before slipping slowly into utter blackness, Catheryn closed her fingers into a tight fist and whispered, "Gerard."

De Brye shouted for his men and waited for one of them

to bring him a lit torch. He then sent the man back out of this chamber and chuckled to himself.

The caves beneath and behind Brezden had proven useful once again. Who would hear her screams from this, the farthest chamber at the rear of the cave? No one but him. He grasped his crotch and rubbed the throbbing hardness briefly.

No, he would not waste himself. He could wait until she awoke. The thought of her cries as he buried himself in her flesh nearly drove him wild with uncontrollable desire.

Impatient, he kicked at her side, hoping to awaken her now. It did little good. The lady slept on, unaware of what awaited her.

Count Reveur and Earl William had taken his woman to Scarborough, forcing his hand. He hadn't planned on acting this soon—not until he was ready to leave Brezden for good.

Raymond had always been certain he'd take his bride with him to France when he left. It mattered little if she joined him on his journey dead or alive. For a while he'd been afraid she had slipped through his fingers, but luck—fate had intervened.

It had been easy to join Lady Cecily's bathing party. That whore welcomed any and all who wished to participate.

When he'd seen Catheryn at the hunting lodge, he'd known his angels had smiled on him. The time had finally come.

Now there was no need for rushing the task he'd so long envisioned. And if the taste of success had been sweet before, it was even sweeter now.

Now he would destroy two instead of one. In one stroke he would kill the Lady of Brezden and in doing so would send the soul of Reveur to the fires of hell.

His actions were justified. Had not the angels told him repeatedly that he was within his rights?

Had not the first Lady of Brezden sworn he could have

her daughter over her own dead body? Well, she was dead—at his hands. He quivered in pleasure at the memory of sending her tumbling down the steep stairs of the keep. He'd stared down at her broken body, knowing that the daughter, Catheryn, rightfully belonged to him and no other.

Unfortunately, he'd not been able to claim his rights immediately. Baron Pike had panicked and demanded that they leave Brezden for a time.

But, even that venture had been fortuitous. Had they not discovered Count Reveur's keep? Count Reveur...the man who had decapitated John de Brye.

The only other person Raymond had ever cared for had died on a bloody field of battle. It was then, holding his brother's lifeless body in his arms, that the angels had spoken to him for the first time.

They had told him over and over that revenge would right the wrong done to him and John. And he'd sought that revenge. From that day forward, he'd lived only for two things.

To make Reveur pay repeatedly for his dastardly act. Finding Reveur's keep had been a stroke of luck. A divine blessing. And he'd made good use of his fortune.

It was an easy thing to force a cleric to write the missive that would call Count Reveur away from his keep. And slitting the cleric's throat afterward ensured that none would be the wiser.

The babe had been far too easy to kill. What sport was a newborn? Lady Reveur, however, had fought like a wildcat; and he'd enjoyed every moment. He'd made her suffer in ways even he'd not known until that day.

De Brye glanced down at Catheryn, and thought of his other reason for living. To find a woman to become his wife. His plaything. His slave.

But the woman he'd so carefully chosen had married his enemy. She belonged to him. Her mother had said so. Yet, she'd become the new Lady Reveur. And his rage knew no bounds.

She would pay for her treachery, in an agonizing slow death. And in doing so would also make Reveur himself pay.

He kicked her one last time. She still did not move. He bent down and brushed a stray lock of hair from her face.

"'Tis all right, sweeting, sleep, rest well. You will need all the strength you can muster."

"Gerard!"

Each time the silent cry rang in his ears, it brought him back to this same spot.

"They have to be in there." After tucking the dream bag safely into his pouch, Gerard crossed his hands over the edge of his tall saddle, leaned forward and stared down the river's steep bank.

He had little fear of being seen. A thick line of brush and trees concealed him and Walter. There appeared to be no need for secrecy. No guards were evident. Now and then a man would leave the cave, patrol the river for a short distance and then return. Either de Brye was a fool, or he was so confident that he felt no need for guards.

Or he was not there.

"Do you have a plan of attack?"

Gerard glanced at his captain. The man looked haggard. In the last four days neither of them had slept more than a couple hours at a time.

It had been a day and a half to Scarborough and another day and a half back. And they'd combed the caves and riverbank endlessly for the last day. He prayed to any God who would listen that his hunch, his odd feelings about her location, was not wrong.

"Milord?"

"Other than getting a look inside that cave and removing Catheryn if she is there? Nay. I have no other set plan."

"Gerard."

He jumped. This time he heard his name outside of his head. And the voice wasn't Catheryn's. He turned around in his saddle, staring in amazement at William.

Gerard directed his attention back to the river. He searched the bank for the mouth of the cave.

"Count Reveur."

"Leave, William. I have no time for your preening games. You are the earl. I am but a count, a lowly baron. I follow orders." Briefly, he glanced back at William. "Does that satisfy your thirst for my compliance?" A bush along the bank moved. After waving the men behind him back, Gerard moved out of sight.

"'Tis not why I am here." William kept his voice barely over a hushed hiss.

Not taking his intent stare from the river, Gerard gritted his teeth, then said, "If you came to take Catheryn back, you will first have to find her." This time when he turned back to the earl, he leveled a steady glare at the man. "And then kill me."

Gerard meant that. He'd not permit William, or anyone else, to take his wife from him again. It should not have occurred the first time.

He waited for a thundering reply.

What he saw stunned him momentarily. William's shoulders fell. The man, only a year older than Gerard, seemed to age before his eyes. "I came to help you find your lady. And to, in some way, make up for the wrong I have done."

If William's appearance had startled him, the man's words left him speechless.

"Cecily was angry with you for disturbing her party and

told me all." William glanced to the cloudless sky for a heartbeat. "I will deal with her later. This is my fault and I offer you my assistance."

A weight fell from Gerard's shoulders. "Thank you, William. I welcome your help."

The earl fumbled behind his saddle with something Gerard could not see. But the instant William pulled the box around; he knew what it held.

"Lady Catheryn left this behind. I thought she might want it."

Gerard opened the lid and lifted the kitten in his hand. Jewel's pitiful cries echoed those he fought to hold inside himself. After tossing his helm to Walter, he pushed back his coif and rubbed his cheek against the cat's fur as he'd seen Catheryn do so many times.

Soon, Jewel's cries turned to throaty rumbles. The cat put her paws on his cheeks and nuzzled his chin. He remembered laughing at Catheryn for teaching the silly animal to hug like that.

It didn't seem quite so humorous now.

He swallowed hard. Then Gerard motioned to one of his men. After putting the cat back into her box, he handed it to the man. "Keep this safe and see that it gets into Agnes's hands immediately."

They weren't that far from Brezden Keep. The man could ride there and back in very little time.

When the man rode away, William asked, "Have you located de Brye?"

"We have searched all the tunnels that I am aware of. I think they are holed up in a cave below."

"What do you plan?"

"I need to get inside that cave to see if she is there. If so, I intend to take her out. Other than that, I am not certain. Either way, I want whoever is inside captured."

William looked from Gerard to Walter. "That sounds

logical. You can do nothing until darkness falls. Sleep. Both of you."

"No. Not until I can share a bed with my wife."

"You will do Catheryn no good if you are so exhausted that you cannot hold your sword. Would you risk her life because you were too weak to defend her?"

Thought of her death sent a wave of blood rushing through his veins. Gerard smiled at the earl. With the speed of a diving falcon he unsheathed his sword and before William could reach for his own weapon, Gerard rested the sharp tip against William's neck. "Too weak to defend my wife?"

At that moment, three men entered the clearing, bringing William and Gerard's arguing to an abrupt end. Two of the men were Gerard's. The other was obviously a prisoner. And by the way he was held between the other two, he was not a well-liked individual.

When they stopped before Gerard, his guard cuffed the struggling prisoner. "Be still. We are not yet finished with you." Then he turned to Gerard. "Lady Catheryn is being held in one of the caverns below us. This lout here," he hitched one thumb at the man, "does not think his master has had enough time to do much harm to the lady."

Red. Pure blood red poured into Gerard's being. It sizzled in his ears and colored everything around him with a haze of reddened fog. It pulsed through his veins; hot and seething with rage.

He dismounted and stood in front of the prisoner. The metallic taste of blood not yet shed coated his tongue. "Who are you?" His words were thick, heavy with the thought of de Brye harming Catheryn.

The prisoner shrank back, stuttering, "I—I am no—no one."

Edyth's dying cry echoed through the haze. He would never be free from the guilt until de Brye's lifeless body lay at his feet.

He stepped toward the man, clenching his fists at his side.

"Gerard!" The sound of Catheryn calling his name ripped through his mind. Tore at his heart.

He was the knight of her dreams. Whether flight of fancy, or visions of her future, it made little difference. And already he'd let her down.

He grasped the front of the man's tunic with a force that tore the cowering knave from his guards' hold. "What harm has already befallen my wife?"

The man turned a pleading gaze to William. The earl walked away with a laugh.

Gerard shook the man. "What harm has already befallen my wife?"

The man shook his head. His tongue stumbled over itself seeking to spill forth the words. "She is still alive. I heard her cries not long ago."

De Brye's death would be slow. Not until he begged for mercy would Gerard permit the devil to die. He took a deep breath before asking, "Then what harm has he caused?"

The man paled visibly in the waning light of day. He held his hands before him and pleaded, "Do not kill me."

Gerard smiled. "You are already dead. But if you wish the chance to save your miserable soul, you need to confess. Now."

His statement of fact terrified the man. The level of fright was noticeable to all when the sound of water hitting the forest floor caused Gerard to look down.

Drawing his amused gaze back up to the man's ashen stare, Gerard asked, "Are all of de Brye's minions as cowardly as you? Is that how he keeps you in his service?"

He waited for a moment for the man to answer. When no words were forthcoming he released the prisoner. "He is useless. Kill him."

As he'd expected, the man's tongue suddenly loosened. "She is battered a little and has been drugged. There is a gash on her forehead. But he has not tortured her as of yet. They leave for France this night."

That admission brought Gerard and William to attention. "France?"

The man shook his head. "Aye. They go there to start their lives as husband and—"

"Over my dead body." Gerard's gritted reply cut off the rest of the prisoner's words. Wife? De Brye thought to make Catheryn *his* wife? Did he think running to France would keep him safe?

De Brye would not be safe if he ran to the ends of the earth.

William stood before the man. "How do they leave?"

The prisoner sank to his knees. "By boat. A supply barge will conceal them until they reach the coast."

"When do they leave?"

"Tonight. After all is dark. The vessel was already sighted downstream."

De Brye had chosen the night for his escape well. There would be no moon to reveal his movements. None would be the wiser.

Or so he thought.

Gerard asked, "Does he suspect he is being watched?"

"No. He believes you are looking for him in York."

Gerard turned a questioning gaze to the earl. William smiled. "My men are combing the woods around the hunting lodge and Scarborough. They are led by a man of your coloring and size. He wears the green and gold tabard you so thoughtfully left at the castle."

Gerard frowned. "I left no clothing at Scarborough."

"No? Then one of Brezden's men visited your wife in her chamber."

Gerard felt the flush heat his face. But he tamped it down

with a curse. It wasn't as if he'd sneaked into a strange woman's chamber. He'd sought a night with his wife.

William dogged the subject. A tactic at which he excelled. "I wonder who it could have been? How do you think the man gained entrance to your lady's chamber?"

Walter coughed and turned away.

"I know it could not have been you, Gerard." William scratched his head in false confusion. "There is this distinct memory I have of ordering you to stay away."

"Cease, William. This is not the time."

The earl cuffed Gerard on the shoulder. "It is the perfect time. You, my friend, are too distracted by worry to think rationally. I seek only to hound you into better clarity."

Gerard ignored William's comment. His mind had already rushed ahead. "What do we have? We know Catheryn is in the cave. We know they leave tonight." He paced the clearing, ticking off the items on his fingers. "We know she has been battered, but not beaten or tortured." He glared at the man still kneeling in his own urine. "But you said she'd been drugged. Is she capable of moving?"

The prisoner lifted his head. "The potions have worn off some, but she is in chains."

Gerard would have snapped the prisoner's neck had William not stepped in between them. "He might yet prove useful. Let him live a while longer."

Before Gerard could answer the earl's ludicrous idea, the prisoner spoke up. "I could help. If you would spare my life and assist me in escaping the devil I serve, I could help."

"How? What could you do?" Gerard towered over the man. "Had you been willing to help a woman in danger you would have done so already." But he knew that this sniveling coward was not a man who would put himself in danger to assist anyone else.

The prisoner lifted his head to gaze directly at Gerard. "I can enter the cave without anyone giving me a second glance. I can obtain the key that will unlock the fetters about her ankles."

William snorted. "And what? Lead her out of the cave? Walk her by de Brye without notice?"

"No." The man shook his head and admitted, "That I cannot do. It would only serve to bring my death and hers."

What he said held a note of truth. He could enter the cave without causing a stir among the others. He might be able to lay his hands on the key. And he might possibly have an opportunity to unlock her chains before de Brye sought to move her to the barge.

Gerard contemplated the idea further before turning his frown to the man. "Why would you do that for the lady? Why should I believe for one heartbeat that you will not rush off to de Brye? What would stop you from telling all to that vermin?"

He watched in amazement as the man's chin began to tremble. Tears gathered in the prisoner's eyes. "I have not seen my wife or youngest daughter in two years. I serve de Brye only to keep them safe."

"Safe from what?"

The man's tears slipped down his cheeks. "Safe from sharing the fate of my oldest daughter." He sucked in a deep breath before continuing. "She was only eleven when de Brye forced himself upon her. I came too late to save her from death or from his touch. But I was able to save my wife and other child by offering myself as slave to the devil's servant."

William remained silent. Walter's strangled gasp was loud enough for all to hear. Gerard bit the inside of his lip to keep from asking anymore questions about the man's family.

Finally, he asked, "You say you are a slave. How many slaves have free run? You appear to come and go as you please. You are not in chains. You do not appear beaten."

After lifting his arms, the man slipped his coarse tunic over his head. Scars, old and new, crisscrossed the man's chest. When Gerard walked around the prisoner he saw the same lacerations on the man's back.

His stomach tightened at the sickening sight. And by the thoughts of what de Brye might to do Catheryn should she be bold enough to open her mouth against him.

Gerard ordered the man to put his tunic back on. Then he asked, "This is how de Brye controls his men? By putting their wives and children under threat of mutilation and death? And by using a whip?"

"It was not a whip."

This time William gasped. "A blade? The man is that good with a blade?"

The prisoner nodded. "Aye. He has a thin-bladed dagger that he handles with ease."

"And none of you fight him off? None of you stand up to this demon?" William sounded appalled and confused at the same time.

"I am but one man. I cannot fight against the chains that hold me, nor the men that assist de Brye willingly." The prisoner glanced at the ground. His brows furrowed in thought before he looked from Gerard to William and asked, "Are you married, my lord? Do you have a mother, or a sister?"

Gerard ignored the man's insolence and waited to hear what else the prisoner would say.

"How far would you go to protect the women in your family?"

Gerard had heard enough. How far would he go to protect Catheryn? He'd seen the horrors de Byre inflicted on women and children. He knew what that demon was capable of doing to Catheryn. How far would he go? To the bowels of hell if need be.

"Get up."

Slowly, the man rose. He bowed his head, appearing to await death.

But this day, he was lucky.

"If you can unlock my lady's chains, I can promise you freedom."

The prisoner lifted his head. A look of hope, powerful, grateful, fell across his face. It strengthened Gerard's hope that this man could be trusted.

"But if you prove a liar, I will make de Brye's brand of torture appear mild." He truly didn't know how, but this man need not know that.

"I will come for my wife after the sun has set. See to it that she is free from her chains."

"Aye, milord." The man fell to his knees and wrapped his arms about Gerard's ankles before disappearing into the forest.

Both William and Walter looked at him as if he'd lost all ability to reason. William asked, "Are you certain that was wise, Gerard? To put your wife's safety into the hands of that man?"

"I am certain of only two things at this moment." He closed his eyes and fought off the nightmares that would not leave him. "De Brye will die this night and Catheryn will be home."

Thunder rumbled loudly in the distance. The sound reverberated through him, lending strength.

Lightning cracked across the sky.

Gerard looked out at the approaching storm. It had also roared around him the night he'd captured Brezden.

Chapter Twenty

The ground beneath her shook with the force of thunder echoing through the cavern. The walls trembled.

Catheryn held her hands to her ears, seeking to shut out the deafening sound.

The rage of the storm matched the one in her heart. De Brye thought to kill her? He thought to make her beg for her own death?

She would risk her soul by taking a life before she'd permit him to accomplish his deeds.

Catheryn had argued with her heart and head about this and had come to an uneasy agreement. Never would she allow de Brye to violate her. If she could not kill him, she would die trying.

She tightened her grasp on the rock she held in her hand. It would be a poor weapon, but it was the only one she could find. While using it to end the devil's existence bothered her, the thought of her own death at his hands bothered her more.

No more tears would fall from her eyes. No screams would be torn from her lips. Bravery was not a trait she came by easily. Over the last few years Pike and de Brye had sought to beat the strength of spirit from her. She was sick unto death of being afraid.

No more.

The sound of approaching footsteps rang out between the clashes of thunder.

She gripped the rock until its jagged edges tore into her palm.

More than one person approached. How would she protect herself? Her heart raced for a painful moment, before she willed it to slow.

The light from the torch blinded her. She held the rock behind her back, waiting for him to come closer. Catheryn knew she'd have to hit de Brye hard enough the first time. There'd not be a second chance.

When the footsteps stopped it was not de Brye's voice that floated down to her ears.

"Lady Catheryn. Please, make no sound."

Her eyes adjusted to the light. The sight of Rolfe was like a feast to her vision. She'd thought him dead. After the way de Brye had cut him the night he'd been in her chamber, she'd been certain her man would have bled to death.

He knelt and twisted a key in the chains about her ankle.

She grasped the front of his tunic. "How do you come to be here? Have I gone mad? Are you a ghost?"

Rolfe shook his head. "Nay. I was left for dead." He nodded toward the other man. "This man saw to it that I lived."

"Then why did you not return to Brezden?"

"We are at Brezden, milady."

Catheryn shook her head. "That cannot be."

"Milady, it is true. The river is just beyond this cave. Brezden is but a short distance from here."

Then de Brye had never left Brezden. He had only gone underground like the snake he truly was.

"I did not return to the keep because I have only been on my feet two days. I have not yet the strength to fight my way out of this cave."

The second man leaned down. "Do not leave just yet, Lady Catheryn. De Brye is close at hand."

At her soft cry, Rolfe covered her mouth with his hand and shook his head. "Take heart, milady. Soon this will be over." His voice broke, proving his weakened condition. He removed his hand from her lips. "Soon we will all be back at Brezden."

"I know this will be hard. But you must wait here until I

signal to you."

"A signal?" Catheryn shook her head. "A signal for what? I don't understand."

Rolfe's companion knelt close to her. "Your husband is nearby."

"No. De Brye will—"

The man cut her off and explained, "He and his men were spotted, but since de Brye holds my family as hostage, he thinks he can trust me. I was sent to scout the area."

Catheryn's heart jumped. Could she trust this man? He could have her, her men and Gerard killed with little more than a hint or two.

"Aye, milady, your thoughts are plain on your face. You have little reason to trust me, but I told de Brye it was nothing more than a hunting party."

"And he believed you?" She found it hard to give credence to his words. "Why?"

He shrugged. "I have more to lose than any other who serves de Brye. Do you think many serve him willingly? He holds my wife and daughter as surety for my obedience."

"Yet you risk their lives for mine?"

"Are you not the Lady of Brezden? Is it not my duty to give my life for that of my overlord or lady?"

"I do not know you. You do not serve Brezden."

A hopeful smile crossed his face. "At the moment I serve the Lord of Brezden, and if all goes well, maybe then I will be permitted to serve you also." His smile faded. "De Brye has already murdered my oldest daughter. I will do whatever is necessary to save the others."

"Milady? You will wait for the signal?"

If Gerard were nearby, why could she not simply rush from the cavern? Even if de Brye took chase, her husband would protect her.

"Why must I wait?"

Rolfe answered. "Lord Gerard is a capable leader. By

now, surely he knows that he is outnumbered. He will not attack until nightfall. If you try to leave now, he is not close enough to save you from certain death."

The other man agreed. "Please, 'tis hard to wait, I know. You must. You will not mistake my signal."

Catheryn grasped Rolfe's arm. "What about the other men?"

He shook his head. "I do not know. We must ensure your safety first."

Without waiting for any further questions, or providing her with any more information, the men left.

Again, she was alone in the dark, with only the roaring thunder for company. This time, however, it mattered little.

How long would she have to wait? Moments would seem like days. She held the rock to her chest. Hopefully she would be free long before it became necessary to test her will to survive.

Or die.

~*~

Rain dripped down his nasal plate. Gerard felt as if he were reliving the attack on Brezden.

Except this time the lightning did not accent a towering keep. It only lit up nearby sections of the forest, of the river and of the path along the river.

He waited. They all waited. A barge had been spotted making its way down the river toward the cave. When it arrived, they would attack.

While de Brye and his men were busy handling the barge, Gerard and his men would take the traitors by surprise.

The waiting was torturous. His mind played games with his heart.

"Cease, Gerard." William's command broke into his thoughts.

He gave the earl a blank look. "Cease what?"

"You are dwelling again. It will do you no good to ponder things you cannot find answers for."

"How did you—?"

William's low laugh rankled. "You may be able to hide your moods from others, but not from me. From the time we studied together in Henry's court I have been able to read every movement of your face. While you learned to read and write, I learned to read expressions. And yours are plain."

This was not news to Gerard. He'd known William's biggest accomplishment was the ability to get inside of men's thoughts. This was why he was the strongest earl in Yorkshire.

Instead of seeking to hide his thoughts, he asked, "Do you think she still lives?" A shivered ran down his spine. His stomach clenched with the thought of her death. No. He would not find her dead.

William sighed and shook his head. "You waste my time with questions I cannot answer. Maybe we should attack now, just to give you something worthwhile to think about."

A sound other than the storm broke the night. The sound of a vessel approaching caused both men to smile.

"Now."

Gerard's heart raced. His mind cleared and focused on one thought. To rescue his wife. After lifting his sword high in the air, he silently urged the men behind him forward.

~*~

"Come, sweeting. 'Tis time to join your parents."

De Brye's voice trailed down the corridor that opened into her cavern. Her pulse pounded loud and fast. The time was nigh.

She grasped the rock and waited.

By keeping her direct gaze away from the torch he carried, she was able to accustom her eyes to the light. Never again would she welcome darkness.

De Brye leaned over her and stroked her cheek. "The moment I have been promised has arrived."

"No one promised you anything." She needed to keep him off guard, until she could choose the perfect moment, the perfect spot to strike.

He ran his hand down the front of her gown. "Oh, but you are wrong. Your mother gave you to me with her dying breath."

Catheryn bit back her outrage. "And who caused her to die?"

With a laugh, he turned toward her feet, to unlock the chain. "It was the only way she said I could have you. I simply obliged the lady."

She lifted the rock and slammed it against the side of his head. Before he could fall across her, she rolled away and stood.

As de Brye fell, he dropped the torch onto the wet stone floor. Darkness engulfed the cavern.

Not waiting to see if he still breathed, Catheryn forced her scattered thoughts to gather. De Brye had fallen forward, toward the center of the cavern. She reached behind her, groping for the wall.

When her fingers brushed against the cool, damp stone, she turned away from de Brye's body and felt her way along the wall, to the entrance of this cavern.

Slowly but steadily she left the evilness behind her. She prayed she could find her way in the dark through the tunnel and to the mouth of the cave.

In her joy at learning of Gerard's arrival, she'd not thought to ask Rolfe or his companion the way.

Her breath quickened. Only then did she remember their order to wait for a signal.

She heard de Brye's shout of rage and picked up her pace. Catheryn trailed one hand along the wall at all times and kept moving.

It was too late for signals. There was no time left to wait.

A shrill whistle split the darkness.

Certain that whistle was her overdue signal, she rushed toward the sound. She hoped she was not following an echo that would lead to her capture.

De Brye rushed closer to her. She could hear his labored breathing. She could almost feel his hands wrapping around her neck, and smell his breath as he gasped for air.

One thought kept her moving. One name kept her from looking behind her to see where de Brye was. The thought of her husband's arms kept her looking and moving ahead.

"You will not escape me."

She ignored the threat yelled so close behind her.

"You will regret this act, sweeting. More than you can imagine."

She would regret her attempt only if he caught her.

"And your men will die too."

Her heart tripped, but her feet remained steady. She would not answer him. He spoke in an effort to frighten her and she'd not let his words have that effect on her again.

Her lungs threatened to burst with the effort she was making in staying out of his reach. It would have been impossible for her to respond to him—she had no breath to spare for words.

"And your husband. I will permit him to watch me violate and mutilate you before I cut his throat."

The image his threats created caused her to stumble. She regained her footing and forced the images from her mind.

"I am adept with a knife. I can keep you alive for days before you bleed to death."

Catheryn covered her mouth with her free hand, fighting to remember her vow to herself. She would not cry. She would not cower before him.

"You will beg for death, the same way Reveur's first wife did."

Catheryn had known, from the little Gerard had told her and what she'd overheard, that his first wife Edyth had perished at de Brye's hands. Until this moment she'd not realized the terrors the woman must have faced before meeting her end.

"She begged for the life of her son too. But it was too late."

His ragged voice was closer.

The nearness gave her a renewed burst of courage. The courage lent speed and strength to her steps.

Still following the wall of the tunnel around a corner, she headed toward the shouts of other men and toward a beacon of light. Even if they were de Brye's men she was certain their wild shouts were because their enemy had engaged them in battle.

But she heard no sound of clashing swords.

"Stop her!" De Brye screamed the order to his men.

The blood rushing through her veins froze. In the glare of lightning she saw the mouth of the cave. Hope unthawed the ice.

Some of the men followed de Brye's order while the others rushed out of the cave.

She dodged, avoiding one man. But another hand grazed her arm and she jerked away from him. They would not catch her. De Brye's curses rang in her ears.

When she reached the mouth of the cave, she ran between two of de Brye's men, then raced down the path and along the bank. Beyond the first bend in the river, the sight that met Catheryn's gaze stopped her flight. She watched in horror as the sachet's dream became a reality.

Battle-clad warriors astride Satan's own destriers raced through the storm toward her.

Mail, as black as the starless sky, covered each battle hardened warrior from helmed head to leather-booted feet.

The mighty war horses with their deadly riders charged ever closer. Ironclad hooves pounded in perfect unison with the heavy thudding of her heart.

Swords, pikes and axes raised, the men rushed nearer.

Catheryn fought to calm her racing heart, forced her trembling limbs to still.

The dream. It had not foretold her *death*. It had been a harbinger of hope and rescue.

He was here.

Her dream knight was here and all she had to do was hold her ground and trust him not to see her trampled beneath the chargers' hooves.

Or murdered by the madman at her back.

There was no where for her to run. De Brye and his men were behind her. Thick brush was on her right. The raging river on the left.

Her only chance for safety, for hope, for life, lay in the brutal force bearing down on her. And in the man leading the charge.

With a hushed voice, she prayed, "Lord, give me strength."

The leader of this pack of death-hungry wolves slowed. He leaned over the side of his saddle and pierced her with his glimmering gaze.

"Hold!"

The command rang in her ears and in her mind. Catheryn's gaze dropped to the beasts charging toward her. Her knees weakened. De Brye would not have the chance to kill her. The strength and weight of the warhorses would destroy her. Her legs threatened to fold beneath her.

She lifted her head for one last look at her husband. What she saw made her stare in amazement. A smile, almost as bright as the streak of lightning above him, lit his face.

He wrapped the reins of his black beast around one wrist and held out his arms toward her.

Another thunderbolt lit the sky. Raindrops rolled down the mailed arm reaching for her.

Catheryn held his gaze with unwavering hope, lifted her arms and gasped as his strong grasp jerked her from the ground.

The remaining warriors rushed by. Their shouts of victory drowned out the roars of the thunder. The air tight in her lungs, she struggled to wrap her arms around his neck as she clung to him.

She was safe. Her heart threatened to burst with love for the man who had ridden out of her dream to take her away from her nightmare.

Gerard yanked on the reins with one hand, bringing his horse to an unsteady halt. He had not expected to literally snatch Catheryn from de Brye's grasp. Not in this manner.

After tightening his grasp around her, he shouted over the din of battle: "Hang on!"

The destrier was fitted for battle. The high saddle was meant to hold him firmly on his horse while he fought. There was nowhere for another rider to mount. Not in front, nor behind.

And he was not putting her down until they were safely away from here.

He pulled his one foot from the stirrup, then hoisted Catheryn high enough for her to use the piece of leather and metal for support.

Gerard turned his horse around on the path and headed away from the battle, toward the clearing where another mount awaited.

William's voice stopped him. "Gerard. De Brye and his men—"

"Can be brought to Brezden."

Without turning around, he waited for William's angry

reply. But it was not forthcoming.

Instead, the earl said, "So be it," before issuing one of his bloodthirsty battle cries and returning to the fight.

Catheryn buried her face in Gerard's neck for a moment, before lifting her head to look at him. "You seek revenge for what de Brye did to your wife and child. You need not let him escape you again."

He found it odd that suddenly revenge did not seem as important as her safety did. "He will not escape. His time will come and you will be somewhere safe."

"But—"

"No. Catheryn, do not argue this with me."

When she fell silent, he asked, "Are you unhurt?"

Her bitter laugh sent a chill down his spine. "I am alive. I am whole. Is that not enough?"

He pulled her closer, resting his lips against her forehead. "Aye. More than enough."

They arrived at the clearing. He lowered Catheryn to the ground and joined her. A flash of lightning flickered off her face. There'd been times he'd thought never to see her again.

Gerard tore his helmet from his head, tossed it to the waiting squire and pulled her into his arms. "Catheryn." His throat closed off anything but her name.

She returned his embrace and asked, "What took you so long?"

Gerard laughed over her feeble attempt at humor. "I was attending a bath party and the days slipped away."

She trembled against him. Was it from laughter? Or from tears?

"Catheryn, you are safe. Fear not, all will be well." Who was he seeking to comfort? Her or himself?

Her choked laugh told him that both emotions ruled her. "If you ever say that again, I will tear out your tongue."

The fierceness of her words surprised him. Then he

realized that every time he had promised all would be well—it was not.

He slanted his mouth over hers. Never had a kiss tasted sweeter. Never had a woman's touch reduced him to tears.

But he knew from the tightening of his throat and the painful twisting in his gut, that it was about to happen now.

After breaking the kiss abruptly, he turned away. What was wrong with him?

He motioned the squire forward and took the reins of Catheryn's mount from the lad's hands. "Come. Let us return home."

"Gerard?"

He wanted to ignore the question in her tone. Instead he turned to look at her. Hurt filled her gaze.

Hurt that he had put there. Guilt made him ashamed. He wished not to linger here. He would rather explore these feelings and emotions in the safety of their keep.

Gerard reached out and pulled her forward. He held her close. Finally, after moments of seeking words, he whispered, "Catheryn, I seek not to hurt you. I only wish to leave this place. To return to Brezden and hold you without the barrier of mail and clothing between us."

He felt her sigh as she patted his shoulder. "You lie, Gerard. It is more than that. Something is wrong, I can feel it. But I too wish to return home."

Chapter Twenty-One

Gerard paced the hall. William and Walter approached Brezden with de Brye and the blackguard's men.

Soon, they would enter the keep. Soon, he would be able to put the past behind him. He would finally fulfill his last promise to Edyth.

In doing so, he would be free to turn his full attention to the years ahead and to the woman resting in his chamber. Catheryn, the woman who was his future.

When nothing but tomorrow loomed before them, he would be able to tell her what his heart had known since the moment he'd first seen her.

"Gerard?" Catheryn touched his arm. "They have arrived?"

He spun and clasped her arms. "Return to bed. I do not want you down here."

"It is my right to be here." Anger reddened her face. "This is my keep. My people were harmed by de Brye's hand."

"Your keep? Your people?" He pulled her toward the stairs, keeping his voice rough. "Tell me, Lady Reveur, have you no husband to carry any of these responsibilities?" He hoped his anger overshadowed his irrational fear for her safety. "You have no rights other than those I give you."

"This is my battle too. You are not the only one de Brye has harmed. I seek my own revenge."

His anger flared. "I will not stand here and argue with you. If you do not return to our chamber on your own, I will—"

She tore out of his hold and finished his threat. "Place me under guard? Lock me in a cell? Where have I heard those words before?"

The commotion in the bailey announced the party's arrival. Gerard pointed up the stairs, yelling, "Now!"

Her complexion paled considerably, but she argued no further. He breathed a sigh of relief when Catheryn turned around and headed up the steps.

Had she remained in the hall, his thoughts would have revolved around her and her safety—instead of around de Brye and his death.

Within a few heartbeats the huge doors to the hall burst open and men poured through them. Some entered of their own accord, while others entered only at the point of a blade.

All came to a stop before him.

From the corner of his eye, he saw Catheryn's maid Agnes slink down the steps and try to hide herself in the shadows. There existed no doubt that his wife had sent the woman to spy for her.

A minor problem easily taken care of. "Agnes." He called the maid forward. The guilt on her face was almost laughable. He ignored it. "Are any of these men from Brezden?"

The woman scanned the crowd. "Aye, milord."

He had assumed that if anyone would recognize the missing men, it would be Agnes. "Good. Take them away from here. See that their needs are cared for and do not let any of them out of your sight until I call for you."

The look that crossed her face told him that she suspected his true purpose—her removal from the hall. It did not concern him.

Left with only his own men and ten of de Brye's, Gerard noticed that the one Walter held at sword point was the one who had helped his wife escape. He would see to it that the man was repaid tenfold. He would be released without anyone else's knowledge. That should be enough to keep his help a secret and what remained of his family safe from retaliation.

Gerard's searching gaze swept over the prisoners. Only one looked directly at him. The returning stare glittered with hate and rage.

When he stepped in front of the man, Gerard understood why Edyth thought she had seen Satan. The pale ice-blue stare shimmered with an eerie fanatical glow. If that satanic look was not enough to freeze the blood in one's veins, the smile would.

Behind the parted lips, broken and jagged teeth appeared pointed. The fangs of a snarling wolf were not as frightening as the discolored teeth this man possessed.

Gerard turned around and approached William. "Milord, all of these prisoners stand guilty of treason to King Stephen and to you. Willingly do I release all but one to your justice."

William lounged idly in a chair, as if he had not a care in the world. He yawned before answering. "They are not fit to dirty my cells. Hang them in the morning."

"But, milord, you cannot!"

Gerard spun around to see who had shouted the denial. As he feared, it was the man who'd helped Catheryn. Gerard strode to the man and punched the fool's chin before he said anything else.

He leaned down to help his captain pick the now unconscious man up off the floor, Gerard whispered, "Hide this imbecile." Aloud, he said, "This man can hang now." He nodded at his captain. "Sir Walter, take him to the bailey and see it done."

After Walter dragged the man from the hall, Gerard returned to the dais. William asked, "What about the final prisoner? The one you refuse to release?"

"You will make no decisions concerning me."

Gerard faced de Brye. "And why is that, de Brye? Are you above justice? Are you not to be condemned for your crimes?"

The sinister smile broadened. "Of what crimes do you speak?"

Gerard felt his blood heat. It rolled and boiled in his veins. Edyth's dying words echoed in his ears. The look of fright on Catheryn's face as she ran from the cave swept through his mind. He forced the memories from him. Battles were lost because men were ruled by emotion. He'd not allow the pain or the rage to cloud his judgment.

"What crimes do I speak of?" Gerard nodded toward William. "We can start with the crime of treason. To your overlord and to your King."

De Brye laughed. "I owe no fealty to William of Aumale. And Stephen of Blois is a pretender to the crown that rightfully belongs to the Empress Matilda."

Gerard moved on. "Then we can add the crime of murder. You did push the Lady of Brezden down the stairs in this very keep."

De Brye shrugged. "She said it was the only way I could have her daughter. I simply fulfilled the lady's wish."

"And the Lord of Brezden?"

As if none of the charges leveled against him mattered, de Brye admitted, "Ah, well, it was a necessary ploy, a planned accident, to ensure Pike's cooperation." He looked past Gerard to William. "I am sorry you never received the lady's missives, but your help was really not needed."

William sat up. "She did send letters?"

"I told you she did." Catheryn answered from the stairs. Her voice rose with each word. "But you would not believe me."

Gerard bit off his groan before turning to her. "Be gone from here."

She shook her head. "No. I will not leave." She looked at de Brye. "How did you intercept the missives? You were not yet at Brezden."

His laugh almost shook Gerard's resolve not to let emotion rule.

"Yes, I was. I came the same day as Pike. For months on end, I worked in your father's stables."

Catheryn gasped, but fell silent.

De Brye addressed Gerard. "Are there any other crimes you wish to place upon me? Charges concerning rape? More murders?" His sinister smile turned slyer. "She was a tasty morsel, Gerard. I was truly saddened that it had to end so. But the babe," He lifted one shoulder briefly. "The babe was no challenge."

"Gerard!" William tried to intercede, but Gerard waved the earl back to his chair.

Obviously, de Brye sought to goad him into losing control. Gerard took a deep breath, seeking to clear the red haze drifting before his eyes. He would not fly at de Brye in a rage. When he snapped the man's neck, Gerard wanted to be fully aware of the act.

De Brye did not give up. "Your current wife is a rather choice piece of flesh too. How did it feel when you discovered you hadn't been her first?"

"That isn't true!" Catheryn shouted at de Brye. She then looked at Gerard. "Why are you doing nothing? Why do you stand there and let this devil lie?"

This was the reason he did not want her present in the first place. It was enough that he fought to control his own temper. How was he to deal with hers too?

She had a right to be angry. Every right to demand de Brye's blood. He would see that her honor and the deeds committed against her and her family were avenged. But not at her instigation.

He kept his voice as level as possible, and ordered, "Catheryn, close your mouth."

"Is it satisfying to know you married a common whore?" de Brye asked. "I myself prefer a fine lady. A lady such as your first wife. Although I suppose a slut does have her purposes."

Gerard heard Catheryn hiss. He knew she was building a fine fire with that breath.

William must have known it too, because the earl leapt from his chair and locked a hand around Catheryn's wrist.

Gerard cringed when Catheryn gasped as she was dragged to the dais. The earl took a seat and held her at his side.

De Brye repeated what he had first said. "You will make no decisions concerning me. If I hang, so does your wife."

"And why is that?" Gerard demanded.

"You cannot hang one traitor without hanging the other one, too."

"My wife is not a traitor. The flimsy evidence you planted in the tunnel is damning only to you. The man and the barge you sent to Scarborough for William to find could not have been arranged by my wife."

"No? You are certain of that?"

"Aye. She never left my sight." Gerard took a step closer to de Brye and repeated. "Never."

De Brye looked toward William. "I demand fairness in this mockery of a trial."

"How can you talk of fairness?" Gerard was amazed. The man was either very bold, or entirely insane.

"I have ever been fair. I only kill when the need arises. You, on the other hand, kill when the urge strikes you."

Gerard frowned.

At his silence, de Brye said, "While your memory lapse is convenient, I remember the day clearly." De Brye's lips curled as he spoke. "You, Count Reveur, were so filled with the urge to kill that you removed my brother's head from his body."

"So that is why you butchered my wife and son? Because in the heat of a battle I killed your brother?" It made no sense. Men died in battle everyday. One did not avenge their deaths on innocent members of their killer's family.

The hairs on the back of Gerard's neck rose when de Brye laughed. "I have only begun to make you pay." He pointed at Catheryn. "She so easily helped to fulfill my dreams by wedding you. Now, none can refute the evidence pointing to her betrayal. I am gladdened to know she will finally be mine—in hell."

Catheryn tried to take a step toward the men, but the earl yanked her back. William leaned forward in his chair. "What evidence do you speak of?" He looked around the hall. "I see nothing that implicates Lady Catheryn in your treachery."

De Brye pinned Gerard with a narrowed gaze of accusation. "You saw the letters found on that barge. Even if she did not arrange the incident, you cannot deny her missive to the Empress."

Gerard shook his head. "I do not know of what you speak. I saw only an act of forgery."

As if looking at someone resting on the ceiling, de Brye shouted. "What now?" He tipped his head like a man listening intently to someone else, before nodding and muttering, "Yes, yes, I know."

Gerard turned to look at the earl. Was their prisoner truly insane? William shrugged and shook his head.

"He has a sword!"

Gerard spun around at Catheryn's shouted warning. But it was too late.

De Brye had already disarmed the man guarding him and did indeed have a sword in his hand. He held the blade steady, with the point directed at Gerard's chest.

De Brye stepped away from the stunned guard and turned his attention to William. "I will not die a common criminal at the end of a rope." He waved the sword tip in the air. "I demand a trial by sword."

"You *demand*?" William's voice sounded incredulous.

With one experienced move of his arm, de Brye sliced open Gerard's tunic without so much as grazing the flesh beneath. "Aye. Demand. If I die, all will be well with Brezden. If I live, the Lady Catheryn hangs with me."

The challenge brought a smile to Gerard's lips. De Brye wished to fight him? The man thought to threaten Catheryn with death? Nay. Never again. De Brye would never threaten, harm or kill another woman or child again. This is what Gerard had long been waiting for. Whether the man was insane or not, he needed to be sent to his maker.

While unsheathing his own sword, Gerard answered. "I accept the challenge."

Catheryn nearly swooned with fear. Fear for her husband and, selfishly, for her own life.

The thought of spending an eternity in hell with de Brye was not a comforting one. It clawed at her soul with icy talons of horror.

William rose and pulled her to the far end of the hall. She realized that Gerard did not need to be distracted by thoughts or even the mere sight of her. Yet, she wished not to be so far away.

The men circled each other; wild animals sizing up the enemy. The guards pulled the prisoners out of the hall. While there would be no help for de Brye, there would be none for Gerard either.

De Brye struck the first blow. His blade rang loud against Gerard's.

Catheryn cringed with each strike of metal against metal. Every blow felt like a stab to her heart. De Brye claimed to be an expert with a blade. What if he was? Would Gerard be capable of besting the devil?

Back and forth across the floor, they fought. Attack and retreat, swinging and jabbing with blades not meant for this type of fighting. Long blades used by a man on horseback.

Heavy swords designed for a quick, clean thrust of death.

Gerard's muscles rippled. Sweat drenched his hair and ran down his face.

"Come, Reveur, kill me if you are able." De Brye's words were laced with gasps for breath.

Catheryn could not stand still. She wrapped one arm across her stomach and shifted from one foot to the other.

She sucked in a quick breath when Gerard backed into a stool. Unable to tear her gaze from the scene that might be her husband's final moment, she watched in mute terror as he lifted his blade before him to ward off the downward arc of de Brye's sword.

To her amazement, Gerard laughed as he regained his footing.

De Brye screamed in rage. He grasped his weapon with both hands, lifted it above his head and rushed Gerard.

After twisting out of the way, Gerard lowered his sword and held it out toward the man racing at him. The end of the blade sliced into de Brye's side.

Blood ran from the open wound. He brought his own blade slicing down Gerard's arm. The linen of her husband's sleeve was no protection against the cutting edge of the sword. Again, blood ran from an open wound—Gerard's.

Fear built in Catheryn's throat. She groaned with the effort to contain her scream.

William jerked on her arm. "Do not watch. Do not make a sound."

The softly spoken words were heavy with threat.

She bit her bottom lip. Nothing from heaven or hell could have forced her to close her eyes.

The fighting slowed as the men tired. Now, life and death would be a matter of who made a mistake and who did not.

Silently, she prayed for her husband's skill to be the better of the two. She begged for God to spare the life of the man she loved.

Catheryn doubted if William would do as de Brye suggested and hang her with the devil. Still, she did not wish to live alone, without Gerard.

Again the men circled the hall. The clashing of swords reverberated off the walls. Winded gasps for air filled the momentary silences.

Gerard's back was to her. She looked at de Brye. His eyes were glazed. They shimmered with an unspeakable evil. An evil no mortal could kill.

An icy claw tore at her chest. Breathing became impossible. She could not force her lungs to fill with air. Gerard would be angry at what she was about to do. While she could live with his anger, she refused to live without him. If the devil were to kill her husband now, Gerard would not die alone.

Catheryn ripped her arm from William's grasp. She ignored his curse and avoided his attempt to recapture her.

She bolted across the hall, then threw herself between the men.

As if she watched from a spot on the ceiling, she saw de Brye's sword arc down and at the same time Gerard's swung up.

All time ceased to exist.

Sharp, hot pain shot tongues of fire down her body. The unbearable agony tore a scream from her throat.

Slowly, like a small pebble dropping to the bottom of the lake, she fell to the floor. De Brye followed. His evil smile still curved his lips as he landed on top of her. Grasping at her, he promised, "You will be with me, this day, in hell."

Gerard dropped his sword. It clattered to the floor. Bile choked him. The heated sweat on his flesh chilled with fear.

Blood drenched Catheryn's shoulder and chest.

De Brye's words echoed in Gerard's ears.

"No!" The shout rose from his chest. It tore hoarsely

from his lips. *No. Not again.* The thought ripped through his heart.

She would not join that devil in hell.

He shoved de Brye's body off his wife's motionless one. Without pausing to see if the devil were truly dead, Gerard cradled Catheryn in his arms and carried her toward the stairs.

An expression of horror filled William's face. That same expression echoed in Gerard's soul.

With a brief glance over his shoulder, he told the earl, "Find her maid." He paused on the first step. "And find Mistress Margaret."

Gerard did not wait to see if William did as he asked. He carried Catheryn to their chamber and laid her on the bed.

He removed the bloodied garments and threw them onto the floor. The reminder of what he'd caused sickened him.

Had he not been so intent on his own revenge, he'd not have accepted de Brye's challenge. Had he thought of his wife, instead of himself, he'd have turned all of the traitors over to William. Including de Brye.

He'd have washed his hands of the devil and taken care of his tomorrows, not his yesterdays.

After retrieving a pitcher of water and some drying cloths from alongside the bath, he carried them to the bed. His hands shook.

He sat next to her on the bed and wiped the blood from her face. He stopped and stared at his wife. She was pale. Too pale.

Guilt kicked him in the gut. Gerard closed his eyes against the force of the blow.

He refocused his gaze on her and bent to the task at hand. For the moment he could do nothing about what happened. He could only worry about this moment. This breath. And Catheryn.

Where was the wound? What caused so much blood? He

worked feverishly trying to locate the source.

"Milord."

Agnes entered the chamber with Mistress Margaret and her bag of remedies in tow.

Never had two old women been so welcome before.

He held up the rag. "I cannot find the injury."

Both women looked at each other before Agnes stuck her head outside the chamber door and shouted for William. At the same time Mistress Margaret waddled to the bed.

She took the cloth from Gerard. "Milord, I need you to move out of my way." She glanced about the room. "Why do you not tend the fire and bring me more light?"

Agnes added, "You could also bring us more water."

It did not take a great deal of thought to know they were seeking to remove him from Catheryn's side.

"I am not leaving."

Again, the women looked at each other first. Agnes turned an overly innocent gaze upon him. "We would never presume to tell you to leave. We need the water and light, milord."

William entered the chamber. His gaze flew from the bed to Gerard and back to the women. "What can I do?"

Agnes nodded toward Gerard. She said nothing.

William shook his head, then grabbed the sleeve of Gerard's tunic. "Come here."

"I am not leaving." Nothing, not even William, was going to make him leave Catheryn's side.

"I am not asking you to." William pointed to Gerard's other arm. "I want to see if this needs stitches."

"Oh." Gerard had forgotten he'd been sliced by de Brye's sword. He tried unsuccessfully to shrug off William's hold. "It is nothing."

The earl pulled him to a bench on the other side of the room. "Humor me."

Gerard dropped onto the bench. The room swam before

him. It was hard to breathe. A weight the size of Brezden itself rested on his chest.

He jumped slightly when William pulled the linen from the already hardening blood on his arm. He removed his tunic and said nothing as the earl wiped off the blood.

These were familiar actions. Many times they'd taken turns tending each other's battle wounds. Gerard doubted if William or anyone could heal the bleeding gash in his heart.

A chill rushed through him. He shuddered.

"You are ill." William's voice was gruff.

"I am fine."

After applying a salve given him by Mistress Margaret, William confirmed what Gerard already knew. "This requires no stitches."

Gerard started to rise. The floor rushed up to meet him. He dropped back down.

William's soft chuckle raced across his ears. The earl repeated. "You are ill."

"No," Gerard insisted, "I am fine."

The earl rested a hand on Gerard's shoulder. "No, my friend, you are sick at heart. 'Tis a disease that befalls many men."

Gerard remained silent.

"Have you told her of this fatal disease?" When Gerard still didn't answer, William sighed. "I will not tease you. Have you told your wife that you love her?"

Shaking his head, Gerard muttered, "No." Instead he'd told her that he knew nothing of love.

"You can tell her when she wakes up." Mistress Margaret called from the bed.

As if torn from a terrible dream, Gerard bolted from the bench. "Wakes up?"

Agnes laughed. "Her wound is nothing but a cut on the top of her shoulder."

He was confused. "The blood."

Both women shook their heads. "The blood was yours and de Brye's. Very little was Catheryn's."

He crossed the chamber, then leaned over the bed and placed his fingers on her chest, over her heart.

"She sleeps, milord. She only sleeps." Agnes's tears interrupted her words.

Gerard sought reassurance from Mistress Margaret. The lady nodded in agreement, adding, "She just needs sleep, milord. I would say she's had a few hard days. Nothing a good, restful sleep cannot cure."

He sank down onto the bed. "Thank you, God." Gerard's voice, barely above a whisper, was as broken as Agnes's had been.

Thankfully, William hustled the women from the chamber, closing the door behind them.

Chapter Twenty-Two

More stars than he could count dotted the dark sky.

Gerard leaned against the window opening for support. A heavy weariness had settled about his shoulders half way through the day. As the sun set the weariness had seeped into his blood, and into his soul.

He glanced at the woman on the bed. She slept the sleep of the dead. No tossing or turning and no sounds broke her unending slumber. She'd been that way since last night.

Gerard rubbed his temples. It did little to ease the dull ache. An ache that echoed in his heart.

After much harassing on his part, Mistress Margaret had finally told him that Catheryn might stay asleep for a long time.

He crossed the room, then sat on the edge of the bed. Jewel crawled onto his lap. The still-growing kitten was as lost as he. And just like him, the animal had not left the chamber for more than a few moments since he'd brought Catheryn up from the hall.

Gerard's laugh rang bitter in the chamber. She had thrown herself between him and de Brye because she cared for him, her husband. Because of that, he lived.

Because of her, he knew what love felt like, and what pain that love could cause. Love was one's heart lightening, nearly smiling when one's beloved walked into a room. Love was this longing, this need that nearly took his breath away whenever he thought about Catheryn.

The pain was living and not being able to do anything to help the one you loved.

Edyth's death had been avenged. She could rest in peace. His only sorrow was that he hadn't loved her. Not the way he loved this wife. For that he was truly sorry. Edyth had deserved better. She had deserved true love.

Gerard picked up the tattered yarrow sachet and smiled sadly. He had thought the bag a young girl's charm. He had thought dreams useless, childish, a waste of time.

How wrong he'd been.

The sachet could foretell true love. Had he not seen Catheryn's face when he had slept with the bag? Dreams were real. It had been so long since he'd longed for something enough that he dreamed about it.

He touched Catheryn's cheek. He dreamed about her being whole, awake and loving him. Day and night he dreamed. She'd once told him that dreams could come true—if one believed.

With every fiber of his being he believed.

Gerard stretched out next to her on the bed and whispered in her ear, "Catheryn, love, wake up."

~*~

Battle-clad warriors astride Satan's own destriers raced through the fog toward her.

Mail, as black as the starless sky, covered each battle hardened warrior from helmed head to leather-booted feet.

Paralyzed and unprotected, Lady Catheryn could only tremble at the coming onslaught of impending doom.

The mighty war horses with their deadly mounts charged ever closer. Iron-clad hooves pounded in perfect unison with the heavy thudding of her heart.

Swords, pikes and axes raised, the men rushed nearer.

The leader of the demonic army ensnared her gaze. Dark, glowing eyes held no sign of mercy. There would be no quarter given if that unforgiving force captured her.

The cloying smell of death permeated the air, broken only by the acrid scent of smoke and destruction. The vile stench seared her nostrils. She shuddered with revulsion.

Catheryn fought to calm her racing heart, forced her trembling limbs to still. She would not cower before her enemies, nor would she kneel in the cold mud and beg for mercy. With a hushed voice, she prayed, "Lord, give me strength."

The leader of the pack of death-hungry wolves stopped before her as the remaining warriors raced past. A thunderbolt lit the sky. Raindrops rolled down the mailed arm reaching for her. These tears from heaven shimmered over an emerald and gold ring on the hand that grasped her shoulder.

No. That wasn't right. He didn't grasp her shoulder. No. He had reached down to save her from the hell at her heels. The hand reaching out to her offered safety and love.

Gerard.

"Catheryn, love, wake up."

In her dream Gerard called to her. She remembered hearing his worried voice many times of late.

The lips touching her forehead were warm. His voice was soft, inviting as he again told her to wake up.

She felt safe where she was. Safe from de Brye. Safe from the dark.

Arms gathered her close. Hands gently cupped her head. "Ah, love, it is lonely without you. Come back to me. I promise you will never know pain or harm again."

Silken threads held her securely in a cocoon of warmth and light. She had no wish to leave.

As he kissed her, she felt a warm raindrop fall upon her cheek. It slid slowly down her skin and across her lips. The rain tasted of salt. Of tears.

She tipped her head.

Tears?

"Catheryn, I love you. I will wait."

He loved her?

Her heart swelled with a longing to see him. To touch

him. To know if his words were true. Catheryn sought her way out of the dream.

She opened her heavy eyelids and gazed in wonder at the man holding her. She'd not been mistaken. It was Gerard. And his reddened eyes shimmered in the flickering candlelight.

"Hello, love."

Catheryn traced his lips with a finger. "I am not dreaming?"

He shook his head. "No. You are not dreaming."

"I thought I heard—"

He stopped her words with a kiss. A slow, gentle kiss that tugged at her heart and warmed her soul.

Gerard lifted his head and met her gaze. "You heard only me. No one but me."

A memory of a fight tugged at her mind. Her breath caught in her throat. "Is—de Brye is he..." Her thought trailed off.

While stroking her cheek, Gerard answered the question she'd tried to ask. "He is dead. The traitors are gone. The entrance to the cave has been sealed."

Something wasn't right. Catheryn stiffened. "How long have I been asleep? What happened?"

"Just a day." He searched her face. "Do you not remember?"

She frowned, begging her mind to work. "You brought me back to Brezden. De Brye and his men were here. There was a sword fight."

"Anything else?"

Catheryn pulled at her bottom lip with her teeth. He didn't appear angry now. Had he been at the time?

At her hesitation, he said, "Catheryn, love, we have much to discuss. There will be many times we argue. But right now, we are in our chamber, our room of truce. No words of anger or accusation have any power here."

She'd forgotten what seemed to her, at the time, a foolish idea and offered a half smile as an apology, before admitting, "I rushed between the two of you."

He laughed softly. "The next time I seek to fight someone, I will lock you in a cell and carry the key with me." His look turned serious. "Never, ever think to do something that foolish again."

"He was going to kill you."

"Yes. And because of you, I live." He rolled off her and walked to a chest on the other side of the room.

He glanced over his shoulder. "Close your eyes."

She did so and waited. Within a heartbeat she heard the herbs and rushes crunch under the fall of his returning steps.

Gerard took her hand in his and placed a kiss on her palm. He closed her fingers over the kiss. Then whispered, "Always remember, that no matter what your eyes may show you, or what your ears may hear, that what I tell you and show you in this chamber tonight is the truth."

He brushed her cheek with the back of his hand. "There is no one else I would rather spend my life with. No other I want to share my dreams with."

The events of the last few days flittered in and out of her still ragged memory. "Why? Why would you wish to burden yourself with one as—?"

He cut off her broken words with a kiss. Gerard knelt by the bed. "I can think of no one as brave, or as honorable as you, Catheryn. Another person would have broken under de Brye's demands. It would have been an easy thing to give him all he asked. You did not. Who else would have thrown herself at a charging destrier, trusting me to snatch her from death?"

She shook her head. "I am not brave. I simply love my husband and could not bring shame to him. My dreams had always told me that you would let no harm befall me. I just did not listen."

"Your slow-witted husband cherishes your love and you. Never again will he laugh at your dreams. Dreams, if you believe hard enough, come true."

His voice shook with emotion. Unbidden, tears gathered behind her closed eyes.

He took her other hand and after softly kissing that palm, he placed something in her hand and closed her fingers over it.

"Open your eyes." He held her hand closed for another moment while he stared into her gaze with a promise that took her breath away. "This I give in token of my love for you."

Gerard released her hand and waited.

Catheryn opened her fingers and stared at the ring she held. An emerald sparkled from a golden band. The building tears slipped down her cheeks.

He held out his own hand, showing her the ring he held. It was identical.

Identical to the ring she still held and to the one her knight had worn in her dreams.

He took the ring from her palm and slipped it on her finger. "The circle of gold represents our marriage. Unending. Always united. The green of the emerald is to remind you that my love will always be as constant as the spring that arrives every year without fail."

She took the ring from his palm and slipped it on his finger. Her voice shook as she repeated his words back to him. "This I give in token of my love for you. The circle of gold represents our marriage. Unending. Always united. The green of the emerald is to remind you that my love will always be as constant as the spring that arrives every year without fail."

Gerard kissed the tears from her cheeks. "You are and always will be my one love."

Catheryn reached up and lightly touched his cheek. "You

are and always will be my true love, my dream knight."

THE END

About the author of DREAM KNIGHT

A firm believer in dreams and happy endings, Alexis Kaye Lynn lives with her husband and petting zoo in NW Ohio. Alexis read books before she rode a bike. She learned early on that if a book wasn't handy that making up stories in her head was easy and much more fun. At first the stories were based loosely on Disney's "Sword in the Stone", until she discovered Kathleen Woodiwiss and an entire section at the book store called *ROMANCE*.

Alexis is a member of Romance Writers of America, MVRWA, GDRWA, FTH and WRW. A newly reformed contest junkie, she has finalled and/or won in RWA's Golden Heart contest, GDRWA's Between the Sheets contest and MVRWA's He/Said She/Said contest.

When not hunched over a keyboard, or daydreaming, Alexis can be found in the dustiest section of the local library with her nose stuck in a research book.

She loves to hear from readers. Please, visit her website at:
http://www.alexiskayelynn.com
 OR her den at http://www.authorsden.com/alexiskayelynn
There you can sign up for her newsletter and leave comments about DREAM KNIGHT.
You can also e-mail her at: alexiskayelynn@aol.com
Or snail mail at: Alexis Kaye Lynn, PO Box 17, Monclova Ohio, 43542-0017

The Gunn of Killearnan
by
Dorice Nelson

To become chief of his clan, warrior Gerek Gunn, Scotland's renowned Beast of Battle, must marry a woman not of his choosing. That's how things were done, so he thought until he met the fiery beauty to be his wife…

Catriona MacFarr had no intention of marrying a man known as the "Beast." The man sounded so much like her father, she was horrified. Such a lifelong disaster could not be, no matter the consequences! Never…

ISBN #1-931696-01-2 (eBook)
ISBN #1-931696-98-5 (Print)
www.novelbooksinc.com/authors/doricenelson
www.novelbooksinc.com
www.doricenelson.com

UNLAWFUL
by
Dorice Nelson

Butchery branded their introduction…
Enslavement parted them…
Deception and deceit compelled a reunion…
Thus began the time for bravery or
betrayal… and checkmate!

Deadlocked by a cursed legend, Kellach must find her mother to remove a Druid's Curse and save her people from the rampaging Norse. Bruic the Badger, must find Irish ports for the Norsemen to save his sons and find his lost Irish siblings. Neither had time for love. Fate and circumstance took the advantage away from both…

ISBN #1-931696-16-0 (eBook)
ISBN #1-931696-83-7 (Print)
www.novelbooksinc.com/authors/doricenelson
www.novelbooksinc.com
www.doricenelson.com

NBI
Check out these
New Releases from
NovelBooks, Inc.

Finders Keepers by Linnea Sinclair — Science Fiction/Romance
When Captain Trilby Elliot rescues a downed pilot, all she wants is a reward. She doesn't want to fall in love. And she definitely doesn't want to die.

Lions of Judah by Elaine Hopper — Romance Suspense
Who can a dead woman trust?

The Gunn of Killearnan by Dorice Nelson — Scottish Historical
Treachery, lies and love...

The Chance You Take by Linda Bleser — Contemporary Romance
Sometimes taking a chance on love is the biggest gamble of all.

Wild Temptation by Ruth D. Kerce — Historical
When a mysterious stranger comes to town, Skylar Davenport must discover if he's really a hot-blooded rancher, or a cold blooded killer...her life depends on it.

Fate by Robert Arthur Smith — Paranormal/Suspense
Compelled by the spirit of a murdered woman, Toronto writer Judy Armstrong tries to save a boy's life.

Winter's Orphans by Elaine Corvidae — Fantasy
Will she save them...or enslave them?

Love and the Metro Man by Rosa Knapp — Romantic Comedy
Forget the white steed...This Prince Charming rides the subway! Two hearts on track for the ride of a lifetime!

Trouble or Nothing by Joanie MacNeil — Contemporary
He was her kid brother's best friend. And now he's back in her life...more man than ever.

Desert Dreams by Gracie McKeever — Paranormal/Suspense
Old World Evil vs. New Age Passion...Can their love survive?

The Anonymous Amanuensis by Judith Glad — Regency
Regency England is a man's world, until one woman writes her own rules...

No More Secrets, No More Lies by Marie Roy — Contemporary
Secrets, lies, and consequences. What consequences does Sydney Morgan pay when all secrets are exposed?

The Blood That Binds by Rie Sheridan — Fantasy
In Ancient Days, when elves were king...
the legends tell of wondrous things...

The Dragon's Horn by Glynnis Kincaid — Fantasy
Three Dragons. Three Immortals. One Choice. But what will they choose? Will they rescue their loved ones, or fight to redeem the world?

Escape the Past by K. G. McAbee — Fantasy
Can they escape their pasts and find a future in each other's arms?

The Binding by PhyllisAnn Welsh — Fantasy
He's an Elf Lord trying to save his people. She's a fantasy writer trying to save her sanity. Chosen by the gods to rescue an entire race, they first have to save each other.

Dream Knight by Alexis Kaye Lynn — Medieval
Do you believe in the power of dreams?

Allude to Murder by Emma Kennedy — Suspense
Balkan smuggling conspiracy entangles two Americans

Mating Season by Liz Hunter — Contemporary
One lucky sailboat captain + His fetching first mate + Hurricane Season=Mating Season!

Unlawful by Dorice Nelson — Medieval
Butchery tainted their first encounter... Enslavement separated them... Deception and deceit reunited them... Thus began their struggle of courage and conquest...

NBI
NovelBooks, Inc.
www.novelbooksinc.com

Quality Electronic Books
❏ Microsoft Reader ❏ Adobe Reader ❏
❏ PalmPilot ❏ Glassbook ❏ HTML ❏

Show how much you loved that book!
Now Available at our CyberShop!

❏ T-Shirts ❏ Sweatshirts ❏
❏ Coffee Mugs ❏ Mousepads ❏
Featuring NBI Bookcovers
and our Illustrious Logo